The Eagle and The Oystercatcher

Holly Bidgood

Holly Bidgood.

Published by Wild Pressed Books: August 2016

First Edition

The Eagle and The Oystercatcher © Holly Bidgood 2016

Contact the author through their website:

https://twitter.com/hollybidgood

Chief Editor: Tracey Scott-Townsend

Cover design by: Jane Dixon-Smith

Paperback ISBN: 978-0-9933740-4-3

eBook ISBN: 978-0-9933740-5-0

Print edition

Printed in the United Kingdom

Wild Pressed Books Ltd, UK

Company registration number 09550738

http://www.wildpressedbooks.com

For my children, Kim and Noomi.

Always remember that creativity is never time wasted.

Acknowledgements

Firstly I would like to thank my parents for giving me the opportunity to experience the Faroe Islands in the first place – without that family holiday this book would never have been conceived. To my dad: thank you for your frequent reassurance that writing a novel wasn't a waste of time; to my mum: your ornithological knowledge has really helped to bring the landscape of the novel to life.

I am indebted to the staff and my fellow students at UCL Scandinavian Studies Department for your support and cooperation in setting up the module in Faroese language and culture during my studies. Special thanks go to John Mitchinson for teaching us. I'm sorry to say I have since forgotten most of my Faroese but hope I will get the chance to rediscover it one day.

I am grateful to the staff at the Taynuilt Hotel for allowing me to nurse the same cup of tea for four hours during many an enjoyable afternoon spent editing the manuscript in the bar. I am also grateful to Hannah and Annick for letting me come round to use the internet when I needed to send/receive an edit.

Very special thanks go to Phil and Tracey at Wild Pressed Books – your dedicated support and guidance during the editing and publishing process has proved invaluable, I have learnt so much; also to my husband Fynn for showing no interest whatsoever in the book but being a brilliant dad to the children and allowing me the time to edit and write. Thank you also to Jane for her striking cover design (and sorry for all the hassle with the eagle).

Last but not least I would like to thank Gail at Homestart Lorn for looking after Kim while I write these acknowledgements!

The Eagle and The Oystercatcher

1

Spring 1940

THEY ARRIVED ON the twelfth of April.

I stood on a low hill overlooking Tórshavn as the two British Royal Navy destroyers pulled heavily into the harbour, hauling their bulks to the island's rocky coast. They were like rocks themselves: cold mechanical rocks, hooking an uninvited rope onto the lives of every islander and dragging us into the throes of the war. The air was heavy that day. It fell in a mist around the mountains, wet upon the low grass roofs of the houses, still rank with the overpowering smell of freshly caught fish. It fell upon heavy expectations and heavy hearts.

I remember the exact spot on the mountainside upon which I stood, and the smell of the damp earth and the shining rocks beneath the worn soles of my boots. I remember what I was wearing and that the buttons of my coat were unfastened and my neck was exposed, chilled to an uncomfortable numbness by the cold rain. Any higher and the three of us would have been lost in the mist, hidden from the scene below us.

I remember the faint rustle of Magnus's great red beard in the wind, and the distant look in his eyes as he surveyed the town, laid out colourfully even below an overcast sky, beyond our stationary feet. And the entire town looked out with him. To the harbour, at those two destroyers as they loomed through the dense mist which clung so closely to the coast, the sea a tempestuous mess hurling itself ferociously against the rocks and roaring like an awakened giant. In the ships' looming shadows the first oystercatchers of spring hopped along the shoreline as though nothing were amiss. I pursed my lips and mimicked their bright call: the comforting sound of home.

The destroyers were bigger than any manmade thing I had ever seen and I was gripped by a shivering sense of dread to think that man could assemble something so large and commandeering; that man should feel the need to. They dwarfed our little fishing boats into primitive insignificance - their masts now matchsticks, their sails tissue paper - and they did not just fill the vision, these cold-blooded destroyers, they grasped the soul.

Destroyer: that was the day I learnt that English word, and I remembered it instantly. Magnus's English was limited - the little he knew he had picked up from trading with Scotland -

but even he knew that word. He spoke it with a fragile caution, as though the sounds themselves might be dangerous, and the typical Faroese spin on the letter 'R' rolled off his tongue, through his beard and into the cool, dense air. Orri and I watched it curiously, that snippet of new knowledge, opening up a world that even then seemed dark and confusing. We could see no reason to trust it.

Nevertheless, Magnus's eyes still shone. They always shone, like stars sandwiched between the foliage of his beard and the matt of hair which was just as red, falling about his ears. He clapped a thick, weather-beaten hand upon my shoulder, and one upon Orri's, but his son's eyes had lost their shine that day. I could see that he was overwhelmed, frightened simply because he did not know whether the destroyers gave reason for anxiety.

But we were young then. I had barely passed my eighteenth birthday, and I suddenly felt as though we were poised on an indefinite, shapeless brink and the whole world was about to happen at once - a cacophonous collapse of control. That gives anyone reason to be scared. Of course, all I could do was watch as everything appeared to be pulled to pieces. I remember the wash of indefinable panic in which I was gripped by such a realisation as I stood on the mountainside; the new word to accompany it; the immense well of sorrow that had begun to open in the pit of my stomach.

And yet I remember little else of that day. I do not even know why we were in Tórshavn. I vaguely recall the smell, the taste; the texture of fish – but admittedly, as a fisherman, Magnus always embodied this smell, and he had little other-related business. I do not know if there was a clamour in the town or not. I hold simply a photograph in my mind, imprinted like a red-hot brand against the inside of my head.

I do, however, remember the blackout.

It was almost unbearable to be in the capital that spring night, one of the longest of my life. We were staying in the small, dank room of an old house fairly close to that dreaded harbour, Orri and I with our anxious faces pressed to the cold glass of the window. Magnus sat by the low glow of the oil lamp at the centre table. Darkness swelled around us like an enclosing hand, filling our ears, our eyes, our choked mouths. It is not easy to forget the silence of such a night. I remember the creases of Magnus's weatherbeaten face as he looked up from his book, and illuminated in the warm glow of the burning oil lamp it was graced by his broad, trademark smile.

'They're still there, boys, time to get some sleep.'

We looked again as the destroyers were swallowed up by the creeping darkness of night, and with a seemingly thunderous rustle Magnus put away his book. I reached out to give Orri's limp hand a comforting squeeze, for he looked exhausted and shaken to the bone, but at my touch he whipped back his hand. I drew breath to apologise – though exactly what for I could not say. His face had become a mask of anxiety. As my apology went unspoken he offered me a weak smile in reparation, his eyes unable to rest on mine.

As we lay awake later that night in the velvet darkness, while Magnus snored contentedly in the second bed across the room, Orri kept himself a couple of inches away from me. He lay stiffly on his back, his arms stapled to his sides as though paralysed. I could see nothing, though I held my eyes wide open to stare at what I was sure lay in front of me – though began now to doubt – but I knew he was awake and that his eyes were open as boldly as my own, unable to let go of the night. For this was the night we first knew, without a doubt, that it was wartime.

I adjusted my leaden body occasionally, moved my arms and legs in want of a comfortable position as they numbed from my restlessness, and every time I inadvertently brushed against Orri's still, alert body he would flinch, draw away into an even greater depth of the blackout. Sometimes this distance seemed so great in the night's disregard for space that I was convinced I was alone.

When we were younger the requirement to share a bed had been an adventure: to us it was a fort constructed from bed posts, pillows and throws, or a fishing boat with a blanket sail atop a wooden sea. We would reel out lines and nets and carry out impersonations of Magnus until we were breathless with laughter and the man himself would call across the room for a bit of peace and quiet. Perhaps we had simply grown too old for games, but in recent years Orri seemed to mourn the loss of his own space whenever I came to inhabit it.

I wished now that we could regress into the comfort of a blanketed den, a safe haven unreachable by warships. Abandoned instead in a seeming oblivion, I could feel my body stiffening, taste the emptiness. But then Orri's shallow breathing would resume, and Magnus would give a loud snort from across the thick dark of the room, and I would take shape again. I drifted eventually into an uncomfortable sleep, the sort of unconsciousness that lies so close to the waking state that it seems almost to be a feat of the imagination; not even that, for in my dreams I found myself in the same room, the same bed, the same company, still stiffly on my back with my head slipping off the hard pillow.

I slid out of bed with numb legs and drew the blackout curtain to one side. The blinding white light from the city's million lamps hit me as profoundly and with as much force as any destroyer would have done, so intensely that the sky was illuminated as though with pure, unspoiled daylight. The buildings themselves were of white stone, and the sea a bright grey, lying as still as a mill-pond, perfectly clear, devoid of anger, emotion or destroyers. Featureless, blank. I realised then that my eyes were not open, and anxiety welled within me for they felt glued shut, my eyelids as blackout curtains. I forced them open, with all my willpower prised them apart. I was met with darkness. I had not moved at all.

2

HOME LAY ON the most westerly island of the Faroes: Vá-gar. We left Streymoy in the small ferry boat in which we had made the same part of our journey to Tórshavn, and the sea swelled its grey fingers beneath us, carrying only an underlying hint of frustration as we increased our distance from what seemed the anger of the harbour.

The mountains rose around us from the sea, boldly and directly yet always with the same silent grace. Sheep watched us from the patchwork fields littering the mountainsides as we pulled eventually into the town of Miðvágur, below a canvas sky blankly washed with grey. The blackout of the previous night seemed already to be a dream, enforced by the exhilarated grin that Orri fixed upon me as our feet touched the dry land of the jetty. His blue Scandinavian eyes sparked again with the vigour I had known so well for eighteen years, as he bathed in the shadows of the bare mountains. He looked upon the clusters of small, colourful houses dwarfed by those mountains to a wonderful modesty, and brightly back to the little boat and myself.

'Don't forget the fish, Kjartan: a boat should never be left empty!' he teased me, for he knew too well my scepticism towards such superstitions.

I regarded him with amusement as my hands slid like cold glass over the coarse knots of the mooring rope. 'Do you think I just carry these things around?'

Orri's high-spirited laughter rang out in the damp, refreshing air. 'A fish for every occasion, Kjartan!' he announced in a deep-voiced imitation of his father, who was by this time standing calmly at the edge of the jetty a couple of metres from us, his hands against his broad hips, his feet rooted and legs parted slightly as he gazed in good spirits across the churning waters. At this he gave a broad, bearded smile, but did not turn his head.

I straightened and drew my icy hands up inside the comforting warmth of my sleeves, and looked at Orri as he unwaveringly kept his eyes upon me.

'Does it bring even better fortune to leave an entire *whale* in the boat?'

His grin widened, and he crossed his skinny arms across his chest and remarked that he was, in fact, in half a mind to leave *me* in the boat, before his father turned from the sea, reached a worn hand inside the pocket of his green breeches and drew out a limp fish. Orri and I watched, speechless, our smiles still lingering around our blue lips, as he threw it in a painstakingly nonchalant manner into the little boat which tossed on the waves. The ferryman smiled to himself as he lit a cigarette.

Magnus, as a man of almost superhuman (as I sometimes thought to myself) confidence, often crossed the normal boundaries of modesty into the realm of showmanship. This did not make him seem arrogant at all; he simply liked to incite wonder and evidently enjoyed watching the intrigued faces of his audience. He was a figure of awe and respect to the young; an experienced businessman to the middle-aged and a sympathetic ear to the old. Magnus was, in fact, somewhat revered in these parts that we called home.

Magnus was a hugely experienced fisherman and trader, responsible for more or less the island's entire fish supply, not to mention frequent trading with Britain. It seemed he owned a thousand boats and employed a million men; he knew the surrounding waters like the back of his huge, weatherbeaten hands. But his popularity and respect did not stem solely from this. The people liked him because he was one of them. In character and charisma, Magnus could not be matched: he knew everyone by name, liked them all. He asked about their wives, their sons and their cows, always in his deeply warm and welcomingly loud voice. I have never met another man with such an unquenchable passion for life as Magnus.

Even following the iron-handed onset of his illness a year later, Magnus's persona became no less endearing, no less eccentric and certainly no weaker; even when his body lost its strength, even when he could not leave his bed.

Now his tall, heavyset frame began to shake slightly with silent laughter at his own exhibitionism, and his son followed suit, although considerably louder, in fitting with his general hyperactivity. Orri's skinny frame was bent almost double, his white-blond hair fell windswept into his eyes, and I could see the light condensation of his breath upon the still air.

The centre of Miðvágur was not so still; it was busily awake with the hustle and bustle of daily life as we passed through in the full throes of the afternoon. We tended to visit the town only on route to Tórshavn, and this came fairly infrequently. Magnus popped into a few small buildings to pay a quick visit to members of his extended circle of acquaintances, while Orri and I tagged along with interest, studying food packets or paintings on the walls. But soon we longed again for the fresh air, and hopped around on street corners, in worn shoes around the gathering puddles.

Eventually we were bound north-west; in a black car along a rocky road. It was a slow, bumpy ride, yet around us the mountains remained unmovable, bare and majestic to either side, as giants to the land, their summits lost in the gathering grey mist. We passed the quiet waters of Sørvágsvatn, rippling calmly in the steady rainfall, its shores as yet unblemished by the rows of iron barrack buildings that were soon to house our wartime occupiers, and at the head of the lake we passed through Vatnsoyri, a village whose houses, conversely, would be evacuated.

Yet for the moment, home was home: the ocean seemed still impassable and the sky remote, for our own sky hung so closely to the ground it could not possibly be traversed by planes; only the mountains reached up into its enveloping dampness, and if the summer sunlight penetrated those grey drapes it would illuminate merely for a few minutes, and weakly at that, before the protective blanket closed in around us once more.

Orri would complain of its imposition; I felt safe.

3

THIS FEELING OF safety was one that I coveted for all the world. The arrival of the destroyers had left me shaken, nauseous, for so indecently had they encroached upon my carefully constructed world. They brought reality, and hurled it upon me with a passion, my own convictions having striven so painfully to blot out all thoughts of wars, weaponry and world politics. For so many years my childhood world had trundled slowly, happily amongst fish, sheep, mountains, the safe and the mundane. Even the outbreak of war in Europe, in those distant, unimaginable lands, had failed to imprint upon this way of life, more or less unchanged for centuries. The only change, it seemed, was in my father.

His middle son had left for Denmark around five years previously – not wishing, as many had thought he might, to join his older brother in Aberdeen. He had left with barely a backward glance to the small islands which disappeared behind him over the horizon. We received letters – my father did – yet we were not graced by even one visit from our absent family member. Only young, I had of course been distraught, emptied of a feeling of completion, thrown face to face with the anxieties of childhood, and the guilt which can only arrive from the lack of understanding in this innocence of age. My father, stripped somewhat of his spirit by the absence of his second-born son, talked often of him, and of his, my father's, intention to visit – and visit he finally did, consumed with worry following the outbreak of war.

That was when the Germans had invaded Denmark; that was the moment at which the war had happened upon me, before the arrival of the destroyers of the Royal Navy, the British garrison, the war had claimed the remains of my family. I did not think they had been killed, not for one moment did I allow myself that possibility. Yet they were segregated, that I did know; segregated from me, and from the Islands. It was not something I spoke about, not even to Orri, and I resented any questioning on the subject on his part. If I did not speak of it, it would not attain to reality – at least not in the busy daylight hours: here I could numb myself. Yet in the apocalyptic darkness of the nights, and the winter ones especially, the uncertainty choked me; I could barely breathe. Everywhere there was space, and a chill so cold it gripped my entire being and shook me until my bones rattled loose in the empty cavity of my body; paralysed, sometimes, barely alive.

For some time before my father's departure I had been anticipating a disaster, an end to all that I knew or held dear. In times of the winter darkness, the soul thinks only of this. It imagines all that could go so wrong, the cessation of all light, the end of the world, the beginning of the war. Admittedly I did not know what would happen, yet I was plagued constantly by fear.

The minute I awoke on dark mornings after little sleep, for every moment of the heavy, exhausting day, with every word, whether spoken or merely half-formed, I would feel it: that overwhelming sense of oblivion. It was before my eyes, behind my eyes, until the whole wretched, oblique world was contained within it. Fear removed my stomach, placed a dead weight over my palpitating heart, constricted my airways until my body doubled-up onto the floor. My head would feel as if it was splitting open, I strove for air with rapid gasps; for life.

I had tried to keep these attacks private, though they were difficult to endure: my head reeled and my burdened heart struggled so rapidly it seemed it would collapse into itself, into the oblivion. Choked up, the tears pressed so insistently against my eyelids, stinging as though my whole body would burst with this, an ocean through the veins. Yet I could not bear for any other soul to be with me at these times, for I did not want to spread the burden, cause alarm, or draw attention to my weakness.

Orri followed me once in my dash for the solitude I knew I had to endure before this feeling passed. He had perhaps noticed increasingly unusual behaviour on my part and he was only concerned, I knew that. But the rhythm of my heart stumbled frantically with his presence, though I could not speak to dismiss him, nor raise myself to push him away, and with each worried exclamation of 'Karri, what's wrong, what is it?' the strain worsened until I thought my body would surely crack and break like china.

Orri himself morphed into the indistinguishable haze of an overbearing presence, and the fear that hounded my soul transcended into pure terror. Even after I had resumed regular breathing and the chill of full awareness, I continued to shake violently. Orri crouched down by my side, though it was some minutes before I could bear to let him touch me.

My father came to notice, of course. All he did was ask me once or twice if I was keeping all right ('yes,' I answered, for I was sure there was no cause for concern), but he did not ask me the nature of my problem. It was not that he did not care for my wellbeing – I knew he did – he simply had his mind on other things. He was thinking of my brother – my brother in Denmark.

It was inevitable, I think, that my father should attempt to contact his middle son upon whom he had not set eyes for all those years, and thus I waited for an announcement to this effect for some time. I could only hold my breath and count the passing seconds, each a hammer to the heart, until those dreaded words made an appearance one dark winter evening: 'Come and sit down, Kjartan. I need to talk to you.'

I had been observing the detachment in his eyes for the whole evening. In the slow, uneasy twilight that darkened as we ate, my father's eyes saw not the splintered wood of our four walls and low, sloped ceilings, nor the freshly-cooked food on the table beneath his nose. I had, as usual, prepared a meal that although fairly standard was always much welcomed after a cold winter's day out in the open. Wind-cured mutton, boiled potatoes and butter: all lay modestly spread out across our small table in the centre of the room. The meal was simple and unadventurous, yet with a fulfilling, homely smell that filled every inch of our one-roomed *roykstova* and invaded our mouths, open in anticipation.

We ate in silence, I with my eyes downcast into the food with which I was playing, stealing often long glances at my father in his solipsistic world of forethought and planning. I could see he was already far from the Islands, from our home, and I knew I could say nothing to deter the course of action upon which he had already decided.

It was not in young naivety that I deliberately prolonged his telling of these plans, for I knew that no matter how long I managed to avoid the subject and keep the words unsaid, his departure would still come to pass. Yet somehow I strove to maintain the fantasy that were he not to tell me he was leaving, this winter night would stretch on forever, the sun never rise and the meat never grow cold. Impossible, I know; but I could not bear to hear those inevitable words spoken aloud as I had heard them so many times in my head – that continuous loop that bore deeper and deeper until embedded, ingrained within every part of my waking state.

I knew he was waiting until we had finished eating. I could see the anticipation in his face, the goal in sight, debating how best to approach it. As the last mouthful disappeared he laid down his knife and fork with a quiet conviction, and I saw that the decision had been reached. I leapt up from my chair and took those few mile-long steps to the stove; stacked the pans, swirled the water collected earlier from the tap outside, adjusted the oil lamp, put on the kettle... anything to keep busy.

But he still spoke. Immediately the warmth of the room left me cold, and my fidgeting hands came to a standstill, though they trembled slightly, regardless of the hot water in which they had been immersed without my paying much attention. I realised suddenly that the water, having found its way straight from the kettle, was scalding hot and my hands burned, pricked with paralysing needles. But I did not move them. I held them there under the pain of the water as it sank its teeth into my arms, and my cheeks burned feverishly. I prolonged the pain as I had prolonged the evening – a distraction.

'Come on, Kjartan; we can do that later,' he said when I did not turn around; instead I inspected every shape, raise and splinter of the wall before me. His voice was warm, caring to my ears, yet too lighthearted in such an atmosphere to pass as natural.

I sat down. My hands were fiercely crimson against the pale scattering of freckles up my skinny arms; my fingers were stiff as though the skin was drawn taut over every curve and awkward joint. I drew the sleeves of my overlarge grey jumper down past my knuckles and curled with some initial discomfort each finger so that they could not be seen and were cushioned by fabric. I felt safer this way.

My father's own hands lay calmly on the table, his fingers linked, locked... no, it was not a tranquil position; this was too strained, attempting to appear relaxed. The fingers were linked in an awkward manner, and I could see that his arms were tense, protruding from the sleeves of his own worn shirt that had been rolled up to just above the elbows. Even this arrangement of shirtsleeves seemed unnatural, as though the fabric was coiled to an extremity, poised to catapult back into stiffness when the pressure eventually became too intense.

At times of genuine relaxation my father had a habit of drumming his long fingers against any available surface, often to a seemingly inexorable internal rhythm. I did the same thing, had the same thin fingers. His hands were not thick-set and weatherbeaten like the seafaring tradesman's fingers of Magnus but rather they were delicate in comparison, dexterous, malleable, like my own.

There was no rhythm now.

'These are difficult times we're living in, Kjartan, these times of war. Of course, you're old enough to realise that for yourself, and all of the implications that come with it. Some people are able to make a profit, especially now given the fishing industry, but for the majority it seems to be a dance with death almost... '

He trailed away, looking uncertain, but upon meeting my intense, steady gaze once more he seemed to be struck by the realisation of who he was speaking to. He shook his head loosely with a smile. 'I'm sorry, Karri, I don't mean to patronise you. You know all this of course... I know you do: you're such a bright boy.' He smiled at me again. 'A bright young man.'

He sighed heavily and leant back in his chair, still surveying me, his youngest son, with a strange mix of expressions, something akin to pride in the well of sadness behind his eyes. 'I have to go to Denmark.'

'I know,' I said, and nothing more.

His eyebrows creased momentarily in thought; then he

chuckled to himself, more in contemplation than amusement. 'Yes, of course you do! You always know these things... ' He took a deep breath. 'It will... it will all be okay.'

'Will it?'

There was silence for a moment. Only the wind howled.

'Karri, please don't think I'm leaving you.' My father straightened in his chair and his eyebrows creased once more with the weight of what seemed like anxiety. His hair appeared greyer this winter than I had ever seen it, strewn with all shades of light and dark; his eyes were tired from his sleepless nights.

On many of these nights I had watched him from the warm comfort of my pillow, the quilts pulled up defensively under my chin. My head heavy, I had observed my father's dark silhouette tip-toe quietly about the room, stand before the window's opaque oblivion; sit thoughtfully on the edge of his bed. I am sure he thought I lay asleep. On one occasion I had got up to relieve myself and he had apologised softly. I all but heard the relaxation of his muscles then from their anxious tension. After I had returned to the warmth of my blankets with a brief 'goodnight', he did the same. And before long I had heard the heavy sound of his slumber.

'It's not my wish to leave,' he continued, almost pleadingly. 'But, you know I haven't heard any news for so long, and I don't know what else to do... this war affects us all... You understand, don't you?'

I nodded, and wished to God that I did not. Ignorance seemed to my exhausted mind desirable: to be a child again, to break out into a screaming tantrum at such a travesty of justice – my father being taken away from my side. To cry with the vulnerable fear of it all until the wells of my eyes, swollen, were dry and empty.

But my grief would progress no further, for he would undoubtedly return. My father was invincible, strong in prowess and intellect, capable in all the languages of the wide world, and never, ever short of words. Words for every occasion, every opportunity, every emergency... with words he would always be safe.

When the anxiety did not pass from his face at my mute affirmation, I smiled for him and said lightly, 'I can look after myself. War changes everything, I know.'

It made me sick to hear myself say such things. With a slight cloud behind his eyes he agreed that yes, I was old enough to look after myself, but this gave no concrete reason for my having to do so.

'You do not need to go through life alone, Kjartan. Independence does not signal strength or maturity; it is not the mark of a great man. Even the strongest people need company. Magnus and Ásdis say you are more than welcome to stay with them, and surely Orri will be pleased to have you so close at hand, the two of you being more or less inseparable even now after all these years.'

Those clouds behind his eyes shifted as he tried to convince himself as well as me that I would be fine.

'And of course the vicar's wife has a room going spare now that her son has moved to study in Tórshavn. She did, after all, look after you from when you were barely a day old, nursing you just as she did her own son.'

A sad smile flitted over his lips: thoughts of my mother were inevitably tied up with recollections of my birth. Another distance between us, since I had no such memories of the woman who had brought me into the world.

'So promise me, Kjartan,' he insisted sternly, with the caring eyes of a father, 'that you won't consider it a breach of etiquette or your own sense of pride as a young man to ask for help should you need it. Or simply just company. Promise me you won't stay here alone, at least not entirely.'

I had expected myself to argue, express indignation, perhaps just for the sake of some negative response; but I could do nothing but smile in acceptance, and nod my head in acknowledgement. I harboured not even an argumentative streak in my thoughts unsaid; all was simply a confusion of ideas and the many sides of reasoning: who was I to act negatively at his going away? Such selfish behaviour was not acceptable, and I hated myself even for its slightest consideration. This was not about me. I was obsolete, and rightly so.

'I should not be gone too long.'

Take as much time as you have to, I wanted to say, but didn't. What difference would it make?

My father looked at me in earnest for a few moments in the dim light of the lamp, as though attempting to read my thoughts. He was always fairly accurate in his interpretation, and now appeared to conclude my reluctance for personal questioning in regard to my feelings over the subject.

He rose heavily, affectionately ruffled my hair, and leaned down to kiss my forehead. I did not look at him. I studied the table through the sounds of his pottering around the stove – the table with all its worn creases, inadvertent patterns etched into its ageing, battered face to create an entire landscape. A world of characterisation whose rough reaches could not be contained within the wooden walls and low roof of one small house.

Not even within the rock-strewn mountains and harbours, rivers and waterfalls of one small island in the now deceptive vastness of the North Atlantic. And across this anthropomorphic expanse of all that could be conceived and understood, over those expressive contours of realistic imagination, would stand the empty chair of my father in the distance.

4

I DO NOT recall the conditions of my father's departure. I must have been in Tórshavn, for I insisted on accompanying him to the harbour in a final attempt to bridge the gap between my irregular feelings of detachment and the events which I knew ought to appear to me significant. My heart was heavy, but my emotions stale, as though I stood in contemplation – as I would soon do once more on the hill overlooking Tórshavn on the day the British arrived – watching it all happen to someone else, someone more important, more real in the eyes of the world than me.

I do not remember looking upon Tórshavn with my own colourless eyes, nor feeling the midwinter weather upon my colourless skin; formless shadow that I was. I do not even remember saying goodbye, though the words must have been uttered from my lips at some moment, for neither he nor I could have parted without me giving him my blessing.

My material recollection dates back to the moment I

stepped from the car into Sørvágur's winter twilight. The winter hit my face with an icy ferocity, tousled my hair and blustered it with snowflakes. It was a bleakness that only a northern winter can muster.

'Good luck, Kjartan!' called Jón, one of Magnus's men, from the car's lowered window. We had driven most of the distance across the island in a thoughtful silence, but now that a destination had been reached, he appeared to have perked up into the friendly disposition with which I was most acquainted. 'You will come and visit us again soon, won't you, lad? Sorry I can't take you any farther in this weather!'

After I had offered my goodbyes and said that I would love to come round soon, he wound up the window against the drifting snow and the car trundled noisily back the way we had come, an ungainly black beetle to be swallowed up into the inhospitable sheet of a dirty white background.

I was left alone on the sparse outskirts of the town, and all was silent save for the barely audible roar of an unseen ocean, and the occasional snatch of a voice from amongst the black, timbered walls of the houses.

I fastened my snowflake-scattered woollen scarf tightly around my neck and nestled into its damp comfort. I drew my bare hands up into my sleeves and set off at a fast, determined walk in the direction of home. It was four kilometres to the village of Bøur; four kilometres of an ill-defined road sandwiched loosely between the tormented waters of the fjord and the steep, rocky slopes of the mountains. Everything about our Islands was steep and rocky, climbing immodestly skywards with little use for the word 'lowlands' and little desire to be anything less than dramatic. The slopes had become hidden under a blanket of snow, barren still, yet now of a different colour.

And I was still awed by the splendour: nothing could detract from these profound razor-sharp rocks and overbearing cliffs; and to be at the foot of it at such a desolate moment did not so much elate the soul – for profundity does not necessarily endow such an emotion – but rather occupied it, dwarfed to a startling insignificance in this grandeur. So it was with numb feet and an otherworldly thoughtlessness that I trudged home, my eyes gliding with exhausted wonder through the surrounding bleakness. The white sky was so extensive that the mountains had been swallowed into the oblique blind-spot that hid the rest of the world, war or no war.

The pain of my numb feet temporarily masked that of my newly absent father. I approached home as the two plagues began to spread and grip my body in a vice of exhaustion. My head ached, my tired eyes stung. I could have lain down in the inviting linen tones of the weather, curled into a foetal position and closed my eyes – tired of the way day followed night and night followed day with endless monotony.

But I tramped up to my door. I had to push it open with my wrists for my fingers were stiff with the cold. I nudged it shut again with a dull thud and a white flurry. I unwound my scarf – sharp with encrusted ice – fumbled with the buttons of my coat, and my hands ached and screamed as I forced them into cooperation, for they would not deign to move even a useful inch to grasp the small circles of my buttons. I struggled out of my coat with some difficulty and it fell wetly to the floor beside my disregarded shoes, my socks, my shirt and my trousers as I peeled off each item of damp clothing. I pulled on some dry trousers that hung from my bedboard, thick woollen socks and the overlarge jumper of which I was ever fond. I did not let myself think; I did not look about the room. Eventually I lay down upon my father's narrow bed, pulled my sleeves down over my hands, and glued my eyes shut.

The bed opened its welcoming fingers and I sank limply into the waiting eternity, still aware of the leaden heaviness of my body. I fell deeply into slumber as the world around me grew dark, and in my dreams I was in a state of suspended animation. Nothing moved, nothing spoke, nothing passed. It was bliss.

5

BUT WE MUST always wake up.

While we were not looking, Norway and France surrendered to the German hand; Russia was invaded; no further news came from Denmark.

The most notable overseas event was what was later termed the 'Miracle of Dunkirk'. This momentous event of history was discussed with some ferocity by the farmers during their frequent social gatherings. 'Three hundred and thirty thousand Allied troops are stranded in Northern France,' one of the farmers would remark. 'The Royal Navy have only enough boats to rescue around four hundred and fifty of these troops, and the boats themselves are under heavy bombardment from all sides.' Someone else would take up the story: 'The shells rain down on sand and sea; all is chaos, and it is chaos without hope; they are destined to become prisoners of war.'

'And then, the miracle,' contributed Floki. 'Over the tormented waters of the horizon and all in between arrive hundreds of little boats, privately owned boats with a heroic British civilian inside every one, driving their flimsy crafts over the tumultuous divide of the English Channel to the aid of their fellows – they had heard the cry for help over the wireless. And do you know what happened? They were saved, the soldiers; every single one was evacuated.'

'Every single one?' echoed Birgir of the farm by Vørðufelli, on his face an expression of disbelief.

'Every single one,' clarified Floki once more, and there was a swelling pride in his voice, and a smile of such to accompany it.

'And how many did you say there were?'

'Three hundred and thirty thousand!' resonated Floki's triumphant answer. It might have been concluded from his tone that the man had engineered the entire evacuation himself.

Birgir leaned back in his wooden chair looking suitably impressed, amazed, it appeared. 'My God,' he said, almost to the air itself, in which his reflective gaze was suspended. 'And in those little boats as well... '

'No,' the hoarse voice of old Ketil the barley farmer piped up from the depths of his chair alongside the fire. 'No, I will not believe it.' Two sceptical, red-ringed eyes peered out from a forest of beard and hair, between whose matted depths little else showed. The voice rasped with old age, but was as set as concrete. 'They'd need proper boats for that. And where would they put the fish with all those soldiers on the decks? And the nets: what'll they do with those? Fish won't catch themselves, you know.'

'Three hundred and thirty thousand,' repeated Floki, no less triumphantly, having either not heard the old man's rasp, or choosing simply to ignore it, most likely because he did not know of what Ketil spoke. Very few people did, in fact. With accumulating years at his back the old man had a tendency to mumble away to himself, perhaps unsure if anyone was listening, but determined to articulate his opinion anyway – whatever that may be. His mind was still sharp, no doubt about it, perhaps even wiser for his disintegrating old age; but whatever it was about which he spoke, the point eluded most people. To listen was like watching a fire die out, or an old car rattle into the distance without ever reaching the horizon; tiresome in a way that drains the soul. There were snippets of coherency here and there, sometimes startlingly profound – admittedly this came only with the shock of his suddenly making sense – and his general mood at these moments was always one of extreme bitterness; a disgruntled blood-shot eye. And it was never fixed upon the uneasy listener, but concentrated upon the nearest material object. In this conversation he may have been talking to the wall.

Birgir – who dealt primarily with cattle – paid the old man no attention, but continued to shake his bearded head in disbelief, leaning back in his chair and swirling his cup of coffee absent-mindedly. 'Sure, that's worthy of our Magnus, that,' he mused with another burst of enthusiasm.

'Worthy of Magnus?' inquired Floki, still glowing into his own coffee. The two had a habit of repeating each other; never before had I heard conversations take such circular forms. It made a man cast his eyes to the sky in the hope of escaping to the heavens.

'Yes, indeed,' sang the cattle farmer, pleased for the attention. 'You can just imagine it, can't you? Magnus in his fishing boat, sailing across the waves... ' He moved his hand through the air as if drawing a heroic picture before the eyes of the others.

'All the way down to Britain, like he does to trade!' chimed another Sørvágur farmer, witness also to the discussion – and thus a claimed witness to Dunkirk itself.

'All the way to France!' extended Birgir, caught irrevocably in the heat of the idea. 'And he could rescue them, couldn't he?' He moved to take a sip of his hot coffee, but with the cup halfway to his beard he appeared to be struck by another thought that required to be voiced, and knowingly raised a finger: 'Single-handedly.'

'Every single one?' inquired Floki, in a way that did not merit his asking, but rather indicated that he believed this to be true.

'Every single one,' said Birgir.

(I wanted to bang my head against the stove.)

From the fireside corner old Ketil muttered something disgruntledly about not having enough room for fish.

'Ah, the fish,' agreed Floki. 'Where would Magnus be without his fish, eh?' The man himself was a sheep farmer, and a very enthusiastic one at that. He knew all there was to know about the practices and logistics of sheep farming, and this knowledge, as he took great pleasure in reminding people more often than was necessary, was the most useful, indeed perhaps the only, knowledge one needed to get by in the world.

To Floki, of course, the world consisted of a sheepfold, an outfield and a cooking pot, and nothing more. Thus a simple philosophy for a simple set-up. With more sheep than was necessarily needed to support one man, both financially and in the digestive sense, the farmer generally considered himself to be utterly independent (even from his old friend Birgir, from whom he received his milk).

Fish, as he would often say, do not allow for any kind of financial independence, for they do not belong to the catcher in the way that a sheep does. Sheep must be looked after, herded, sheared, and shared out when butchered; they are a full-time occupation, part of the family, very much the same as owning a bed, or a car (though far more beneficial, of course); the fish are dead the majority of the time. The fisherman does not have to make sure that the right fish are allocated and confined to the right pasture in the right outfield outside the right village.

Sure, if it wasn't for Floki all the town's sheep would be running wild, on the mountains, on the roads, in neighbouring pastures (God forbid); parents would have to lock the doors of their turf-roofed houses to keep their children safe from the tearaway sheep of Sørvágur.

I remember acting out this scenario in the presence of Orri one May, just after lambing, while he fell off his bed in unquenchable tears of laughter. For although 'vagabond sheep' might be a step beyond reality, the preliminary assertions were of Floki himself, in all self-belief. And although the man carried with him – like the others – a sublime respect for Magnus and his trade, he considered such reliance on fish to be somewhat of a weakness. Well, this is what he liked to think at any rate; but we could all smell the undertones of jealousy, albeit they were weak and effectively innocent, even if the man himself could not.

Birgir sucked the end of his pipe thoughtfully. 'Where would *we* be without Magnus's fish?'

The table was quilted with low murmurs of agreement.

The pipe end made a gestured reappearance into the stifled air of the wooden-walled room. 'Can't fish and rescue soldiers at the same time.' More similar murmurs.

'Not at the same time,' reinforced Floki, who liked to think he always came upon ideas first. 'Mind you, the British must owe him already for all that fresh fish he supplies them with during this wartime: twenty percent of their entire fish consumption, they say! Can't expect him to supply fish *and* evacuate all their troops from a foreign country; now that's just too much to ask of one man.'

Birgir agreed in all seriousness, a stony face at such an unimaginable thought, pouring himself a glass of alcoholic *akvavitt* as though this might steady such possible injustice. Once achieved, he thought aloud to no one in particular: 'Nice lad, that son of his. He'll make a good fisherman, like his father.'

'Or sheep farmer,' added Floki, in ever adamant support of his own trade.

'Oh, aye,' agreed the remaining men at the table, 'nice lad, indeed.'

Listening regularly to the musings of these conversations, I was always struck with an amazed hilarity by how quickly the talkers would revert back to local matters. It always happened in this way: one minute the discussion would concern the political disruptions in Europe, or the apparent climate in the southern hemisphere; and the next minute the topic would have somehow progressed, without any noticeable hitch or joint, to the best way to carry a hay stack back to the farmstead without damaging one's back.

I always listened with sparkling interest from my usual position in the kitchen area from where I kept the coffee in supply, striving to see if I could pinpoint the precise moment at which the conversation turned. But no matter how attentively I listened, this changeover continued to elude me, a hidden join which added a similarly obscure element of mystery to the seemingly narrow-minded conversation. Another resonating theme was the illumination of their friend and colleague, Magnus. There seemed to be no huge leap, as would normally be expected, between his being rightly respected and being regarded as some sort of divine superpower. I admit to slight exaggeration, but the likening of Magnus alone to, for example, a horde of boat-owning heroic civilians was by no means a rare glorification. Also, the interpretation of the fisherman as singlehandedly supplying Britain with twenty percent of their wartime fish struck me with a similar sense of wonder as to why our district's civilians, knowing full well that Magnus was far from being a sole provider, liked to absentmindedly harbour this illusion. He, Magnus, seemed like Father Christmas.

As well as providing for our district Magnus did often trade with Britain, of course, and trade had multiplied considerably given the war; but he was perhaps more involved in ferrying fish to Britain from Iceland. All this before he fell ill, at least.

Sometimes Magnus would be sitting amongst them, discussing matters just as intently as the other farmers, a farmer himself, in a way. And at these times they would treat him no differently than they treated each other. However much respect they held for this prominent man, he was first and foremost an honest man earning a living from the land, just like every other man of the district. His disposition was somewhat raucous at these times, perhaps exaggerated by the copious amounts of akvavitt that always accompanied the coffee, though he was not anyway a quiet man by nature.

He would talk fixatedly with the rest of them about the benefits and disadvantages of the new machinery that had found its timely way into our agriculture, and debate passionately whether individual ownership was more preferable than our more common practice of shared sheep ownership and thus shared profits and divided responsibilities.

These late-night discussions of all matters serious would, at lighter moments, become punctuated by bursts of piercing laughter, particularly as the akvavitt did the rounds. They would all throw back their beards, slap their thighs, the table; ordinarily one man would be left looking sour-faced in response – a joke at his expense, no doubt. But this brief indignation would be duly forgotten, and the coffee would continue to flow, and the room to fill up with smoke – a rich tobacco smoke, the smell of which bored into the wooden walls and damp rafters even after the foggy tendrils themselves had long since dispersed.

At first, as the smoke began to curl below the low ceiling, my eyes would water and my throat would become dry, but after some time I would become accustomed to it, to its smell and its texture, almost comforting in a way. It called to mind the consistencies of the day now passed, the familiarities of daily life. Within the smoke dwelled the smell of fish, the excitement after a catch. Or the aroma of wet hay in the steep outfields, as the sheep bleated forlornly through the misty rain. A picture overseen by the grey blend of the mountains and the sea.

There would be the cry of the kettle as water came to the boil. Under the low rafters these familiarities of our ways of life engulfed the soul and warmed the heart, still we were glad to be locked away in this smoky world for the time being. Safe, and now with the scope to appreciate that which lay outside the walls. Then, once the doors to outside had been thrown open, the smoke began to clear and these memories would be rekindled back into life; the smoky world itself suddenly no more than a lingering aroma of wood and snippets of conversation.

Of course, worldly matters were not always discussed in such a way; serious turns inevitably occurred, happenings so dark in consideration that even the distance of overseas could not be maintained, even the mind could not be comforted by the safety of home. The skies above Britain were aglow with the fireworks of the Blitz; for fifty-eight nights the bombs rained down as though they would never stop, as though the Germans would never run out.

One night in London, I learned, a total of three thousand people lost their lives – more civilians than servicemen – *in just one night*. All eyes were red-ringed that day; we barely spoke, hardly looked at each other; all food turned to ashes in my silent mouth. Such a grand scale, such an extremity of fear... such appalling things darken the soul of anyone, geographical position regardless.

That night I seemed to hear the howling of the bombs as they dropped, leaden weights through paper air; I imagined the force as they hit the ground, as they hit my stomach and tore a deep hole through my torso, pierced by shards, burning.

Fire raged through every building as though they too were made of paper. I heard the screams of the afflicted, felt the eternal despair like concrete in the lungs, saw the rows upon rows of lifeless bodies on the decimated ground. And I pictured the families belonging to every one, to hear the news... what would become of them? It did not seem possible that life could continue as before, in any way: the world was a changed place.

The farmers, similarly, sat in silence around the table, each in his own thoughts behind his pipe. No one touched the coffee. The room, as always, filled up with the same thick smoke, but the taste was bitter, the smell suffocating. Laying down the coffee pot I ran outside and retched violently by the side of the deserted road. Having swallowed nothing but ashes I succeeded only in vomiting up a little bile. And the icy blackness of the midwinter night sank its claws into the bare skin of my arms.

6

Late summer 1940.

IT WAS NOT long before those soldiers whose arrival had caused such a stir in the harbour that April day appeared in our little town, and not much longer before their presence was considered to be the norm.

It is said that the only thing necessary for survival in the village of Sørvágur is a fishing road and a pot in which to cook the fish. Needless to say, in this respect Magnus played a vital role, for the fishing industry in the town was the most dominant of the island. This, in a way, was his territory: Magnus ran his boats from the harbour. Magnus and the community; the community and Magnus.

Such was the inherent success of the industry that Sørvágur boasted an extremely popular fish market. It was a vibrant occasion, more so every week, and as the British garrison continued to arrive, the crowd swelled and multiplied, demand for fish rose, and the profits with it.

I loved this time of the week: I felt as though I had purpose. We would get up early, Orri and I. In the winter it would still be dark, the sun nothing more than a faint glowing suggestion on the horizon, and the mountains would tower dominantly around us, casting long and gradual shadows over the sleeping houses as we assembled the stalls with Magnus's men throughout the early morning, our scarves fastened tightly around our necks against the morning chill, and the smell of fish almost overpowering in our nostrils.

The sky on that particular day was an endless blanket of opaqueness stretching back forever. It seemed impossible to imagine that the same sky could also hang over a world ravaged by war. The landscape beneath it was illuminated in a strange, bright daylight that glinted off the bare rocks of the mountainsides and all but radiated from the calm waves of the sea. I could see clearly all the way up the steep-sided fjord to the open sea and the bold, mountainous rocks of the Mykines, which rose ruggedly from the waves off the shore. And the foreground swelled as a sea also; the ebb and flow of faces and voices, punctuated often by bursts of shrill laughter, which made themselves known like smoke signals over the chattering heads of the crowd.

I peered through it with interest, catching snippets of conversation and seized social opportunities amongst the market-goers. The fishmarket setting provided an endless supply of these. Everyone knew everyone else more or less, but here we all had one utterly indisputable common connection: fish. It did not matter whether you liked fish or not; whether you knew by heart the intrinsic qualities of small or large-scale fishing, or the fish themselves; whether you could even spell 'fish'; there was always scope for conversation: 'So, what's your favourite type of fish?' or, 'My grandfather was a fisherman, you know.' The possibilities were endless. And if they became exhausted, then there was always the topic of the weather.

I caught all sorts of examples in my scanning of the crowd; their capacity for intense discussion of one and only one subject never ceased to amaze me. They engaged each other with a vigour that could I never seem to muster. I kept myself at a good distance from the crowd – any crowd, it should be added. It is true, however, that maintaining a station behind one of Magnus's fish stalls could hardly be classed a reasonable distance from a fish-orientated crowd, each and every one of whom would inevitably buy some fish from me, ask me for some information about the particular types of fish on sale, or generally just shout 'Fish!' at me in a loud and excitable voice (admittedly, the latter of these occurrences had never actually come about, but each week in the melee it seemed all the more likely).

The reason I enjoyed the position behind the fish stall, aside from the aforementioned early morning preparation before capacity swelled under the mountains, was because I was still involved, without becoming swallowed up and drowned in the sea of the crowd. Behind the stall I was at the heart of the gathering, intrinsic to it, and every question or observation directed at me by the townspeople would, without question, contain my particular fish stall as a subject. Thus there would be no need for snatched small talk, nothing personal, no reason to give anything away; I knew the answers before the questions had even taken shape. Fish, you see, we all had that in common.

I watched the British troops in particular this week. They seemed to have taken quite a liking to the young women of the town; or the young women had to them. Some of those women were still little more than girls, yet they flicked their hair in the wind and batted their eyelashes until they all but dropped off.

I cannot deny that it was for one pair of fluttery eyelashes in particular that I searched, knowing full well that inherent disappointment would strike when, as usual, they were not to be fluttered in my direction. I could not envisage what I would do if such a thing were to happen. It was entirely likely that I would blush crimson to the tips of my ears, mutter something incoherent and turn and flee in the opposite direction (were my knees not too weak to carry me).

I saw her then in the company of a tall khaki-clad suitor, and my knees did go weak, and my heart made a hop-skip-jump sort of a movement, and I wondered what they could possibly be communicating about given the language barrier.

I was gripped with a strange elation as I watched her, as the blood coursed through my body with an electric current and my limbs felt as though they were not my own. I watched her clasp her hands behind her back, place them self-consciously on her hips; twist her fingers around each other, cross her arms over her chest... I watched the rise and fall of her breath, the quiver of her lips into a demure smile, the gentle billow of her skirt in the breeze.

I watched as she readjusted a pin in her red-orange hair when she thought the soldier was not looking, and when he did not turn back to her immediately I saw the flicker of her lashes as her eyes wandered, perhaps inadvertently, over the market..

Before I knew quite what I was doing I had thrown myself down behind the barrier of the fish stall, hidden from view, away from wandering glances. My head reeled. A few moments passed before I was able to get my bearings, by which time Orri had crouched down beside me. He looked up and around, as though taking in his surroundings, though his eyes sparkled with a hint of his usual mischief. Then, fixing me with a gaze of mock seriousness, he asked, 'So, err, for what reason are we hiding behind the stall?'

'It's safer here,' I whispered, feeling my cheeks going hot. He nodded, seemed to consider this a reasonable argument. His fine hair stirred in the wind. 'Is it maybe time to venture back out there, do you think?' I could tell he was trying not to laugh. 'Just, err, just in case anyone's wanting to buy a bit of fish?'

I bit my lip. 'I think you should go first.'

He rolled his eyes, grinned broadly, and was gone. With a sigh I followed suit, standing up in one swift movement to find myself facing one of the garrison troops. He was taller than me and looked a little lanky under the tightness of his black leather belt. If I was taken aback by our sudden encounter, the young man nearly jumped out of his skin. My first thought was whether this could be the same soldier I had seen conversing with the red-headed girl (the one I could not shake from my thoughts) but it seemed unlikely he would have torn himself away from her side to go in search of fish.

The soldier held up a finger with apparent embarrassment. He pointed to a collection of white fillets, then held up the finger again, this time adding another two. He smiled in an apprehensive manner, the corners of his eyes creased. I noticed how his ears stuck out slightly under his cap. 'Three pieces of cod,' I clarified in my best English. The soldier looked surprised.

I supposed he must have considered the scripted response of 'you speak English?' before deciding against it as a fairly pointless one (since I obviously could).

I tossed up a couple of cod pieces, wrapped them loosely in the customary brown paper, feeling their solid weight, reassuring in my cold, bare hands. The soldier watched me in suspended animation, as though thinking deeply, and I found myself asking hesitantly, 'Are you, err... having a nice time?'

Jón had berated me on more than one occasion for failing to engage customers in conversation. It did not come naturally, and I suspected that any attempts at small talk on my part only served to worsen the situation to an almost unbearable level of awkwardness, indeed there were only so many fish-related questions I could ask; it was no wonder I felt compelled to drop down and hide behind the stall.

When I watched Orri in his exchanges with the customers he seemed to embody the very essence of life itself. He would joke and laugh, or be earnest and compassionate when the situation called for it, as though he and the visitor were the oldest friends in the world – which, admittedly, they quite often were – and not once was there an awkward moment or a passage of silence that dragged on for longer than one could stand. Orri was as light as the breeze and as welcoming as the sun.

Luckily the victim of my attempted small talk gave a broad, friendly grin.

'Oh, aye,' he pronounced, 'it's no bad.' I was unsure whether he referred to the bustle of the fish market or to garrison life on the island as a whole.

'Oh,' I said. 'Good. That's good.' Feeling I ought perhaps to say more I gestured with the parcel of fish towards the low-lying mountains around us, their summits lost once more in the damp descent of grey clouds, and the far reaches of the fjord engulfed by creeping mist. How quickly the weather could, and would often, change. I remarked that it was really quite nice here, when it wasn't raining. And if only, I added, it didn't rain most of the time. As if on cue, the first few drops of a misty drizzle lighted on my bare hands, the opening notes of a continual drone that would undoubtedly persist for hours, perhaps for days.

For a moment my customer seemed unsure as to the seriousness of my response, searching my face as I handed over the brown paper parcel for signs of the tongue-in-cheek remark I had intended it to be. I almost kicked myself for my ill chosen tone; Orri's amiable way of communicating in such circumstances was never as deadpan as mine. But the soldier's reply was in keeping with my remarks. 'And ah thought the Scottish weather was bad enough,' he said. 'Ah was hoping for a wee bit o' sunshine for a change. Hoped they might send me south, tae the continent perhaps.'

'Actually,' I said. 'I think there is a war on down south.'

He laughed, a short burst of genuine amusement, before leaning towards me over the filleted fish in the manner of one about to confess a guarded secret, as though my self-conscious attempt at humour had cemented a bond between us. 'Ah wouldn't have minded, if only they'd sent me to a town whose name I could actually pronounce... '

Grinning, I obligingly spoke the name of the town. I could not help but erupt into laughter as he made a garbled attempt to mimic the sounds, although – I tried to explain as, still laughing, I made a hasty apology – it was more his look of intense concentration and bewilderment that I found so entertaining. By his broad, self-mocking smile, it would seem he was not too offended. He made another nonsense interpretation, then we worked through it a few times, syllable by syllable. Orri looked on with an amused frown, recognising in our exchange the deconstructed Faroese sounds.

The young Scotsman muttered the name to himself a few more times, as though imprinting it in his memory, then thanked me. 'Ah'd ask you for your name, but ah suppose we've no got all day.'

I spoke it anyway, and for a second time he furrowed his brows and asked me to repeat it. After he had tried out the sounds a few times, I informed him that it was perfectly acceptable to call me 'Karri', a nickname he agreed was a lot easier to pronounce. Then he held out his hand, warmly shook my own, and introduced himself as David. He laughed again when I had little trouble repeating the sound of it. He asked for my friend's name, perhaps eager for another new word to try out, and upon being introduced, Orri shook the man's hand with gusto, grinning mischievously.

'Welcome to Faroe!'

'He's been practising that for months,' I explained, and Orri scowled at me, rightly suspecting that I was making a joke at his expense.

'One of us ought to make him feel welcome,' he reprimanded me in our own language, though he smiled still, and the icy blue of his eyes glinted and danced behind the curtain of grey drizzle and the wet wind toyed with his hair. 'God knows they'll be here long enough.'

7

Winter 1941.

THIS PARTICULAR MURKY winter morning I had become plagued, after an indefinite stretch of timelessness, by a pulsating, irregular rhythm. *My heart's gone wild again*, I thought, *my airways are constricting.* On a few occasions I had woken up in the throes of an attack. But this rhythm appeared not to emanate from my heart, but rather to govern it: I was simply a heart on the bed, beating strongly against the blankets, pondering the oddness of my non-existent limbs, for last night I was sure they had been there; how else could I have returned home?

Eventually I drifted into the awareness that there existed a ribcage against which my heart beat – a newly discovered life force – and presently all else followed until I attained the status of entity again. And I realised that the staggered rhythm was not internal to this particular entity, but seemed to originate from the door. As I regained full consciousness, it stopped. There followed a moment of helpless silence as I attempted to remember the correct procedure for an occurrence of this kind. Quite a regular occurrence. Another timely knock, then:

'Karri! Karri, it's me... hello?'

Ah. I rolled off the bed, quickly pulled on some clothes, and opened the door as my name began to roll off his tongue again: 'Ka – oh... hi, Karri.' He grinned. 'I thought perhaps I'd got the wrong house.'

I frowned at him with the squinted eyes of early morning – there were precious few houses in Bøur, and one of them belonged to Orri and his family; he had lived there for nearly twenty years.

'The door is unlocked,' I said in a hoarse voice.

His eyes continued to shine out from under the brim of his woolly hat with a brightness that could almost blind me this side of my awakened consciousness; it was like looking directly into the sun. The sun gazed back. 'I know,' he said, airily, 'but I can't very well just burst in uninvited, can I?'

'That's never stopped you before.'

He considered this. 'No,' he said presently, 'No, I suppose it hasn't. Anyway... err, good morning.'

'Good morning.'

I stepped back from the door to let him through. He was

encrusted with pure, white snow. While outside it had glistened, once inside he looked a little dejected as he pulled off
his thick, icy jacket with newly exposed pink hands, his head
bowed and his blond hair flattened by his hat to fall limply
across his forehead. I thought I perceived an undertone of sorrow, the kind that persists as a lining for all other emotions
and lingers there like the painted, immovable background to a
work of art. Then as he spoke he sparked up again, noticing
the unceremonious pile of last night's wet clothes. I looked at
them too, lifeless and disregarded, and was gripped with the
strange sensation that it was me who was lying there.

'Honestly, Karri, I've been gone for twenty-four hours and
the place is already a mess.'

We had few possessions, barely enough to cause what could
rightly be considered a mess; at any rate my father always kept
them all in their rightful place, his books in particular. I looked
wearily about the room to see if anything had escaped its confines, but all was as I remembered.

The room was suspended in a dim light, for although the sun
had long since risen our window was small and singular, situ-
ated above the stove at the far end of the room. The sloped ceiling began about three feet from the wooden floor and peaked
just above this window; the beds were tucked cosily against the
wall, one at each side and a third, long since empty, standing
end-to-end with my own. I had adorned it with various things

– half finished knitting works in all colours and sizes, a clothes' chest, a few of my own books purposefully left open in certain places, and any things that I found lying around that I had been able to borrow for this purpose until my father reclaimed them – so that it no longer resembled a bed at all. Not really; not if I half-closed my eyes and willed it to be so.

With his woollen socks sounding soft on the old wood of the floor, Orri lit the lamp that stood on the table, and the room was bathed in a glowing warmth. He ruffled up his hair, somewhat restoring the familiar vibrant energy of his disposition, and took it upon himself to light the stove. 'This house,' he declared whilst rubbing his hands together over the welcomed heat source, 'is freezing.'

I noticed that there was snow piled up against the window. 'I've almost run out of peat,' I answered. I was still standing by the door. Although the door was closed, the chill remained.

'You dig it out of the ground,' Orri pointed out, helpfully.

'I've run out of *dry* peat.'

'Did you not buy some from Birgir? The man's a one-man peat factory.' A kettle appeared in his hand. 'In fact,' he added, for Orri was apt to think aloud, 'I'm surprised Olafur didn't organise it for you before he left: to ensure that he didn't get back from visiting his son to find that his other one had frozen to death.'

'I think he meant to.' I shuffled over to the stove and extended my bare hands to absorb the meagre heat. 'But things didn't go entirely to plan really, did they?'

Orri drew his hands back slightly from mine, far enough to avoid their touching, though not so far that he thought I might notice. I did, of course, though I did not want to ask about his motives. I had done so once before, and his discomfort had transcended into plain view. He shifted his feet. 'So you haven't heard any news, then? From Kálvur, or... ?'

I shook my head. A closed answer. I had not heard from my brother since he left, nor from my father since the postal connections with Denmark had been severed. And Orri knew this.

'Still,' he said airily, as I gazed at my feet, 'if you haven't heard from him – or from either of those brothers of yours – then that's nothing new. Nothing's changed. Which means they're probably fine. Georg will still be cutting up people's arteries and attaching them to other organs, I expect. Or whatever it is he does for a living.'

I smiled to myself: Orri employed his own special flavour of optimism, contagious simply for being slightly ridiculous. 'He's a surgeon, Orri; not Doctor Frankenstein.'

Orri was laughing: his eyes shone out like ever-present stars. His skin had become flushed, not the previous rough pink it had been from exposure to the harsh weather but now warm;

he had natural colour in his cheeks. The gentle light of the oil lamp fell about his face, smoothing the contours of his cheekbones in a way that caused him to appear younger and his eyes larger and rounder. He ran his fingers through his hair again and it lay tousled in all directions, as always.

'Do you know,' he began as he handed a mug of boiling hot tea into my grateful fingers (having assured me that all I needed was a cup of tea, and the entire world, to the farthest stretches, would heal itself. Or something to that effect). 'I think I'm going to enjoy having you around. Do you have any milk?'

'I – what? No, no milk. Peat and milk – completely out now. What do you mean? I've been around for years; you've barely been able to get rid of me.'

'I mean,' he explained as he sat cross-legged on the bed beside me, a smile playing about his lips, 'while you're staying with us, it'll be good to have you there.' I detected a faint blush of colour at this confession. 'I've no desire to get rid of you.' He took a thoughtful sip of tea. 'Not yet.'

My reaction momentarily delayed by my scrutiny of his colour, I was able to give a more tamed response than my initial desire to assert my independence would have allowed. This, I reminded myself, was not the main issue which fuelled my reluctance to answer. I had spent indefinite stretches of time with Orri and his family in the course of the preceding year, yet worried always that I might be overstaying my welcome. I had therefore on each occasion retired back to my own little house amid sharp protests from Orri. 'Thanks,' I began in as warm a manner as was possible, 'but I'm staying here.'

As I should have anticipated, the boy did not subject me to questioning on the matter, but laughed wholeheartedly. It was always as if he were laughing at some inner hilarity known only to himself; this impression enhanced by the knowing sparkle in his eyes. 'You're not staying here, Karri!' he pronounced, almost spilling his tea. 'You have no peat and no milk, and God only knows what else you're missing and can't provide for! How long will it be before the roof disappears as well?' Another bout of giggles followed. He shook his head and now with a degree of seriousness, said, 'You can't spend the rest of the winter here alone.'

I protested anyway, if only for my own conviction: whether I went through it alone or not I wanted to establish that it was at least possible, that I could manage if I wanted to. Or had to.

'I don't have to be self-sufficient in everything; we live in a community after all: we all provide for everyone else. Peat from Birgir, like you said, and he's a dairy farmer as well. We may not own a family cow, but–.'

'But it's snowing!' Orri exclaimed, pointing a long finger towards the gathering snowdrift against the window. This was by no means a startling revelation, or indeed a particular cause for concern: snow generally did tend to fall during the winter –

it was expected. The only possible harm of the weather was to the livestock. Perhaps in Orri's eyes I bore a close resemblance to the sheep in the outfield pasture. I pointed this out to him, and once more he fell about laughing. I could not hold back the smile that pricked the corners of my mouth.

'Karri, I could barely find the house today.' He had managed to compose himself successfully enough to harness speech. 'The snow fell so deeply last night. I arrived at a vaguely building-shaped mound of snow where I was sure your house had stood yesterday, and for a good twenty years before that, and I thought: 'My God, it's been *bombed*!' He beheld my bemused – albeit entertained – expression, while still keeping his vigour of speech. 'You'll get snowed in.'

The house's old-fashioned turf roof did in fact stand rather low to the ground and the floor *was* partly sunken, as though it was gradually disappearing, to be lost within the turf of the fields.

'At least then I will be warmer.' I swallowed a wonderfully hot mouthful of properly brewed tea – only Orri could make it so.

He had been watching me as I in turn stared absentmindedly at the wall, with all its arbitrary patterns and twisted shapes, ingrained faces and suggestive scratches. Every inch had become so personal to my eyes, for as a young boy I had imagined that within the wall there were people, words and stories, so vivid and imaginative was this detailed, private world. Upon my turning to look at him, Orri's eyes continued to sparkle for an extended moment, as though the action of my looking had not quite clicked in his perceptions yet; then a warm grin spread over his features.

'I'm not convinced,' he admitted. Nor was I. But I could not take up so warm an invitation simply because it appealed to my desire for company and a place of safety. I had no wish to encroach upon the lives of others for it was unfair to those who suddenly found themselves required, or obliged, to look after me. The thought had always made me uncomfortable.

'Oh, Orri,' I said, dejected at the loss I must suffer. 'I can't, I really can't; I mean... you've got enough on your hands looking after Magnus.' I ran a finger around the warm, familiar edge of the mug. 'I'd just get in the way. And I'd never wish that responsibility on all of you.'

'Kjartan.' Although he still smiled, the laughter had subsided and his speech was now more in earnest. 'You always say this and I always tell you the same thing: you will not be getting in the way!' He flapped his hand in exasperation. 'And Magnus being ill doesn't change anything; hell, he'll be glad of the company of someone other than his immediate family, who won't bloody leave him alone – he's trapped in the house with us. I mean, an interesting selection of locals drop round all the time with little presents and various anecdotes concerning fish, but they only stay until the tea's gone cold. They have their own agendas. And anyway, you know how fond he is of you. You're practically part of the family.'

I bit my lip: how dearly I wished this were true.

'We could turn the bed into a fishing boat?' he suggested, following a moment's quiet. 'Like we used to.'

I sighed, let my eyelids fall shut. 'Orri... '

'Or you can curl up in the tin bath for a night's kip.' He sounded a little exasperated now. 'Or with the chickens. I don't care. Just come for a little company at least, stop letting me worry myself sick about you.'

I nodded, drew in my long legs and wrapped my fingers more tightly around the cup. The walls entwined themselves around me, simple and plain – in the way that only wood can be – yet adorned with so much detail, mind-imposed order and character, anthropomorphic. Sometimes it did not matter to me what happened outside; sometimes I was sure that not a single thing came to pass and nothing existed. And this was comforting – for what, then, was there to worry about?

'We can go later,' Orri said quietly. Almost apologetically I only nodded again, struggled to meet his eyes. 'Magnus wants to talk to us about something... but I suppose he's not going anywhere... '

I heard the deflation in his voice, and my heart ached. 'What does he want to see us about?'

He shrugged; then all at once the grin took up its next-to-permanent residence, and it was undoubtedly genuine. 'Fish, presumably.'

8

IT WAS NOT that I was leaving home, for Orri lived all of one hundred metres away, therefore I was able to return whenever I liked. This I intended to do, for I could not take all of my books with me. I chose a couple with great difficulty and packed them into an old bag with a few items of clean clothing, my notebook and pen, and more pairs of socks than I could possibly require – to be on the safe side.

'You can survive anything,' I explained to Orri at his inquisition into this extravagance, 'as long as you have dry, comfortable feet. It is the basis of northern civilisation.'

Personal survival kit accounted for, I was accosted nevertheless with a strange finality as to my actions. Perhaps my mind was away in Denmark with my father, or drifting across a cold, grey sea as now he must surely be, within the cold, grey mechanics of a thoughtless war.

The snow had fallen deeply overnight, though positioned as we were, exposed to the open sea and all its desolate winds, the winter's blanket was unlikely to linger so fully for much longer before it gave way to the more familiar claws of frost and the harsher hand of the season. The village lay especially pretty in the pure whiteness, helpless and unmoving; it was already late in the morning and for most people the daily rituals had long since begun. The turf roof of my empty house glistened, the snow-drift piled up most deeply against one outside wall. The door gazed back at me somewhat forlornly as we trod Bøur's narrow streets between closely-knit houses, under the ashen sky and the framing presence of the two adjoining mountains which met barefaced and unremitting in the valley behind the village.

Open and shallow, the valley cut a thickly meandering path away into the low clouds. Into this the carefully separated fields were sewn in as patchwork – full of sheep and bare of crops and hay for the season, increasingly they attained a higher gradient until they lay all but vertical. It was a wonder the livestock did not simply drop off them.

With its back to this rugged splendour, facing modestly out towards an endless sea, Bøur lay near to the head of the fjord, on the north side, nestled like a small clump of rare flowers growing from the bare rock. An insignificant cluster of small houses that, as a boy, I had feared would one day slip quietly into the water, unnoticed. The colour of the painted wooden walls would wash away with the tormented waves, leaving only dispersed traces, like blood in the wake of a whale hunt. To the south side of the fjord, characterised like most of the Islands' coasts by its immense, vertical cliffs, stood two absurd islets in the path of the waves: Gáshólmur curved as an inelegant arch, a vacant centre through which could be seen the open sea, the world imagined; and Tindhólmur –

'Earth to Kjartan.'

'What?'

'We're here.'

'Oh. So we are.'

'Well, are you going to come in?' Orri asked as we stood windswept on his front doorstep before a doorway that gaped open towards the sea. 'Or shall I leave you out in the snow?'

'Err... I think I might come in... ' The doorway was low, lower than I remembered, lower even – so it seemed – than at the time of my last visit a mere three days earlier. It was, however, a very accommodating doorway, and to my recollection always had been; a larger point of entry would doubtless fail to instil such a homely feeling. As usual with little thought, I stooped slightly and entered the house.

Orri, in his emphatic demeanour, had been known on many an occasion to forget this simple act and had thus hit his excitable head against the top of the frame. This time he managed to remember and as I dawdled uncertainly, he hopped from one foot to the other in a process I assumed to be a special way of taking off his shoes: his long legs flitted in and out of his own control and his left hand flattened intermittently against the wall in support. The shoes were followed by the woollen gloves, the coat and the hat, which he ruffled his hair with on removing.

His things lay disregarded on the wooden floor of the narrow hallway and the boy himself had skipped with impatience away through the kitchen, leaving behind an encouraging grin. By the time all this had occurred I had managed only to remove my hat, having stood dumbly for some time with the thing in my hands, and my hands clasped before me as Orri danced that most peculiar of dances and with it occupied most of the hall's space. As he disappeared from sight with an unseen gasp of, 'Hi, Mum, I've got Kjartan – he's in the hall doing an impression of a hat stand,' I hung my coat from one of the pegs along with Orri's discarded belongings.

'Thanks, Kjartan,' said the small, blonde woman now standing in the dim hallway. 'Heaven knows when my son will learn to do these things for himself.'

I made to answer in the vein that Orri possessed a vivacious drive to do everything and anything all at once and thus all things escaped his grip like a fresh catch; but as she continued speaking I got the impression her prior remark had simply been to fill in the time or make known her presence, I don't know why. Something about her apparent reluctance to meet my gaze. She was already turning away as she asked, 'Would you like a cup of tea?'

I answered yes and followed her into the kitchen, again ducking my head marginally to miss the door's heavy beam. She busied herself immediately at the stove. Once more I sensed that her asking had been merely a matter of social courtesy as opposed to a homely gesture of welcome. I shifted with discomfort on my slightly damp, woollen-clad feet, for she seemed grudging in her movements to accommodate me. Her lips were pursed, her deep-set eyes with wrinkles about the corners were fixed on her task. Her arm movements were pronounced and deliberate as the pots and the kettle clanged tunelessly.

Eventually two mugs of tea were delivered into my waiting hands, though still she did not meet my eyes. I gushed my gratitude to her for going to such trouble, trying not to begrudge her for the stiff, vacant smile she gave me; after all, she had her mind on other things. I must surely be getting under her feet. Ásdis had always been a rather reserved figure, never a woman open to hilarity and free-spirit like her unquenchable son and his father with all their good humour.

As if on cue I heard an explosive peal of mingled laughter from father and son. It came rushing down the short, narrow staircase that rose almost as a tunnel from the opposite end of the tiny kitchen, next to the cowshed door. The bedroom was positioned over the cowshed and the heat emanating from the livestock served as under-floor heating, as was the traditional method. The resultant vague earthen smells were soon experienced as nothing more than a background aroma, not unpleasant once the nose had grown accustomed.

I managed the steep, narrow steps below the low ceiling whilst balancing two mugs of tea with only a little spillage. The steps turned out to be the easy part, for as I moved through the amalgamation of bedroom and living area and entered Magnus's private room through the adjoining door, the voice of the man in question called out in such an enthusiastic manner that it took all my self-restraint to stop myself from hurling the mugs across the room in nervous surprise.

'Morning, Kjartan, lad!'

It was a strong voice with which he spoke; still a strong voice, though perhaps not as powerful as it had once been. It seemed nonetheless remarkable that a man in such an advanced stage of illness as to be confined more or less constantly to his bed should still possess such a full, jovial manner of speech. I had previously considered it impossible for a man of Magnus's stature to waste away but the growing difficulty with which he rose, walked, or even moved his weakened muscles had become increasingly apparent.

In painfully tangible time, with his belt tighter and his cheeks looking hollow, Magnus had retired, resigned himself to his permanent bed. He was persuaded to rise occasionally, with effort, and was helped to tread the few stairs and ultimately achieve the goal of reaching the front door. There, wrapped in coats and blankets against the talons of winter which were as sharp as those of the illness, he would sit and breathe the fresh air. On a good day he might also make his slow, stumbling way around the walls of the house, unaided if he felt this to be at all manageable. Some days were better than others; some were cripplingly worse; eventually they became indistinguishable more or less.

I could not help but feel, though I truly despised myself for such a thought – that we were caught in a waiting game. Still, what I lacked in intrinsic optimism, the man himself made up for in spirit. A figure of blunt realism, he would most likely affirm with bright eyes and a grin of acceptance that the whole of life itself was a waiting game, regardless of additional personal misfortune – *all part of the experience*, he would say cheerfully.

Magnus lay propped like a limp straw doll against what could possibly be the family's entire supply of pillows, tucked in with woollen blankets. I could see that on the miniscule table by his bed there stood some form of hot drink in waiting. Its smell was unusual, medicinal; I had not known Magnus to accept medical treatment of any kind before – *this new sorcery, lads: more folk have been harmed than cured. Fresh air, mind, now that'll do the trick good and proper!*

Perhaps now he thought differently. Or not...

'Ah, real tea!' he exclaimed as I handed Orri his mug. 'The drink of kings, lads, surely – at least that's how it seems now that I'm denied it... Can't be doing with this newfangled hocus-pocus.'

He eyed his own medicinal cup with evident distaste. 'Chuck it out the window, will you, lad? So she'll think I finished it.'

Orri, whom he had addressed, leaned confidently back in his chair with an air of humorous disapproval, and stretched out a pair of long legs to rest on the side of his father's bed. 'Just learn to drink the bloody thing.'

'And make a sick man even sicker?' Magnus scowled, though still with good humour, into his beard, the one aspect of his body that appeared to have gained strength and vigour. 'Vile stuff, that modern medicine, Orri lad, vile stuff. *Poison.* I could piss in a cup and it'd taste better than that.'

His son clicked his tongue with just enough incredulity to suggest he might possibly agree, unwound his legs and picked up the cup, then hurled its contents with satisfied gusto from the snow-framed window which he had pushed open. The claws of December crept over the sill before he had closed it again.

'Good lad,' congratulated the sick man. With quiet glee and an air of success, he rearranged the collection of blankets about his chest before clasping his large hands again in so firm and conclusive a manner as to suggest business. His eyes appeared to gaze inwards at some idea that wished without delay to be communicated. 'Now then: sit down, you two... ' His voice bubbled with undertones of excitement, the sort of pleasure that arises from the ability to impart knowledge, teach in the ways of trade, and ultimately plan out courses of action and ideas.

I looked around at the sea of chairs before me. The act of sitting down ought to have presented little difficulty but as the chairs were so many and the room so small I found myself at somewhat of a loss as to the best way to negotiate this labyrinth, even had I a choice of chair in mind. The space between Magnus's bed and the bookcase by the window – in essence, the room – was impassable; I had needed to reach over the throng of furniture, balanced precariously, in order to successfully deliver the cup of tea.

'Err... *where* should I sit, Magnus?'

'On a chair, lad!' came the reply, in annoyance that business proceedings should be further delayed. 'There are plenty of them.'

I chose one by hopping over a couple of others, spilling tea on a couple more, and sat down. Orri was as usual poised on the brink of laughter. Magnus frowned, one bushy eyebrow dipped and the other raised along with the corresponding corner of his upper lip. He was evidently in confusion as to why I should take so long to find a seat and effectively prepare myself for the undertaking of business discussion. Truth be told, I knew vaguely what to expect, or at any rate was capable of hazarding an intelligent guess: his profession could not be disregarded or made redundant (as with most other previous features of his daily life) in the wake of crippling illness. It was a business and fish must be caught and fish must be sold, come rain or shine, come Magnus or no Magnus.

In these times, of course, there was no Magnus. So the responsibility had required to be transferred to another levelheaded person of equal if not simply potential capabilities. At first I had thought that Orri might be handed the crown, from father to son and heir, as it were. But of course Orri was too young and inexperienced; this was no longer homespun local fishing: the war had caused an unbelievable increase in trade, in prices, in requirements for fresh Faroese fish to be shipped for rationed English consumption.

But they wanted fish, and we had fish to offer, an abundance of fish at our fingertips. Funny how one people's despair is another's profit. Given this, the responsibility had been awarded to one of Magnus's longstanding men. And given Magnus's immense popularity with both his men and the local people, Jón – the 'lucky man', so to speak – regarded Orri as a son of his own. Indeed they were all fond of Orri, and even more so since the continual deterioration of Magnus. Thus Orri was still involved, still played a useful role and I with him, as were the insistent wishes of the man in charge from the bed that was now his office.

Can't have you sitting down and reading all the livelong day, Kjartan; books won't feed a nation, you know! Boy of your age needs to keep his hands busy, learn himself a trade, get some experience under his belt, isn't that right, lad?

And so had the weekly fish market followed. I was thrilled to be involved, even if I lingered somewhat on the outside – a pretender, often a fraud, but keen to learn nonetheless. And in no way had it been a complete disaster, for Orri and I had been awarded further smaller tasks in a pattern that revealed itself increasingly more frequently. Thus I came simply to expect another task, perhaps this time of a more permanent nature given the fisherman's attitude of stirring anticipation – 'Now then, boys, I have a little favour to ask... '

9

I HAD BEEN for some time plagued by a recurring dream. It came and went like the tide, like the Island's low clouds; it filtered through my semi-consciousness like liquid trickling into the cracks. I began to doubt the possibility of escape even in the hours of waking, such was the strength of its impression.

I am resting at the base of the mountain – standing, sitting, the state is inconsistent – and over me it casts its long shadow, caused by a sun so low in the sky that it cannot be seen. I have been following it, the sun, for so long, trying to find the place where it rests above the horizon, a heavy orb, seconds from being extinguished. It remains always just out of sight, as though it anticipates my approaching steps and mimics them so that the distance between us is constantly maintained, and although I am exhausted and fatigued to the point of utter hopelessness, I have effectively moved not a mile at all, not even an inch.

The mountain's shadow is as solid as the object itself, over my head in an opaque canopy. It follows me wherever I go, and the places to which I move seem to be all the same place. There are people there, people I have known throughout my entire existence who are close to me, mean something to me that is irreplaceable. But in that place they are malicious in character; we have fleeting conversations that I cannot recall but I am tortured by their words, in a helpless rage at their backs which are turned to me in dismissal.

I know that I deserve this, and as a result I am gripped by an anger that transcends to uncontrollable hysteria. I hear screams, I hear shrieks and whispers and moans, possibly uttered by me, but of no effect upon the ears of my assailants. Sometimes they laugh, their faces twisted in shadows, and their mouths contorted in teasing malice, ugly and terrifying. And when I awake my lips are always salty with the lingering taste of fear.

After a long eternity of a night, the morning dawned. I was dully surprised, my perceptions curiously misplaced, for through the irretrievable depths of a dark night it had seemed that the sun would never rise. That there was no sun of which to speak, for I had forgotten its warmth, its rays; its colour.

Each time I struggled helplessly into consciousness the silence did not simply *meet* my ears, it tore at them with an abrupt cessation of cacophony. I only became aware of the screeching voices that had assailed me once they had leapt to a sudden stop. Thus it seemed the void of the night had been dropped on me from a great height, and impaled me to the bed.

Day still managed to break through, however, and with the sun I rose also. I made the mandatory cup of morning tea in Orri's kitchen, then put on my coat, my hat and my scarf: all of winter's paraphernalia. I shuffled outside in my thick socks and boots and smoked a cigarette, sipping tea while ruminating on my dreams until I deemed the morning sufficiently advanced as to constitute the breaking-in of a new world.

The snow still lay as a blanket on the ground, though less heavily than on the previous day, and with a greyer hue. My little house peered, as always, between the black timber walls and turf roofs of Bøur's other houses. It seemed to ask me, 'Well, Kjartan, what's the matter? What were you expecting?' And I shrugged as I stubbed out my cigarette, for I did not know.

I brewed another cup of tea, lit another cigarette, and resumed my position. And I waited; waited for a light to reveal itself and explain to me how I ought to feel.

Surely, it had only been one year since I had said an empty goodbye to my father at Tórshavn harbour, but already I was having difficulty remembering him. He did not seem like a father of mine any longer, though I missed him sorely nonetheless. It was as though he had left the face of the planet, and I was abandoned, and everything had sparked into a vibrant, non-linear sort of life that required my undivided attention. For if I did not award it this, then I would lose a foothold on reality. I would lose my way, dead to all but my own solipsistic understanding. It was this thought, perhaps, that caused me to look upon Tindhólmur with a different eye that morning.

The islet would loom into view every morning as I left the house and it appeared unusual even at the best of times. During the night it had acquired an anthropomorphic character – Tindhólmur had invaded my thoughts as soon as it had been uttered from the lips of Magnus the previous day.

Tindhólmur rose from the destructive sea a short distance from the headland at the opposite side of the fjord, and Bøur looked directly upon it. It was an islet of towering rock, one side of which sloped at an increasing incline to a five-peaked summit. Each peak was jagged and razor-sharp, nearly three hundred metres high. On the other side the peaks fell away again as a sheer cliff face of bare, torturous rock.

The islet could appear two-dimensional on some days, as though crudely and roughly hewn out of paper and pasted onto the grey seascape. The waves hurled themselves against it, refusing to let it stand peacefully, for it cut both the sea and the sky into fragments. It was inhabited once, apparently, or according to legend at least, but so easily does legend become history.

This particular segment of history concerned a family; a father, a mother and a child. For some reason they had thought it a good idea to settle on the unforgiving slopes of Tindhólmur, battered by the sea and screamed at by the wind. While the father was out fishing one day an eagle swooped down to instigate, as eagles do, a theft. It was the child that was taken. The eagle, grey wings against a grey sky over a grey sea, stole the child away to its nest atop one of the peaks; and the distraught mother followed, climbing all the way up those turrets of rock, up to the highest point to rescue her poor child, only to discover that the eagle had pecked out the child's eyes, later causing it to die from its injuries. And so the couple moved away from Tindhólmur, and everything remained unchanged.

The story had borne unto me no significance or cause for thought until now – stories are fiction after all. Though of course once the subject of the fiction is brought to one's attention it becomes suddenly an intrigue, and the ideas that one has encountered in passing amass into a homespun curiosity that calls for some form of clarification.

Now that I came to think of it, one of the peaks was named '*Arni*' – Eagle...

'... And *Ytsti, Litli, Breiði, Bogði*.' I recited the names of the others as I finished my cigarette.

10

I PEERED IRRITABLY into the encompassing mist around the peaks. A long time had passed since I had seen the summits clearly; at least, I think it had been some time: the details of my memory were even less distinct than the rocks themselves. I could see them intermittently as our little boat drew closer, though only as obscure shapes and dim shadows that seemed to flitter about with the curling of the mist, never stationary, never definite, trying always to slip from the senses as though they were never there, as though they desired to mask some deep secret.

It was impossible to determine when these low-lying clouds had first taken up residence as curtains to the towering peaks, the Islands were so often shrouded in the northern weather's sulk. That wispy cloud coverage over all highest points was liable to come and go like the tide, or linger indefinitely for as long as it pleased as simply a featureless extension of the grey northern sky. But I was certain, as I cast back my recollection with more than a degree of desperation, that these clouds in particular had withstood many a coming and going of the tide, many a day of otherwise clear sky, dispersing not an inch, and effectively masquerading as a permanent landscape feature, indistinguishable from all else around them.

Perhaps my imagination was running away with itself due to lack of meaningful sleep and the subsequent tendency to dwell on the border of the unreal, but as our boat approached Tind-hólmur's base, through the low clouds lingering some hundred metres above us, I caught a suggestion of colours and structural shapes on its slopes, entwining themselves through the tendrils of mist. Only for one fleeting moment, before it was lost to the damp precipitation, and my hair was plastered to my forehead, the sea roared in its consistent way and my feet were uncomfortably damp.

'Do you not find this a little strange?' I inquired of Orri, my voice hanging forlornly in the heavy air. I was sitting at the blunt rear of the boat, which was barely two metres long and constructed of wood painted a faded, earthen green. Despite its expert craftsmanship, I could not help but distrust the safety of the boat in such disagreeable weather.

'Find what a little strange?' Orri asked from the boat's prow, where he clung tightly onto the sturdy oars, forcing them against the waves.

'*Find what a little strange*, he asks.' I was all the more irritable for being wet and uncomfortable. '*This*, Orri; I mean, what is it we're *doing*, exactly?'

'What Magnus has asked us to do,' he answered curtly.

Orri was not one to ask questions or inquire into his father's judgement or actions. I was not prone to this either; but ordinarily they made at least *some* sense, and I was able to see the reasons and benefits for and of such actions. My trust in Magnus was not so great though, that I would carry out any utterly incomprehensible request without a fair amount of free thinking on my part, whether or not I put my thoughts into words.

Orri had voiced upon casting off from our home island that common enquiry: 'Are you okay?' I had replied in the affirmative with the kind of smile for use when one has no appropriate response to employ, though perhaps I was not as convincing as I might have been for he kept throwing me long, drawn-out glances, laced with concern.

Maybe he wanted to ask me how I was managing in my father's continued absence, but was somehow afraid to; each time it seemed he was about to speak he would divert his gaze in a troubled thoughtfulness and continue to row monotonously. Whatever the case, I was determined not to allow the inquiry to arise again, and to focus attention instead upon something more worthwhile.

'There can't possibly be anyone *living* over here,' I thought aloud. 'Can there?'

Orri shrugged between strokes of the oar. 'For fear of child-snatching eagles, you mean?'

I was not in the mood for facetiousness. His tone was forced, as though he might be hiding something.

'*Is* there anyone living here?'

'I don't know, Karri. Does it matter?'

'But Magnus knows.' My tone was accusatory. 'And yet he wouldn't tell us – *why* is he insisting on keeping secrets?'

'I don't know, Karri,' Orri repeated. 'Perhaps he wants us to find out for ourselves. Essence of adventure and all that. You know what he's like.'

Sure enough, when I had pestered Magnus upon the allocation of the long-term task for an explanation, he had replied simply with a knowing smile and a sparkle in his eyes that was barely contained. He had positively brimmed over with something akin to excitement. With Magnus everything transcended into excitement, there lay interest even in the most mundane of things.

I hopped nimbly from the boat to secure it to the rocks of Tindhólmur's shore. The mist was so thick and low that I feared if I straightened my back just an inch, my head would become enveloped and lost within it, such was its disregard for dimension. The bite of the air was icily cold, and pure white snow lay on the lower slopes of the islet, the only part which remained visible to the eye.

As I threw the bag of fish, milk and other nondescript food-stuffs upon the ground a little way up these slopes, I was gripped by a fresh burst of restless perplexity. 'This has got something to do with the garrison, hasn't it? No one in the *village* has mentioned anyone living on Tindhólmur. Have they stationed some of the troops here?' I opened my arms in exasperation. 'Here on this uninhabited and uninhab*itable* lump of rock?'

'Who knows, Karri?' Orri sighed from where he had remained in the boat, his bare hands still grasping the oars. 'No one can possibly know what they are up to, and what they are doing on our islands. Can we go now, please? I'm cold.'

As I clambered back into the boat, clumsy in my irritation, I was hit with force by another thought: 'He's been doing this himself, hasn't he?'

'Who has?'

'Magnus! He's been rowing out here himself twice a week for... for who knows how long? But no one ever thought to ask, no one even *noticed* or deemed it worthy of noticing, because it's Magnus, and we know he always has a reason for everything he does! In the name of business, normally, and who are *we* to understand that as well as he?' I dropped my arms and let out a deep sigh. 'Well, they're all going to ask questions now, aren't they? They're all going to notice, now that it's *us* inexplicably rowing out here rather than Magnus; and they'll ask why we're pottering around Tindhólmur in a little boat... and what will we answer? We'll tell them we don't bloody know... '

'Who's 'them', Kjartan?'

Orri's voice carried no hint of annoyance; but rather was soft, and his eyes were wide and friendly as they beheld me. Was there something unnaturally contained within his gaze? A fear of upsetting me further, maybe? As he shifted his eyes I perceived in them an emotion resembling compassion. I faltered, and in the weak search for the point I intended to communicate, the best that could be located was: 'Everyone!' The tail end of the word drifted away into deflation and once again I could do nothing but sigh deeply.

Orri smiled and brushed moisture from his hair and face with a languorous determination. 'Do you really care?'

I opened my mouth silently, shrugged before giving up altogether on trying to instigate a response when I did not know what I wished to communicate. I hung my head dejectedly.

Orri, conversely to his father's enthusiasm, was exhibiting an uncharacteristic lack of interest in our task. His silence suggested more than unconditional trust in Magnus and his judgements; it was as though he had known what to expect from his father, as if there was no secrecy between the two of them. I was the one who must choke on the frustrating mystery of the situation, and for this I could not help but feel hurt.

Obstinately I said nothing as we rowed back to the island. Orri did not offer any explanation. His discomfort was plain to see.

***

True, it was of no issue what the townspeople said in respect of our bizarre trips to Tindhólmur. Yet the inherent pointlessness of the proceedings continued to plague my fragile sense of displacement to the extent that I viewed all fish – or even their mention – as a cause of anxiety and contempt.

'*So, what do we have today?*' I was asked in the fish market the following day, and I replied bitterly: 'Fish.' A small pause. 'Any you can recommend?'; 'Well, in the corner there we have some white fillets of an indiscriminate nature, perhaps we could call it cod; some stockfish to the other side there. More cod. And if that doesn't catch your fancy then might I suggest emigration?'

I was unable to close my mind to the fingers of insecurity that crept in uninvited. This was a different home, a different set of world affairs, different company, and a different winter. And I was cautious, for it seemed that everything might suddenly dissolve – one morning, one moment, without my realising, and I was helpless against it. And if this changed world was on edge, poised on an unforeseen brink, then so was I – for how can one stand firmly on a ground that shifts through all possibilities, and is in essence nothing at all, if not just itself a possibility?

I dreamt often of a distorted, otherworldly interpretation of Tindhólmur, a distortion that, given its increasing vividness in these moments of light sleep, came to seem ever the more real. More so in fact, than the genuine article that had stood before me, inanimate, for nearly twenty years. And I had stood looking back at it in the same manner: inanimate.

These snatched dreams served to realign what seemed to me more and more out of place the greater the degree with which I straightened my head to inflict upon it a long, searching look.

I was sitting on top of Tindhólmur's highest peak. Its dimensions were exact and I stood no taller or larger than usual so as to be able to wrap both of my hands around that jagged turret upon which I was placed. Yet, dreams being inconsistent with reality, our dimensions, both human and mineral were obsolete and thus the two of us were of a similar size, though we each fluctuated between all ratios. With my hands of human size, I smoothed out the mountainous summits, teased their paper-thin, scissor-hewn edges into smooth, direct points towards the sky. I unfolded every inconsistency, every corner, ironed every crease with my fingertips; concentrated in earnest upon my task.

The sky gave me a blank look, a mournful insistence of oblivion behind its gaze, and absorbed all else into nothing more than mirrored fragments of its emptiness.

And, broken, I wept with the sky and all: at everything, nothing; that was left.

11

Spring 1941.

THE ARRIVAL OF springtime is inevitable: the seasons will change as the sun rises higher and higher in a desperate grasp for air and in anticipation that it might look over its thawing world from the high seat of the heavens. As the colours disperse under the frost's retreating claws, the world draws a deep breath. But for the world itself in the depths of winter, devoid of an exterior viewpoint from its own frozen claustrophobia, spring seems almost a myth.

Maybe the season will change in name, yet the bite of the air will remain, neither abating nor lingering with a vengeance, for such displays of drama are unnecessary for a realism that knows it has already won, already come to dominate. The frost and the snow will not commit themselves to deepen, but will simply remain eternal in the everlasting monotony of the season; the sun will hang its head low in the sky and, ashamed, will not look upon the world it has abandoned to savaged decomposition.

Then, suddenly, it all comes to an end. What had been lost springs into a new life. Overnight, it would seem, as though nothing had happened and nothing need ever happen again, save for the sorts of things that can easily be rectified, easily coloured in from the assumed, listless grey.

I awoke on this sudden spring morning as though an electric current had been passed through my lightly sleeping body. My heart hammered with uneasy energy and I sat bolt upright under the dislodged sheets of the bed before I had even come into full consciousness. I thought perhaps I had been called to life by the brief screech of a noise or maybe it was a sudden movement, but the room appeared unaltered. Orri lay peacefully asleep, his hair curled wildly about his pale face, contented in slumber. One white arm lay limply over the edge of his narrow bed as though pointing to the middle of the room where he had left the book he had been reading, having likely dropped off to sleep while reading it. The door to Magnus's small adjoining room stood dimly ajar, and I could hear him snoring vigorously, all but drowning out the more gentle breath of his sleeping wife in her makeshift bed on the floor. She insisted on continuing to sleep by her husband's side despite the apparent discomfort of her pallet. I thought of all the losses she had suffered, the unborn children and the sickly daughter whose little face I could only dimly recall. And now it was Magnus who lay dying. How scared she must be.

In keeping with the overbearing monotony of winter, the fisherman's condition had not worsened, nor had it improved. He had barely left the house in the previous months and as a result the room had become more confining. Magnus seemed smaller. Even his beard had succumbed to the claustrophobic diminishment of all things within.

There had been the usual spate of winter illnesses among the townspeople, though they had all recovered with a surprising vigour given the debilitating lack of natural daylight, even the most elderly patients for whom the winter was especially difficult. It was wonderful, of course, that they all should regain full health. Admittedly – and oddly – it was even better health than they had embodied previously; a fuller health than those members of the community who had not contracted the illnesses of winter. It was the ones who had remained 'healthy' who now appeared to be sick with their pale winter skin.

It seemed somehow unnatural, this excessive recovery, for ordinarily the season would not allow for this, at least not with such speed. Regardless (as we heard both from gossip and from the proud Danish doctor of Sørvágur), it happened in more or less every case in the district. Unfortunately Magnus was not one of those incredibly recovered patients. The man himself put the community's health down to 'these good, old-fashioned remedies; none of this new medicine rubbish.' He did not seem bitter.

Having dressed as quietly as possible that morning I tiptoed across the room, causing Orri to stir only slightly. I padded down the rickety stairs to the kitchen. It was brighter here for lack of curtains, the daylight so unusually soft and inviting that the stupor of sleep soon left me. Light glinted tranquilly from the pots and pans that hung from the wooden walls. The silver ladle beamed at me, whilst the squat stove sat quietly asleep. I devoured some bread left over from last night's meal, for an empty stomach does nothing to mar the chill of the early morning air, and concluded that my cup of tea must wait until I had returned.

The morning air did not disappoint me: its bite was as deep as the winter's, for this had crept away so quietly and so suddenly that some form of residue was no doubt inevitable – a reminder of the time when the world was clutched, struggling, in its grip. Although there was a brightness woven below the clouds, there was no sunlight, and the sharp hills were cut out in a strange patchwork of grey and brown. The sea and the sky were also grey, the latter a featureless sheen stretching back to infinity, and the former tempestuous.

I loved this time of the day. It had barely dawned, and I could hear nothing but the crashing of those slate waves against the jagged rocks a short distance away; there was not a soul about, not even the early-rising fishermen. I indulged in the feeling that I might be the first person to ever have the fortune to breathe this air. It bit into the bare skin of my face and ruffled up my hair to lift off the weight of sleep.

Barely minutes later and I was halfway along the road to the town of Sørvágur, my bike flying with an unbridled energy and the air stinging the inner expanse of my lungs. It was busier in the streets of the town as Sørvágur contained more people for the morning to coax out. Many more, in fact: the British troops had been continuing to arrive on our island of Vágar throughout the year and in the last few months had taken to visiting many of the houses in the town, so often were they invited.

Magnus was of course included in this socialising, and often I would return from a busy day in the open air to find the house full of uniformed troops involved in some eclectic card game, drinking tea and laughing with good humour. Orri would greet me, grinning, at the door, drunk on social encounters and the liveliness of his household, and generally a glass or two of akvavitt. He had even taken to practising his English and was improving rapidly, a cause of great excitement to him.

**

I cycled breezily through the sparsely populated streets, nodding an English, 'Good morning,' to the troops who had newly emerged for their day's work. A few of them I recognised from our frequent card games.

The post office stood just around the next corner. It was of typical Scandinavian design: timbered walls painted black and a corrugated iron roof, built as a house initially. The front door had been painted a bright red and though now a place of business the post office retained a homely atmosphere with practical and comfortable furniture and heavy, patterned curtains drawn back for the morning. Paintings by local artists hung on the worn wooden walls. The inside, as always, smelt of coffee: one could not last five minutes in the post office without being offered a cup of coffee, for within these four walls it had established itself as a very particular way of life, an absolute necessity, and only the very best coffee would suffice.

'Morning, Kjartan. I was just making some coffee, would you like a cup?'

'Thanks, Elva, that'd be lovely.'

I could not stand the taste of coffee, yet I was determined to carry out all that was required in order to attain comfort in the presence of another human being, the sort of 'comfortable' whereby conversation flows more or less readily to the lips and to the ears, and does not fill one with an overwhelming desire to break all contact and hurl oneself through the window to escape the discomfort involved in social discourse.

I always seemed to be at a distance of some sort, feeling like a fraud in conversation and in my general demeanour. I would read the body language and expressions of my peers, assess the tone of their voice and conclude ultimately that I was not wanted, for my inherent shyness no doubt made them uneasy. Thus, to drink a quick cup of coffee with Elva would essentially constitute a point of focus, a shared, common interest. Two mornings a week we would sit, without fail, at the post office desk, fiddle with stamps, sip coffee, and exchange a few words, generally concerning the stamps and the coffee.

'Good coffee, this,' mused Elva, in the spirit of things already. She adjusted her skirt to keep her hands busy. 'You'd never think there was a war on,' she continued brightly, 'with good coffee like this.'

I agreed with her, though I was not altogether clear on why the happening of a war should entail bad coffee. I could not discern, similarly, if the coffee was as good as was claimed; the taste was vile to my tongue whether there happened to be a war on or otherwise. I swallowed down another sip with pursed lips, enjoying at least the comforting heat of it. My companion made a similar move, but paused thoughtfully with the cup halfway up to her mouth. 'I don't suppose you'll have heard from your Olafur?' she inquired, though it would seem she knew the answer already.

I shook my head as I attempted to stomach another sip of coffee without my expression mimicking my insides. 'No,' I clarified, in case she had missed the movement of my head, for I was never sure how much attention she was giving to the conversation: she seemed only to make eye contact at times when she herself was the speaker. I was met with a nod of understanding, coupled with a sip of the coffee. I took the opportunity to ask her how her own family were keeping, so ardently did I desire to hear about her daughter, the captivating redhead, the girl I longed to see each time I visited the post office, the girl I always feared to see...

And then she appeared in the doorway.

If I had up to this point managed to subdue my desire to make a leap for freedom from the nearest window, then now my strength was tested. She appeared even more beautiful than the last time I had seen her. *Beautiful* not being a word I was given to employ often, the girl's unexpected appearance gave little leeway for vocabulary more fitting. And so this morning she was beautiful: thick red curls around a delicately pale face, waves of it falling over her slim shoulders and the curved shape of her breasts, down to a round waist, her clothing neatly arranged even at this otherworldly hour of the morning.

Automatically I reached up a hand to my own dark hair, anticipating full well the state in which it was likely to be lying after a restless night and the morning breeze. I brushed it out of my eyes with as subtle a movement as possible, decided that this would have to suffice for the time being, and turned my attention back to the coffee after the polite smile I offered her was returned by a sincere look of non-amusement, (a scowl, in my interpretation).

Her mother did not possess the attentiveness for such minor details, and thus proceeded to think aloud: 'Perhaps Kjartan will be kind enough to show you the ropes of the business, Asta.' (I blushed fiercely into my coffee.) 'You'd have the time to spare for that, wouldn't you, Kjartan?'

'Err... yes.'

'I don't need to be shown how to do my job,' said the girl. She threw me another scornful look from the doorway in which she stood with her white hands on her waist, one hip dipped slightly. I could not help noticing that her skirt rested just above her knees, a little shorter than was generally condoned, and her blouse lay undone, exposing the flawless hollow at her throat. I studied the ends of my nails ferociously and with burning cheeks.

'But of course you do, love.' Her mother was undeterred by the dismissive nature of Asta's posture and expression. 'And who better to help you with your experience than Kjartan? He's been with us for... is it nine months now, Kjartan?' She turned towards me with an air of thoughtfulness. I was given no time in which to answer. 'Nine months now,' she continued with firm intent, as though imparting to her daughter an in-disputable line of reasoning. 'And he's never put a foot wrong since he's been working for us, have you, Kjartan?' (Again, not a breath in which to hazard an answer.) Then, to her daughter: 'Now, don't look at me like that, love. You know he really is a lovely young man... '

I cast my eyes around the room for the nearest window. Asta sighed impatiently and I noticed her breasts rising and falling in one sweeping movement. She threw a hint of a smirk in my direction, accompanied by a raised, mocking eyebrow. I had never encountered such a proud and dominant girl, though I was given to wonder if this could partly be the reason for my infatuation, since she appeared to possess the traits and qual-ities I condemned myself for my inherent lack of. Perhaps it was my lack of self-confidence itself that predisposed me to in-terpreting every look she afforded me as a message of scorn. The little self-confidence I did possess seemed always to be plundered by her mannerisms, leaving me, in my weakness, at a greater degree of uneasiness than I had initially stood.

I pulled the sleeves of my scruffy grey jumper down over my hands and curled my fingers inside.

'... And you'd love to help Asta out, I'm sure, wouldn't you, Kjartan?' Elva puffed out her chest in pride at having organised a course of action. She gave me, of course, no time in which to even nod my compliance.

The girl's look was of pure poison now, I was certain. My overworked heart hammered painfully against my ribcage and I hated myself for possessing the ability only to incite this sort of negative response in such a beautiful girl.

No, it was not that she was beautiful, this was not the issue, for my heart was not in the habit of striving uncomfortably after beautiful girls; it was that she was *her*. I could not keep my eyes off her, I could not help but be drawn to every curve of that slender body, her graceful voice... and all else she embodied that conjured an inexplicable assertion of all that I longed for. She seemed to me unique, otherworldly in her beauty and magnetic in her attraction, and within me I carried a heavy heart for I knew I could never deserve someone so perfect. And so real. With intense, sharp eyes she knew more than I could ever hope to understand; in those eyes I no doubt appeared a useless, naïve boy from the village, with few words to pass my lips. I made to extract myself from the glare she had turned upon me, excuse myself from Elva...

'Would you like another cup of coffee?' the woman asked of me in earnest as, half-way up from my chair, I opened my mouth to speak. 'Err... no thanks, Elva.' I took a brief moment to collect myself. 'It's about time I delivered the post... '

⁕⁕⁕

The morning had still not begun at Magnus's family home as I positioned my bike against the outside wall, its worn tyres slipping slightly over the night's covering of snow. I peered through the window into a dim, lifeless room, and ran two fingers along the slight jut of the lower frame, brushing the snow over the sharp edge with glassy fingers and feeling the icy cut of the smooth wood underneath. I could see the condensation of my breath on the windowpane, a blank, misty canvas, sharply defined in the clear morning. With a numbing fingertip I formed *HELLO* backwards on the cold glass. All other words escaped me. I watched the fog disperse for a moment, then pulled on my woollen gloves, drew my scarf more tightly around my neck, and set off at a fast pace towards Gásadalur, dropping my feet at a heavier step than usual to loosen the bite of the cold snow through my boots.

The brown satchel bounced rhythmically from my right hip with every step, and with the same rhythm the letters inside made an ominous papery noise, oddly in harmony with the soft crunching of the snow that accompanied it. There was no fish to deliver today, and for this I was thankful, for I could not abide the faint, lingering smell from those brown paper parcels at this time of the morning. It was a long walk in which to be plagued by such an irritation.

Gásadalur was our neighbouring village, an even smaller settlement than Bøur: barely ten turf-roofed buildings, home to around fifteen inhabitants. Plenty of sheep, of course, in steep outfield pastures lining the bowl of the mountains which towered over the hamlet like the cupped hands of a protector. There was no road, for how could one hope to hew such a thing from the rocks of the mountains that lie at the head of the fjord?

The isolation of the place required me to cycle along the road from Bøur to Sørvágur, and back, in order to collect the letters from the post office. I had to head first through Bøur to deliver the first letters, then to walk around the mountainous head of the fjord, above the sea, to reach Gásadalur. Admittedly there was only a small amount of post that required to be delivered to the hamlet; the people of Bøur, in fact, should they need to contact their neighbours here, simply gave me the letters in person rather than visit the post office. Most of them, I expect, wrote these letters merely to give me something to do, to make my trip worthwhile, even if the correspondence was of no grave importance. But I did not mind, for it kept the channels of communication open, nurtured relationships and the sense of community. Through these written words flowed rivers of colour, ideas and imagination in their most secure, beautiful form; an entire world contained in the rhythm of words.

With this thought I glanced absentmindedly to my left, across the waves to Tindhólmur. Its unusual rocky peaks were still hidden in a shroud of opaque grey, as were my thoughts and inquisitions on the subject. I had looked in this direction a hundred times, surveying the crisp, clean, open morning in its season, but this time, within the veils of the permanently descended clouds, I definitely saw shapes.

Or at least, I thought I saw shapes: dark, indistinguishable shapes peering and dancing through the mist, which curiously appeared to be thinning around the jagged tops of the island, as though the sky were breaking into fragments around its sharp edges.

In a sudden burst of inspiration I clumsily pulled out from amongst the letters in my satchel the binoculars I carried to feed my vague interest in the birds of the island. The binoculars were of poor quality, but I fixed them on the distance all the same: as the mist cleared from the islet's upper slopes it struck me that they were much greener than I remembered, deeply so against the grey of the sea and sky; a shape hinting of red, perhaps, and... *Is that a chimney?*

Without my acknowledgement, or even permission, my feet sprang into action, skidding through the crunching snow down grassy slopes. The slopes were followed by narrow streets, defined by stone walls, through which my sprung feet carried me at a hectic run the short distance back to Magnus's black-timbered house, and through the door. They carried me past the kettle, past the sleeping stove, up the narrow steps to

Orri's side, and gently I shook him into consciousness. 'Orri! Orri, wake up! Quickly, come on, come with me!'

He groaned, his eyes half opened and trying with difficulty to focus on me.

'Karri, what the fuck? What time is it?'

'Just get up,' I urged in a strained whisper. 'You have to come and see this. Quickly, come on!'

I grabbed his hand as he rolled uncertainly out of bed, and led him anxiously down the narrow stairs and in the direction of the front door. He was still half asleep and unintelligibly murmuring, but managed to catch his coat as I pulled him out onto the front doorstep.

'There, Tindhólmur: do you see?'

He peered ahead into the distance through tired eyes.

'Do you see? It's – oh.' I caught my breath suddenly as, looking with Orri towards the subject of my agitation I saw the beginnings of rising slopes from the sea... and then a shroud of mist. There were no shapes. Surely the angle at which Bøur looked out upon the islet was not different enough to that of my previous position to warrant such a changed outlook. Or unchanged, as the case seemed to be. The summits, the slopes had hidden themselves again; the grey sea and the grey sky formed their blank, bleak canvas over my illusion.

For one long moment my thoughts were utterly lost. Feeling warm fingers intertwined with my own, I realised I was still clutching Orri's hand, and weakly let it go. My own fingers tingled heatedly, and I curled them back into the sleeves of my jumper. 'I saw a house, Orri, I'm pretty sure... There *is* someone living there.'

I continued to stare into the mist. When finally I turned to look at Orri I saw that he was lighting a cigarette, his coat now donned against the morning chill, sleeves pulled down over his knuckles. The cold air seemed to have woken him up. His fair hair was tousled haphazardly, and his light blue eyes were sunken and tired, yet still emitted the intelligent brightness with which I was so familiar.

'Like you said before, it's probably just something to do with the garrison.' He spoke through climbing tendrils of smoke. Though his words sounded nonchalant I saw the thoughtfulness behind his gaze, as though he, too, was attempting to make sense of the situation. But perhaps he was right: perhaps I was making a fuss about something over which we had no control, and no understanding. We had never known war, after all. 'You're right, Orri,' I conceded. 'How can we know what the garrison are up to?'

He watched me with intensity and the cigarette in his hand burned away slowly. I watched the falling ash, like snow in the still air. He must have come eventually to follow my gaze, for as if waking from a dream he lifted his hand up awkwardly to draw on his cigarette, realised it had burned itself out, and struck another match with fingers that seemed somehow diffi-cult to control. It was my turn to watch him. Finally he made eye contact. I was certain he must have thought that lack of sleep had robbed me of my senses, that I was confusing fiction with reality, legend with history: seeing the eagle's eyrie on Tindhólmur's peak, and even the ruins of the deserted family home...

'You'll come straight back afterwards, won't you? I'll make you some breakfast.'

I was unsure why he had asked, for there was no reason for me to linger around in Gásadalur once the post had all been delivered. I nodded anyway, for he seemed to have warded off any further discussion. With heavy movements he handed me what remained of his cigarette, and with a tired smile, disap-peared back inside and closed the door.

It was with leaden legs that I began the renewed ascent of the mountain path. The morning was progressing rapidly, and I began to hurry my steps, for although there was no pressing need to complete the job quickly, I enjoyed it only when I was entirely alone. Above the crashing of the sea, out of sight of both lower villages – Bøur behind me, Gásadalur over the mountain before me – there was only the mountain and me.

No people, no fish, no worries. And during the lambing season even the sheep could not be seen this far afield. The mountain and I got along wonderfully, each at home in the company of the other. I completed the tiring journey to the neighbouring village without once looking behind me to Tind-hólmur, leaving the letters and packages on each doorstep so as to avoid having to attempt conversation with the recipients, then I had no choice but to face the islet. As I came again to the open top of the mountain, the only place I could ever truly breathe, Tindhólmur came so obtrusively into view that even this loose comfort was taken away from me. I tried my best to turn a blind eye. All was beautifully silent.

12

BØUR HAD AWOKEN by the time I returned, cold but re-freshed. On my way back into the village I stopped outside the church for I liked to read the notices displayed outside. They offered lessons in this or that and informed of social occasions. There were also personal messages and other things related. The church itself was small and simple, modest but with a sense of low-key profundity. It was built, like the houses, from black timber, its roof of grey slate that shone darkly in the fre-quent rain, and its short spire was white. Inside there was no décor, simply a few rows of wooden pews on either side of an aisle, lit dimly by the constant welcoming glow of oil lamps.

I entered slowly – the small door was always left unlocked – and stepped carefully across the floor, enjoying the quiet, hollow tapping of the soles of my shoes on the dark wood beneath my feet; the only sound, the only movement. I laid down my almost empty bag on a pew near the altar, sank down onto my knees, clasped my hands together, and began to pray.

I was not a firm believer in God; did not even know if I was in fact a believer at all. I was not ordinarily given to such open practices of faith. But recently it had seemed right, as long as I did not question but kept my mind serenely closed – and provided I was alone. I prayed for the fishermen of our district and their continued safe return; I prayed that the war might soon be over, and for all those it was affecting, hurting, killing. But most of all I prayed for Magnus, and afterwards my knees were weak. But this was an honest fragility, an openness, intertwined with a calm feeling of hope: that no matter how bad things might seem, or become, there was always... well, this I did not know, but nonetheless it gave reason not to be afraid. Whether I doubted my faith or not, the church still seemed to constitute a place of sanctity, perhaps simply because it lay always quiet and enclosed, calm, and usually empty.

It was not that the place allowed me to think straight but rather that it did not demand that I think at all, and did not compel me to do so. I could allow myself to sit quietly and without thought, and it did not matter: the church was entirely separate from the rushes, panics, responsibilities and constraints of everyday life. Aside from the mountain, perhaps, I could think of no better place to be.

However, I could not help, when absent from this place, but question the religious connotations and my own beliefs. This was not least frustrating because of my tendency to indecisiveness, but also because I wanted more than anything the peace of mind to simply accept things without question, to simply accept and be happy in the face of any external adversity. But I was compelled by my own enemy of a conscience to practise the opposite, for there were too many assertions to the contrary of what I thought I ought to believe; too many reasons to doubt; inconsistencies, waves of the unintelligible and downright painful in any attempt to comprehend.

The horror of the war, needless to say, though so far away, did all it could to exacerbate this lapse of faith in universal justice and all that was eternally good.

As I left Bøur's little church, the doubt, uninvited, began its questioning. A deep unhappiness churned in the pit of my stomach. I wanted to take the weight from my numb legs, lie down on the ground that I could not feel, curl up against the intrusive wind, close my eyes to let nothing in... I stopped still for a moment outside the church. My eyes were closed, I breathed deeply, tried to concentrate on nothing else but the icy bite of the wind on my cheeks. Despite my best efforts, a voice still drifted in through my senses:

'Morning, Kjartan.'

My eyes snapped open to a bright world: a woman was watching me from the doorway of the house that stood adjacent to the church. The weak light of the morning glinted warmly from the soft contours of her open face, and from the greying strands of her dark hair. She smiled at me in a way that seemed intended to make my newly fragile heart weep for the love of another human being. Especially this one.

I was embarrassed at being caught leaving the church, as though it was a sign of weakness, but as my catcher was the vicar's wife, I hoped that she might understand. It was not the first time, after all. Sure enough she chose to ignore the questionable stance in which she had found me – stock still, eyes closed – and proceeded without delay to offer me a cup of tea.

'How does life find you this morning?' she asked by way of greeting as she led me inside her black timber house. I responded positively, the prescribed answer. But before I had a chance to return the inquiry she took me by the shoulders and peered into my face, into the depths of my sunken eyes, the dark rings I knew were there, and my colourless skin. I thought I might wither away into the sweeping wind outside, or sink into myself, deflate.

She looked unconvinced by my standard answer; she had known me too long to feel the need to employ small talk. This woman had nursed me at her breast, a poor motherless creature, as she had done her own children.

'You look exhausted.' She brushed back the hair from my forehead. The hallway of her house was stiflingly warm.

'How have you been sleeping?'

'Err... not too well... '

She clucked in a motherly sort of way, stroked my hair and ushered me into the kitchen. In reassurance that the apocalyptic nature of my nights need not disturb those day-to-day matters in which one can always find ritual solace, she filled the kettle with water. I sat down at the table and recalled the many times I had watched her do just that, enveloped in the warmth of maternal care and domestic security which my child's mind, upset even then by the injustices of my own family life, had coveted.

I could have cried as she set a cup of tea before me, followed closely by a plate of bread and butter. She also took up a piece between her fingers, savouring a mouthful, a cup in her other hand. She shifted the chair slightly with her hip before taking a seat opposite me.

'Am I disturbing you?' I was hit by a sudden anxiety that I might be encroaching upon time she had envisioned spending upon the pursuit of a different task, perhaps in other company than mine. She looked a little surprised, fittingly since she had not given any indication that my presence was ill-timed. She smiled and licked the butter from her fingers with the enjoyment of a child in such a simple thing.

'Don't be silly, Karri, you know you're always welcome. The house is so quiet since Kristjan flew the nest.'

I could not help the burst of laughter that escaped me: I had never heard the youngest of Guðrun's children speak in anything more than a whisper, he was quiet as a mouse. She laughed, too, when I told her this. Only two or three years older than me, he had recently moved to Tórshavn to train as a vicar, like his father; and as a sharply bright young man, analytical and thorough, had taken to the study of theology like a fish to water (an analogy of Magnus's). He did, however, lack a certain amount of common sense at the most crucial of times, and tended subsequently to give the impression of being utterly and irretrievably *up in the clouds*. I had always liked him. His sisters had also moved to the capital. I wondered if Guðrun felt similar to myself in this respect, adrift in an empty house that had once been a home to others, to loved ones.

'You'll have to come and stay at Orri's as well,' I said, tongue-in-cheek. She smiled in response but I caught the suggestion that she kept something back, something unsaid. She hesitated, almost for longer than I could bear.

'And how is... how is Ásdis treating you?' she asked carefully. There was a forced lightheartedness that could not mask her concern. I answered that while she did not exchange many words with me, Orri's mother had certainly not made me unwelcome. Guðrun nodded, her eyes not quite meeting mine.

'She's not said... she's not had you bed down with the chickens, then?' She attempted a smile. I wondered if she shared my apprehension, my guilt, at accepting hospitality from a woman who needed to care for her dying husband. Before I had the chance to apologise to Guðrun for my inexcusable lack of compassion and breach of privacy (having not yet summoned the courage to apologise to Orri's mother herself), Guðrun continued quietly.

'And is Orri happy... to have you there?'

I nodded; of this at least, I was certain. 'He says the house feels less... upsetting. Magnus encourages us to make as much noise as possible, to liven things up, he says.'

Again I thought of Ásdis, and those children born dead or dying, whose absence seemed to invade each corner of the quiet house and could be perceived in the possessive way in which Ásdis mothered her only son. Did her animosity towards me stem from my having lived while my mother died? I caught the impression that she would gladly have given her life that her own children might have lived.

Guðrun smiled warmly, breaking off from her apparent bashfulness and the thick silence of things unsaid. I wanted to ask her for her own interpretation of Ásdis's quiet hostility towards me, for it was evident that she, too, had picked up on this, that it was not simply a feat of my imagination, borne of the guilt that I suffered at accepting hospitality from the household. Yet there lurked a nagging discomfort within me that prevented my asking and advised me instead to hold my tongue.

'But you're still not sleeping well,' Guðrun surmised after a pause. I shook my head. Embarrassed, insecurities laid bare, I clutched the mug to my lips as though behind it I might find a place to hide.

The compassionate look I received from Guðrun was enough to make me despise myself for inviting sympathy, worry and attention. For confessing to weakness when I should be stronger; for admitting another into that corner of my consciousness whose contagious darkness could only cause upset and trouble.

'I don't suppose you'll have heard from your father?'

I shook my head. She was silent for a moment. I would not meet her eyes; instead I studied the inside of my cup, watching the rising steam curl around it.

'Is he often in your dreams? Is that why you're not sleeping well?'

Again, I shook my head. 'No.'

She studied my face, Guðrun always knew when I was lying – and I swallowed uncomfortably and attempted a meek smile, the sort I prevailed on in the hope of raising the mood and deferring intense personal insights.

'I'm sorry, Karri,' she said, not to be fooled. 'I didn't mean to upset you.'

I only nodded as if in acceptance and drew the thread of a new topic from thin air, one that I knew she would happily discuss: 'How is Kristjan?' As expected, Guðrun laughed, accepting my divergence from the previous subject of conversation. 'Ah, yes, my son... '

I received a long, detailed account of her son's latest 'escapades' in Tórshavn. I listened carefully, nodded, laughed in all the right places. Currently, I was told, he was learning to play the organ, and had met a girl. She erupted into laughter. I loved to listen to Guðrun's stories; I could have walked to Gásadalur and back a hundred times just to hear them. And perhaps it was this, but not exclusively, that led me, following the arrival of her husband into the kitchen, to agree to be involved with the church service in Bøur the following Sunday.

I had not intended to allow myself to be persuaded into doing something which would inevitably cause me so much worry, but the welcoming smile and enthusiasm of the vicar as he entered the room and posed the question were so strong that I found myself agreeing with little outward reluctance. Inside, however, my organs twisted around each other in discomfort.

As some of the British troops were expected to attend as usual, the vicar had got it into his head that someone was needed to give a reading in English, and this someone was to be me, because: 'You come to our church quite often, don't you, Kjartan?'.

'Yes,' I replied with less than a hint of conviction, though it went unnoticed. I wondered how God would feel about a useless and despairing agnostic such as myself openly praising and serving him in public. I did not even know whether or not I qualified as a fraud. That seemed worse.

13

IN THE COURSE of the following days I lost far too much sleep over the matter of my appearance in church. It manifested itself as a restless discomfort, present even in my best efforts to concentrate on anything else but that.

It was early spring and the first lambs were beginning to arrive, mostly through the nights, which were still unavoidably dark; a lingering homage to the still-recent winter. Orri and I spent a few hectic nights with Flóki and his sheep; Orri virtually passed out on his side on a makeshift bed lining the floor, dead to the world for as many hours as was permitted or could be utilised for this purpose. I lay uncomfortably awake beside him, or sitting up with a heavy head, or pacing the floor quietly in a manner reflecting the restlessness of my thoughts, until we were called to action in the early hours of a dark morning.

We pulled on coats, hats, scarves, and touched a flame to the wick of the oil lamp, which shone as a single ball of light through the opaque air as the livestock bleated with the pain of birth. I was gripped by an unbearable discomfort, so reluctant to subside that even during the daylight hours my soul and vision were filled with the distressed darkness of these nights. Had the night I came into the world been this dark? I wondered. My father had never spoken to me about it; he would not have wanted to remember the pain of his wife being taken from him.

Orri was always beside me, his blue eyes heavy and dark-ringed from exhaustion, yet still glittering in the singular light of the lamp, enthralled by each creation of a new, bleating life. He would give my arm a squeeze in his own warm grip but could barely bring himself to speak, and on the brief occasions that he did so, his voice was no more than a whisper.

Sometimes the ewe would give painful birth to a lamb already dead, and with this Orri's eyes went dead also. Flóki himself was never struck dumb by the stillbirths – he was experienced after all, he had learned not to give a second thought – but in our own young minds we were profoundly tortured. The ewe would stop its cries, we would stand uncertain, plagued by unanswerable questions, and all would be silent except for the howling of the wind, the pattering of midnight rain, as the lamb lay limp and lifeless on the ground. The first time was the most disturbing. Even Orri did not sleep that night and I knew that he, too, was lost in thoughts of his own mother and her losses.

Luckily the weather held out, more or less. It was grey and cloudy but brighter beneath, and this meant the possibility of good fishing, bad weather having the ability to cripple the trade at his time of year.

On a short and unsuccessful trip taken by Jón with Orri and myself in tow, I was scolded for turning our small boat anti-clockwise against the sun. 'It must always be turned clockwise, Kjartan!' Jón stressed. "*With* the sun, always: it is only turned widdershins when taking a body to a funeral, you know that."

I swore at him, in no mood to be cornered by such narrow superstitions.

'Please don't swear at me, Kjartan: I'm just trying to explain.'

I threw down my oar in frustration. 'Explain *what* to me, Jón? Explain that *I'm* to blame because we haven't caught any fish? I am sorry, Jón; sorry that I've single-handedly caused the collapse of the entire wartime fishing industry!'

As I was confined to a small fishing boat a good distance from land, I simply sat down heavily and contented myself to sulk for the remainder of the day.

***

We ate our evening meal sitting around Magnus's bed. He

himself ate very little, talked much more in a voice hoarse and cracked, but always bright. After a good while of mindless chatter, the usual sort of mealtime conversation, he addressed me directly with what I surely recognised as a teasing smile.

'Reading in church tomorrow, eh, Kjartan?'

The thing that always held true with Magnus was that he was under all circumstances sharply perceptive, almost as though he possessed the ability to read minds. But with this perceived knowledge he remained quiet, smiling knowingly, and would draw light to it only with small hints, always teasingly and unfailingly subtle. With this hoarse remark I saw that familiar knowing glint in his eyes, and was convinced that he could read my anxieties therein. Perhaps he was even more aware of them than I was.

Upon first meeting Magnus, when he was in full health of course, one would by no means suspect him of such intimate perceptions: he was a loud man, always welcoming and friendly. He had such gusto of gesture and temperament. But it could be seen in his eyes, when the time was taken to look properly, even during his illness, the fierceness of his intelligence. I saw no point in attempting to hide my misgivings regarding the subject he had just raised, and subsequently found myself at a loss for the appropriate reaction. 'On request of that mad little vicar, I suppose?' This was not a question, more an accusation. I laughed: Magnus was a very religious man, of course, but liked to praise God in his own way, specifically in the appreciation of the bounty of nature and the more naturalistic aspects of ordinary island life. He was, needless to say, not much of a fan of the vicar's own gusty and grandiose approach to religious worship in a tightly-knit community. He found it, quite reasonably, over the top. *God is not prevalent in the hopeful and apologetic babbling of communal praise and prayer; He is to be found and appreciated in the perfection of the natural world, unshaped by man – we are merely granted use of it*, he would say. Magnus's praise existed in the cultivation of that which he had been so kindly granted; he required no church.

'He noticed I'm a regular churchgoer,' I clarified, tongue-in-cheek.

Magnus's ghost of his former full-bodied laugh showed he had understood. He scratched his beard delightedly and slapped his other hand weakly against his side.

'Then you must sing to the heavens with them, Kjartan lad!'

***

Every pew in the church was filled. Small though the place might have been, it had become a crowded hall; I was sure the walls had grown. Everyone knew everyone else except the British troops, though their acquaintances were often numerous. There were a good many of them, dressed in immaculate uniforms, sitting quietly in the back rows as the Faroese congregation enthusiastically gossiped amongst themselves.

Orri and I took seats at the front, directly in front of the altar. Orri straightened the collar of his shirt and attempted to flatten his blond hair, though to no avail. He looked flushed and expectant, his bright eyes darted searchingly around the room.

'What are you looking for?' I asked with interest, and as his eyes came to rest on my own he smiled, and I was sure it was a knowing smile, though I was unable to question this further for the gossiping congregation fell suddenly silent.

All eyes turned to the altar, to the vicar. He stood with his hands clasped before his chest, surveying the congregation and wearing his usual condescending, sugar-sweet smile. He always wore this smile, even when not in sermon. The 'smile of brotherhood' Orri and I called it, not without a certain degree of flippancy. It was a frustratingly calm, empathetic smile, accompanied by intensely soft eye contact and phrases such as, 'bless you, my child', spoken in a sing-song voice so smooth it could have cleaned a rock.

He began with a short welcome speech, an opening prayer, his voice singing out. We were invited to pray with him in Danish for the continued good health of our community. All the while my heart pounded like a drum; surely it was audible over the prayerful silence? It sank, finally, into my stomach as

I was called up to the front. I hated public speaking, regardless of the language I was required to speak. Orri gave my shoulder a supportive squeeze as I left my seat and bowed to the altar. I took my place before the thick, leather-bound English Bible, facing the congregation.

For a moment not a single word of the text made sense, but after a deep breath I was able to read aloud. It was a beautiful verse, full of meaningful imagery and designated to lift the soul, and in this, a proper setting, the words seemed effortlessly more real compared to my earlier dispirited rehearsal to an empty hall.

The British troops looked delighted with their newly acquired comprehension. As I considered this, however, I was struck by a sudden sour taste in my mouth and a hectic skip of my heartbeat. The war was growing consistently worse, people were suffering beyond belief. The world was a horrible place, gripped in utter terror and turmoil, yet I stood preaching sugar-sweet assurances of justice and eternal harmony, babbling a message of goodwill to all mankind. What awful words at such a time. Yes, they gave reason to live, reason to put up with this bitter life... yet they were hollow, patronising, a crippling lie.

I long so desperately for these promises to be genuine that I am washed with a deep hurt, and I despise them for their beautiful appeal, for they will do nothing but offer false hope. I feel betrayed, sick, on the verge of tears. It is all I can do to stop my voice from shaking... As the congregation say 'Amen', I walk, almost run, down the centre aisle, through the church door. I push it heavily to a close behind me, lean forward by the side wall with one hand pushed against the cold timber, and I am sick. Violently sick.

I sank to the ground, weak and light-headed; for a moment I was certain I would pass out. The world, the air, felt like a suffocating fabric around me, and would not allow my eyes to open. Then the heat of a body warmed my side; a hand presumably belonging to it conjured a tissue into existence, and with it wiped the tears from my cheeks. I recognised her comforting scent.

'Poor Kjartan,' murmured Guðrun. 'You are in the wars, aren't you?'

She pulled me towards her, held my head against her chest so that I could feel the beating of her heart, and stroked my hair for what could have been seconds, days, or weeks. Eventually, with a deep intake of breath, I sat up, and put my head in my heads.

'You need some sleep, Kjartan.'

I could not subdue my surfacing irritation. 'I *know* I need some sleep, Guðrun.' My voice was hoarse from the acidic sickness that stung my throat. For a moment she sat in silence, her arm wrapped around my shoulder. I drew in my knees like a vulnerable child.

'Look... Karri,' she said suddenly, and too uncertainly for my comfort, 'I'm going to give you something... I had not planned to, not yet; but I think... I think you need it.' She reached into the pocket of her coat, then took my hand and pressed into the palm a round, gritty, fabric-like object. Opening my hand, before my blurry eyes I saw a tea-bag. 'Just brew it as you would a normal cup of tea, before you go to bed. It should help. '

I thanked her, lacking the spirit to question such a seemingly pointless gift, and instead I simply buried it in the depths of my own coat pocket. Shakily I rose to my feet and once Guðrun had returned inside, for a few minutes I wandered aimlessly outside the church. No sun shone in the sky; it did not even hang there. No rain fell, no wind blew through the unruly mop of my hair, which was badly in need of a trim.

I stood in the midst of the sort of day that seems unreal, as though time has come to a stop and all that is left simply *is*. These clear grey mornings do so much for the soul: they do not lift it nor dampen it; they simply calm it. I breathed deeply, quite unable to articulate the feeling of grounded elation which wrapped itself around me now as I stood alone beneath the mountains. Perhaps it was because such mornings instilled within me not the slightest desire for thought. The mountains sank into the land and into the sea with melting sighs of acceptance. Their edges were ill-defined, as though soft, quite unlike the coarse, disproportionate contours that abounded beneath my feet when ascending the path towards the sky.

Despite the cold bite of the air I began to warm up inside, though my legs were still made of jelly. I lit a cigarette. Orri was the first of the congregation to leave the church, and he did so like a kicked football: bursting through the doors at an impressive speed and making a dash directly to my side.

'Karri, are you alright?'

Bobbing up and down on the balls of his feet, he took my shoulders and looked unwaveringly into my eyes. '*Are* you alright? Guðrun said you'd been ill – said you *are* ill. What's wrong? Have you been sick? Should I get you a glass of water?'

I could not help but laugh. 'Orri, calm down. Everything is fine.'

He brought his arms down to his sides, continued to study my face. 'You look awful.'

'Thank you.'

He smiled at me, seeming a little embarrassed. 'No, I meant tired. Really tired. And a little green.' Uninvited, he took the cigarette from my fingers and put it to his own lips.

***

Sundays always gave rise to gatherings. Immediately following the service no one would have any plans or commitments: for the calm of Sunday afternoon the fish could be left to grow fatter still, the barley could be left to drink up the rain, and the sheep could look after themselves. And we could talk. We did so freely; friends and family through generations.

Orri was especially loved by everyone in the area, and since the onset of his father's illness he had been no less than adopted by almost every family in the village. Ashamed, I could not help the small bite of jealousy that crept into my thoughts. Orri was looked after by many, they paid him gentle attention, though this was not from pity; he did not wallow in his misfortune or worries for his father. They treated him as a son, as a friend: he was lively and companiable, charming and energetic in the most welcoming and wonderful of ways. He was always smiling, laughing, asking after people, utterly compassionate... I was jealous, perhaps, because my own relationship with the townspeople seemed somehow different, more subdued; less open. I did not talk as much as Orri. I remained painfully shy, self-aware. Maybe it was that I longed to have Orri to myself, for without him I drifted directionless, as though I had been stitched onto the outside of things. It often crossed my mind that he might prefer the company of others, for when with me he was not always so lively.

The lull of the crowd came to fit perfectly the still, clear brilliance of the grey morning light and the damp air, refreshingly cold against bare skin. I watched the people in subdued silence, their voices washing like waves over my cold ears and through my head, blurring into one continuous note of a gentle sound. My eyes were half-closed. I watched Orri; surrounded, animated, until once more he came over to me. He studied my face and informed me I was in dire need of some fresh air.

14

BEFORE LONG WE were up in the bare hills. We climbed over fences, our shoes wet in the morning grass, and the year's first lambs, small and muddy, stumbled away from us over the harsh curves of the land, bleating forlornly in a way that managed to sound heartwarming as it drifted through the clear and empty air. The clouds were low, lingering in thin white wisps above us, and although the rain did not fall, by the time we reached the mountain's summit, overlooking the sea, our hair, faces and hands were sodden.

I stopped and looked down at Bøur, lying below. I breathed deeply, my hair was plastered to my forehead; drops of moisture caught on my eyelashes. Exhausted but happy I saw the natural world, felt it in my lungs and against my skin, felt it rushing through my head. My hands were cold as ice. As we stood there, hearing only the sounds of the sheep through loose, wonderful silence, the rain began to fall lightly around us and soak into the mountain.

We arrived back home in the early hours of the evening, fatigued and drenched to the bone but nonetheless quite content. It is a wonderful feeling to be wet and tired when there exists the imminent luxury of a warm room, dry clothes and a hot drink. I clutched my drink with both hands, fingers barely visible from the ends of the sleeves of one of Orri's jumpers in which I had wrapped myself, and I sank into the heat of the fire. But despite this thoughtless relaxation, sleep still would not visit me. I lay awake that night while Orri slept, and I drowned in waking dreams. Around me the world adopted new sounds and textures; I traced my fingers over objects that were not there, all of them distorting and stretching in a way that ground against my teeth like long fingernails across a blackboard. Holes opened up in everything. In darkness I fell backwards into a fluctuating oblivion; a cottonwool silence. My heart did not beat; it only skipped and stumbled.

I snapped suddenly into the true reality of the night. Everything seemed strangely silent and hollow. With the same jerking movement I sat bolt upright in the bed and looked across the room to Orri. He was still there, lying on his side, sleeping deeply. One hand rested limply next to his pale face. I did not know why I had thought he might be absent. I climbed carefully out of bed and pulled on a jumper against the low temperatures of the spring night. Such a night was not as dark as in winter, and I could perceive shapes just clearly enough to allow me to light the lamp beside my bed. Its glow, though dim, was warming. Orri did not wake.

Lightly I trod down the steps to the kitchen, put the lamp on the table and a pot of water on the stove, having stoked up the embers. Then I sat down and placed one of my oldest brother's so distant letters open in front of me; the one he had written from Scotland only shortly after the beginning of the war, the last my father and I had received from him. Outside I could hear the lightly falling rain.

I had read Georg's words a hundred times, yet I did not grow tired of them. Sometimes they played a continuous loop inside my head throughout the waking day: the Blitz, the civilians, the soldiers, the destruction, the pointlessness of it all. I appeared always to be searching for clues within his words, clues from which I could deduce the exact nature of all happenings, and what would happen in the future of all this insanity. My imagination ran wild.

For the hundredth time I laid down the letter, as the water on the stove came to the boil, and I was struck with a sudden thought, of something I had forgotten. I tiptoed to the hook from which hung my coat, still damp, and reaching into the pocket I withdrew Guðrun's teabag. I brewed it in the newly-boiled water, as Guðrun had instructed. It did not smell like tea. I took a sip, and another, and another. I encountered no taste, simply a feeling; a material sensation that took hold of my body.

I drank some more: my bones were now heavy as rocks, my head filled with an overwhelming, dampening heat, my leaden eyelids dropped... *Outside I heard the rain fall upwards, towards the sky.*

***

'Karri... ? Karri... !'

I heard my name repeated over and over as a dull and distant whisper, first through deadly silence, then through the crashing rain which crescendoed to an almost deafening point that pounded the very inside of my head. Then the pounding receded and I heard the voice more clearly. I encountered some difficulty in opening my eyes – they were glued shut, full of sand – and when I finally managed to do so they ached painfully as though someone had placed a brick behind each one. I squinted at Orri as I raised myself up onto my elbows.

'Karri... ? Karri... err, what are you doing?' His voice sounded like a hammer in my skull. My back ached from the hard surface beneath it and I realised that I was lying on the kitchen floor. The oil lamp had long since burned itself out.

'What's wrong?' Orri said. 'I woke up and you weren't there. So I came in here to look for you and found you passed out on the kitchen floor.'

His voice was diminishing again. I snapped my eyes open to quell a spiralling descent back into sleep. I pushed myself up into a sitting position, my knees tucked under my chin, and my hands in my hair as if to massage my brain into cooperation.

'I'll get you some water,' said Orri, and did so, returning to sit by my side and place a comforting hand on my shoulder. 'Kjartan, I'm worried about you.' He hardly ever called me by my full name.

'Don't be,' I managed to articulate. After a sip of water and a deep breath I struggled uncertainly to my feet, placed the glass on the table, mumbled, 'Fresh air,' and stumbled hastily from the room.

Orri followed me outside and waited patiently by the door while I threw up. I struggled to breathe. My throat was unbearably dry. Droplets of cold rain ran down the back of my neck, streamed down the bridge of my nose and splashed around my bare feet. Orri followed me with his wide blue eyes as my ice-cold feet carried me back. With a weak smile I said, 'I think I feel a little better.'

He reached out a bare, skinny arm, ruffled my wet hair and led me back inside. I dried myself and dressed quickly, reluctant to move any slower for fear that my eyelids might once more insist on closing and the waking world would slip away.

The new day brought with it the responsibility of another

trip to Tindhólmur. This time I was required to carry out the duty alone, for Orri had been asked to help Jón the fisherman with (presumably) something fish-related. Orri was now reluctant to allow me to brave the water alone, adamant that I was in no fit shape to do so in a tiny rowing boat. 'I know it's not exactly across the sea,' he insisted, following the declaration that it was akin to sailing to Scotland and back, 'but I really think you should go back to bed.' He grinned. 'Or back to the kitchen floor.'

In the process of pulling on my shoes with a closed determination and the speed of incentive, I informed him, without looking up, 'I'm going. It will do me good.'

'I'll come straight home this evening,' he said after a small pause. 'Will you be here?' In his voice I could hear the attempt to sound bright. I stopped and looked up. More than anything else I could see that he simply cared for my safety and wellbeing.

'Yes,' I replied, wishing today did not have to happen; wishing it could be evening – any evening: always the evening. Then I would not have to leave the house. Responsibilities or no responsibilities, daylight compels a person to venture outside. Orri insisted on walking with me to the harbour. I had not asked him to do so, at least, I did not remember asking; I did not remember even leaving the house. I found myself suddenly at the harbour in the pouring rain; face sodden, legs like jelly, and with no recollection of having taken the necessary path that had brought me to this place. It was freezing. I pulled my hat further down over my ears and squinted out along the bay: the clouds were low, the rain thick, and visibility was extremely poor, though not dangerously so. For the Islands this weather was fairly standard and so must be endured. No one complained.

Despite further protestations from Orri I bid him a slurred goodbye, before performing a movement that felt like drifting, rather than clambering, into the boat. I experienced the sensation that I was sitting on the air several inches above the bench, yet still I began to row. I chartered the entire distance of the bay locked in a determined concentration. I seemed to have rushed headlong into it with little reasoning, like a drunken man with a set task to carry out, whilst trying to give the impression that he is by no means drunk. Indeed, my head reeled as if I had attempted to walk along the straight white line at my haphazard feet.

As I left the shelter of the bay I soared suddenly from my deadlock of concentration into the openness of a fiercely sensual world. Here the oars cut rainbows through the waves which shattered against the boat in slow motion.

The rain does not fall, it glitters and dances over me and my boat on an empty sea. Against my skin the rain feels so real. My skin is a canvas, delicate, so fine it can float away with the wind,

fly over the waves to distant lands where the waterfalls flow to-
wards the endless sky and the trees grow with their roots in the air.
Because this is how it should be.

I climb to my numbed feet in the prow of the dancing boat and
pull off my coat, my jumper and shirt. The soft rain plasters as a
rhythmic blanket around my chest and my arms, my neck... I can
hold the rain in my fingertips, watch every droplet as it falls, and
inside each one I can see the world.

The boat lurches but I am steady on my feet, for I am not re-
ally standing here; I am floating, suspended over the waves like a
cloud, like a bird, like... like nothing. The sea, the sky have become
as one: a tempestuous, endless capsule of grey; so many colours and
shades of grey, fluctuating and rolling. I stretch out my fingertips;
stretch out my bare arms and prepare to fall effortlessly into the
inviting waves, into the rolling sky, to be gathered up within those
grey arms. I see the shimmering colours so closely, so tangibly be-
fore my own eyes. I close my eyes because here I do not need them.
My skin embodies all my senses; my entire body can feel every-
thing as though I am intrinsically wrapped within these glorious
sensations. I close my eyes and let my body fall...

Just before I drop from my suspension a deep tremor runs
through the boat, through my previously unfeeling feet and up
my legs, gripping them in a sudden leaden heaviness quite contrary to the disembodiment of a moment earlier. The shock
passes through my feet and causes them to tip backwards,

stumble uncertainly on hard rocks behind them. I see the steep, rocky slopes of Tindhólmur, pressing down against all senses. I see the dense clouds of wet mist above me. Directly above me, for there is unyielding rock against my back and underneath my head, which screams at me and throbs painfully. I lose myself in the shapes of the mist – it forms mountains, trees, animals and faces that watch me as they grow larger in blurred vision and fade indefinitely to black; the darkest black.

I have a dream so vivid it could be real. The rain is falling all about me, cascading; a refreshing waterfall just intense enough to wash away all fatigue. I am standing alone at the summit of the mountain overlooking Bøur – but the village is absent. Instead I see before me an endless tumultuous sea of mist and waves. The houses of the town still remain, but they are merely suggestions of houses: flittering shapes through the wonderful greyness of an abstract sea. It is impossible to describe or understand how, but I can see the sense of everything; I can see how the whole world fits together. And in seeing this I know there is no reason to be afraid. No reason to feel lost anymore.

15

I SAT UP. I seemed to have completed this action before fully waking, yet I remained unsure as to whether I had in fact regained consciousness at all. Again I lay on a floor. Yet this was not a floor I recognised: its surface was of panelled wood, sleeker, smoother than that of our little turf-roofed houses, and at one time quite well polished, although now it was beginning to appear worn. The floor was adorned with faint footprints and was scuffed by shoes, while the reflecting daylight from a small window nearby showed many other scratches, marks and stains. I pushed myself to a half-sitting position. Feeling the irritation of pain, I examined my hands and saw that they were scraped and sore, brown from the earth. I looked from them to the rest of my surroundings.

Tables and counters lined the wooden walls, and some ranged across the spacious floor, and each stood cluttered with an impressive variety of objects. There were pots and pans, tins and cups, strange glass beakers, bowls and paperweights, needles and string, and, for some reason, many kettles. Some of these objects were arranged in neat piles, or organised by order of size; some seemed to be grouped together in a certain place, looking ready for, or already engaged in, a specific purpose. Most things, however, were simply strewn around haphazardly and had, in many cases, found their way onto the floor. I moved a foot, and something clattered ominously.

I lay bathed in a soft grey light emanating from the room's small windows, through which a haze of grey shades peered down into my face and shadowed my bare chest. At the other side of the room a solitary lamp burned with a full flame, casting a long light on the clutter and the shadows of paraphernalia, creating a strange, artificial twilight. I strained my ears but could hear no sounds of life. I craned my neck in an attempt to peer through the wide crack in the door that gaped open in the opposite wall but I saw nothing save for an indistinct grey atmosphere.

As I sat up something warm brushed against my straightened arm, taut against the floor in support of my weight. I gasped, my pulse hammered in my forehead. A cat stared back at me, standing on silent paws, its eyes piercingly curious. It regarded me judgementally for a moment, then it appeared to make a snap decision as to the nature of my character and sidled up to me, purring contentedly.

My seemingly displaced heart continued to throb painfully

behind my temples, torn from the emptiness in my chest. It completed another double-beat as the door at the far side of the room was flung open in the most flamboyant way possible, and a man entered. He did so in a lighthearted manner, almost as though he ought to be whistling jovially in accompaniment, yet also with a sense of focussed determination in the face of an important task. He strolled through the doorway, shoes light on the wooden floor and an old, rusty kettle in one hand. As he made a fluid move to place it on the surface of one cluttered table, he caught sight of me.

I sat staring at him, unmoving. My eyes felt as wide as saucers. I was equally as lost for words as for breath, as my brain, quite fruitlessly, tried to keep up with what was happening as well as attempting to recollect how I had arrived here – wherever 'here' was. Why was I not wearing my jumper? I wondered what had happened to the boat. I was sure I remembered a boat...

The man, similarly, wore a look of surprise at discovering me on his floor. He dipped his eyebrows in confusion. I could see the wheels grinding thoughtfully behind his searching gaze. Silence reigned. Then something clicked into place and he nodded, it seemed to himself, as a quiet exclamation of, 'Oh,' escaped his lips. He held up a long finger, then skipped breezily from the room. The cat followed.

I continued to stare at the empty doorway. Seconds later

the man returned, the kettle still in one hand while the other grasped what I recognised to be my own grey jumper. He practically skipped across the room to my side. Pots clattered noisily under his feet. He reached down and handed me the kettle. I took it stiffly while my eyes snapped back to his: he had paused, appeared to be still in thought, a little lost. Neither of us said a word. Then briskly he reached down again to take the kettle from where my arm remained outstretched, and replaced it with the jumper. I was offered a lopsided smile along with the words: 'I've dried it for you!'

He was speaking English. I wondered if I had simply heard him incorrectly. I shivered from the cold bind which gripped my chest, and pulled on my jumper, gladly appreciative of the new warmth around my skin. I tugged my sleeves down over my curled hands and bunched them up against my lips. The man was busying himself noisily around the stove. 'I'll make you a cup of tea,' he told me cheerily, over the clatter, 'It will make you feel better!'

Still sitting on the wooden floor, I observed him as he worked. Of a tall stature, the young man's height was not matched in physique, for he was as skinny as the cat was round. His legs were long, and his forearms emerged like sticks from the rolled-up sleeves of a brown shirt, displaying also a pair of pointy elbows as he reached in various directions. There were cupboards above his head towards which he had to raise himself up on the balls of his feet. When he had gathered whatever he had been looking for, he curved his lanky, pipe-cleaner body over the stove.

At the collar his brown shirt lay loosely open where a couple of buttons were missing. He wore the shirt untucked; his braces hung down by the patched-up knees of his grey trousers as though he may have forgotten to attach them properly when he dressed himself that morning. I deduced from his appearance that the day had kept him occupied with thoughts other than of his attire.

The cat returned on stealthy feet and pressed against my side. With little prior warning, the claustrophobic heat from its textured fur prompted a return of my stomach's sickness and an urgent need to locate the nearest bucket – which I thankfully found empty atop one of the counters as I struggled to my feet, before my insides were torn uncomfortably to pieces. With my elbows on the counter-top, I put my head into my hands and groaned.

'Don't worry,' the man said. In the cessation of clattering his voice sang out as a reedy tenor. 'It's just a side effect of what you drank last night... That, and the hallucinations, of course... '

He sounded light and breezy; even chuckled to himself in cheery acceptance of a mistake. 'It was just a prototype, really, that one: not meant for consumption just yet! Still needs a few little amendments... '

Had he taken the drink in question himself, I was sure he would not have sounded so nonchalant, or have been in any state to arrive by my side so energetically. 'Here, get some of this down you: it'll help. We'll sort that bucket out later.'

In no state to be discerning, I took a few sips of the liquid I had been offered, scalding the inside of my mouth in the rush for peace of mind. The taste was subtle, light, in no way medicinal. I caught the suggestion of fresh air and damp earth, overcast skies heavy with impending rain, under which the world lay brightly illuminated; an absence of gravity... something about leaves... It seemed as though my legs evaporated, yet I held my upright position, leaning against the counter for fear they might give way entirely.

'Good lad,' the young man encouraged as I drank with an unbridled vigour. 'Much better now, eh?'

Almost instantly my stomach was settled, banished of upset and nausea. There followed an elongated second of relief and ecstasy at restoring balance, before the mental confusions, finding now an unobstructed pathway to my stomach, rudely overturned it. Once more my head buzzed painfully. A few sentences sprang to my lips, but were unable to progress any further, for in the overwhelming desire to express all my thoughts at once, not one of them could be formed coherently.

'Now,' announced the man before I had uttered even a single word, 'why don't you sit down and tell me what you're doing here?'

I stared at him. 'What I'm doing here?' I echoed hoarsely in his own language.

The man grinned. 'Well, you must have come here for a reason.'

'For a reason?'

The grin across his features was insatiable. 'Are we going to make a conversation from this repetition?' His eyes sparkled and with this I was suddenly hauled down to earth, waking from a muddled dream. My hands opened outwards in barely containable exasperation. He regarded me with a teasing expression until my skin itched with irritation.

'You look as if you want to ask me a question.'

'Where do I *begin*?'

'You could start with the basics?' he suggested, a knowing smile hanging off his face.

He knew exactly, and to every word, my imminent questions – that much was evident – yet he appeared to be taking great delight in prolonging the process of enlightenment. My body writhed with restlessness.

'Where am I?' My heart quickened with unease, my airways began to constrict in the way so familiar. My head swam.

He assumed a mildly puzzled expression. 'What do you mean?'

It was too strange. I stumbled to the opposite side of the room and leaned heavily against one of the cluttered benches, knocking astray a couple of noisy pans in the turmoil. He did not follow, did not move an inch, but continued to watch me. The smile was gone; he looked concerned and said nothing, perhaps to allow some form of calm to be restored.

'Okay,' I began breathlessly, still leaning with shaking legs against the opposite bench. 'I was on a boat... I think... in the sea; it was raining. Then I woke up here.' I gazed up at him searchingly. He offered me a calm smile. 'But what was your reason for coming here?'

'Coming *here*?' I echoed again, quietly. 'No, I was going to Tindhólmur... to Tindhólmur to take Magnus's fish... '

'Ah: you're one of the boys who bring me fish.'

I paused. 'Brings *you* fish?'

'Do you want to see where you are?' He spoke in little more than an excited whisper. 'I'll show you.'

He pivoted immediately on his bouncing soles and exited the room like a gust of wind. On trembling legs I followed, caught in the whirlwind, to another room, small and cosy. A table stood in the centre with two chairs. Upon it stood a couple of unwashed pans and a set of cutlery. Daylight flooded in over every inch of the room from a large yet simple window...

I stopped still, my eyes having only briefly scanned the rest of the modest room before becoming glued to the window. My stomach gave a sudden lurch, and I was gripped by uncertainty of that which my eyes had at first believed in that split second of an initial glance.

The window was plagued by mist, a grey and watery fog that curled through the air languorously and suggestively of shapes and colours, variations on the theme of grey. There was a hint of green, looming through the spreading tendrils of mist. As it slowly cleared I saw the earthen-green lowlands and the rocky reaches of the mountains opposite, the incredible patchwork of steep fields that adorned their sides in curves and contours, larger than life. And the small clusters of colourful houses huddled into the mountainside across the deep cut of the bay, dwarfed into modesty. I saw the insignificant snake of a path, a rickety fence, a tumbledown stone wall. Sheep milled around the cliff tops above the shattered waves that broke upon Sørvágur, Bøur...

I swore in my own language. Pressing a hand to the cold glass, I almost felt the drizzling rain against my skin; almost heard it patter so quietly and calmly against the damp, fresh-smelling earth. I sensed the melancholy bleating of the sheep through the mist, the sweet song of the birds, and the occasional shout of an excited child, or a farmer to his sheep. Laid out so openly before me like this, my island had never looked so beautiful. The stranger appeared silently at my side, smiling.

'What do you think?'

I looked at him. His face was a thin oval shape from which strong cheekbones stood out against hollowed cheeks. A mop of dark hair fell into brown eyes, a hint of sallowness about the surrounding skin. Deep set as the eyes were, they shone out piercingly bright, yet I thought they seemed troubled.

'So that's one of your questions answered,' he said when I failed to express my thoughts.

I was awed into silence by the view from the window and the subsequent realisation of where I must be – upon the slopes of Tindhólmur. He let me stand for a few long minutes at the window, my arms heavy at my sides. 'How... ' The word caught in my throat, and I had to swallow. '... How are we here?'

'It's not such a difficult journey,' I was told, still brightly, as he peered with me out of the window. 'You just take a boat... then the walk isn't difficult; just a fair amount of climbing... '

I explained myself more fully. 'I mean... how can you build a... a house here? On Tindhólmur?'

'Just look at where you build your houses.' He indicated Bøur, grinning. 'The land is uninhabitably steep; the village looks as if it might slip out of existence. All huddled together just where the mountains meet the sea; on the edge of the cliffs... halfway down cliffs. Each house is like an extension of the land with those turf roofs – it is possible to build a house anywhere! Once it has been built, it becomes part of the land itself.'

I had never considered our local architecture in such a light. He let out a laugh. 'Your fields are almost vertical.' He turned abruptly from the window and offered me his long, spidery hand. 'Thomas.'

'Thomas,' I repeated quietly, with the typical Faroese inflection I had which never failed to irritate me. Before I knew what I was doing I had shaken the proffered hand. This was the moment in which I was required, by the graces of social etiquette, to divulge my own name. Yet I seemed to have forgotten it.

'And this is François.' Thomas gestured to a table leg next to which the tabby cat was sitting, contentedly licking its fur. He cooed something in an elaborate language that I had rarely heard spoken, and in response the cat bounced to its feet and trotted over to the man, who nudged it affectionately with his toes. 'He's French,' I was informed.

'Your cat is French?'

'French, yes... a French cat. *Miaow*!' This last appeared to have been addressed to the cat. Thomas stood looking down at where the animal lay on its back. He stroked the fur of its underside lightly with his worn shoes. 'So you were just bringing me my fish then, eh?' This sentence seemed to be addressed to me.

'Yes,' I rushed out in imperfect English. 'Fish, like I am every week... I'm sorry, how do you know your cat speaks French?'

'How do you know your livestock speak Faroese?'

This had sounded like a rhetorical question, yet in its wake he stood looking at me expectantly, the glint all but leaping out of his eyes. My mouth decided to attempt an answer: 'I, err... well, they live here, in Føroyar, for a start... '

'And what makes you think my cat hasn't lived in France?'

I spread out my hands in another exasperated gesture. 'I'm sorry,' I began in the manner of one who is bemused to the point of irritation (and is thus anything but apologetic). 'I am not here to discuss your cat.'

'Ah,' he exclaimed, taking me a little by surprise, 'So you are here for *something*, aren't you?'

'I don't even know who you are. I didn't know anyone lived here; I didn't think anyone *could*. You can tell me your name, but how does that help me?'

'Why don't you sit down?' he suggested. Dazed, I moved to do so, but was struck by another question. 'How did you know I speak English?'

'Sit down,' he repeated, half-way to the door. I noticed he still held the old kettle in his left hand.

'But I asked... '

'Just sit down, you look as if you might pass out.'

He padded quietly from the room, and I fell onto one of the rickety chairs and leaned forward until I could rest my forehead on the edge of the table. The loose pain in my head fluctuated: I could feel its movement, feel it expand and contract; my head itself a bottomless chasm, in which the whole world was contained.

And behind my eyes dance all the colours of the rainbow, with such intensity that they disperse into an encompassing force of white – a white light in which exists everything together and nothing at all. There is both silence and cacophony... I fall into it, behind my eyelids. I know that my skin has folded and my bones have evaporated. Into oblivion I fall with no speed at all.

'Come on, lad, wake up.'

It was a now familiar voice coaxing me as a hand shook me by the shoulder. I groaned. I was on the floor again, this time mostly under the table. Its scratched mahogany underside faded in and out of my blurred vision until it was replaced by changing walls; bathed in a grey daylight, as I was helped onto unsteady feet and back into the chair from which I had fallen. My head screamed, perhaps I had hit it against something in the sudden descent into unconsciousness. A cup appeared before me. 'No,' I groaned. 'No. I'm not drinking any more of *that*. Let me be.'

'It's just tea.'

'Just tea?'

He laughed. 'There's no need to be so wary!'

'You tried to poison me,' I rested my heavy head in my hands and my eyes remained closed.

'Poison you?' He chuckled. I heard him take a seat opposite me. 'That was not my intention. You'll be fine, lad, no need to worry: the effects are only temporary, they'll wear off.' I glanced up at him through the web of my fingers. 'I blended it a little too strongly,' he explained, though I had little idea of what he was talking about. 'It seems to have provoked a sort of temporary narcolepsy.'

'Narcolepsy?'

'Sleeping sickness.' The insatiable grin did not wane. 'Nothing serious, mind. Your body just needs to catch up on a bit of sleep. Give it time and you'll feel good as new. Sleep it off, eh?'

'You know... ' I began hoarsely, finding difficulty in mapping out a sentence, 'you know that I drank that... stuff?'

'Well, I saw you passed out on the rocks. Half-naked, very wet, missing that bag of fish... I recognised the symptoms.'

'You call those symptoms?'

He gave a shrug. 'Well, I could see what had happened. Had you passed out for the usual reasons – illness, for example – you would have looked terrible. A bit like you do now in fact. But you had colour in you when I found you. You looked peaceful; curled up just out of reach of the waves.'

He leaned back in the chair, fingers looped around each

other. I watched him cautiously with my head still clutched in my hands, and my elbows against the hard wood of the table. He looked thoughtfully at his fingers.

'I did not think it would be dangerous, even though it's not quite blended correctly yet. You could've ended up sleeping so peacefully at the bottom of the sea, though. I suppose she shouldn't really have given it to you.'

'Guðrun? You know Guðrun?'

He looked mildly surprised. 'Well, yes, of course... has she not told you?'

'Told me what?'

'I thought that was why you came here... '

He scratched his tousled head and frowned into the near distance.

'Look, I have already told you,' I said, my voice breaking. 'I came here to leave the bag of fish, like I do every week... like *we* do every week.'

My heart lurched at the recollection of Orri. No memory in particular – just Orri. Gripped by a melancholy desire to return home, my heart seemed to be stuck uncomfortably in my throat; my eyes stung. I screwed them shut against the thick air of the room.

'No, but you must've known... ' Then Thomas faltered. 'Maybe this isn't the best time for all this. Come on... '

16

AFTERWARDS, I COULD recall little of the journey back to my island. There were rocks under my feet, there was rain on the end of my nose; there was the whispering cacophony of the waves beneath the gentle rising of the boat, all under an endless grey, featureless sky. I looked into the waves, and from their unyielding surfaces they scowled back at me, cold claws of spray from a blank chasm beneath, ripping at the sides of the boat, trying to pull me into the depths. There was a deep chill in my soul. I recalled seeing the cliffs, catching the scent of wet grass in fresh rain...

I am six years old, gathering hay in the spring as it sticks damply to my shoes, then chasing sheep over the contours of the mountain, my oldest brother laughing from the near distance through the musical patter of the rain: 'Kjartan, let them alone.' His hands are stained with dark ink, revealing the patterns of his fingerprints and skin.

I have tripped on the church path and am sobbing uncontrollably until Guðrun kisses my knee better and puts me to bed.

I lay in that bed now, sinking into the peace of nothing. The sound of my breathing resonated like thunder in my head, deep and regular, hypnotic. I waited for the final breath, for the last gasp of life before I would pass into a peaceful oblivion... And as each breath came I felt instead that I would breathe this way forever, immortally regular; unconscious yet deeply alive.

I dreamt passionately, although the subject of my passion was unclear. The lucid hallucinations of childhood faces and tangible weather slipped slowly from focus and recognition until I was faced only with shadows. Occasionally I became plagued by sudden bouts of discomfort, an inner restlessness, as though my brain had been attempting to wake up, to bring me to the surface. In these moments I witnessed flashes of colour, sharp and burning. Long nails dug into my skin and scratched horrible noises against the surface of darkness before me. There were shapes behind my itching eyelids which fluctuated between the size of needle-eyes and entire planets. In these moments I experienced an awareness of my physical presence, but my body was numb, paralysed.

As I floated into consciousness, however, I lay at peace. My body felt heavy and the blood flowed hazily through my veins, as though I was filled with hot air. I breathed deeply, feeling my eyelids fluttering.

I was as familiar with Guðrun's house as with my own. Outside the rain still fell, and with its gentle drumming I was yet more at peace. Although my form lay leaden and as if filled with a dense cottonwool, it was a pleasant sensation nonetheless; and with every waking breath I felt it slowly clearing, dispersing, replenishing. Eventually I raised myself into a sitting position on the edge of the bed and was mildly surprised to discover that I was naked. I did not remember undressing. I scoured the surrounding room for any sign of my missing clothes, but finding none I pulled a thin blanket from the bed and wrapped it around my waist until I deemed myself sufficiently and modestly covered, and was marginally warmer.

I shuffled through the low doorway and proceeded towards the kitchen. The light outside was of late morning, clear in the rain. It shone warmly onto the walls, the stove and the table – and in the same manner onto Thomas. His booted feet rested up on a chair and his right arm stretched lazily towards a mug of, presumably, tea, that stood on the tabletop. He drummed his long fingers against that same surface to a silent, internal rhythm.

'Morning!'

I tried to complete the mental jigsaw in the woolliness of my head. 'Are you still here?'

He laughed. '*Still here*, he says.'

I was on the verge of giving up and going back to bed, when

the front door opened and through it stumbled Guðrun in a flurry of raindrops.

'Kjartan! I knew you'd wake up eventually; didn't think we'd sent you into a coma.'

A low chuckle. Surprisingly, she spoke English. True, we often spoke the language together to practise, or simply as a small change to the mundanity of daily routine but this time I suspected it was for Thomas. 'How do you feel?'

'Err... I'm not really sure,' I said in Faroese.

'English, Karri, English,' Guðrun chided as she passed me on the way to the kitchen. She laid down her basket on the table. 'I like your sheet. What's the occasion?'

'I can't find my clothes.' I clutched the sheet around my waist. As I expected she would, Guðrun smiled.

'You were soaked to the bone, I couldn't leave you in wet clothes now, could I?'

I raised a hand to my burning cheeks. Guðrun laughed. 'I used to give you baths, Kjartan Rasmussen, there's nothing I haven't seen before. Sit down, I'll make you a cup of tea.'

I wondered, not for the first time, if this was the legitimate solution to all life's problems. I sat down. 'Shit!' I exclaimed suddenly, in English. Two pairs of eyes flashed in my direction. 'It's Tuesday, I was supposed to take the post this morning. The fish will be rotting in the post office by this hour!'

'Today is Friday, Karri: you've been sleeping for four days.'

'Four days?' My body was suddenly leaden, weighed down with rocks from the mountains.

'Don't worry, love, Orri filled in for you.'

'Did he?'

Orri. I swallowed. The heaviness lifted slightly. 'What about my duty as an insomniac: has he adopted that as well?'

Guðrun laughed. 'Well, let's see: he knocked on my door in the first light of Tuesday morning, with a pale face and watery eyes. He seemed half-asleep on his feet. "Guðrun," he said, "I'm having an appalling dream that I've been up since some ungodly hour of the morning, scrambling over mountains to deliver irrelevant packages to irreverent neighbours – would you be so kind as to wake me up?" He's got his father's sense of humour, that lad.'

'Where is he today?' I asked hopefully.

'In the outfield with Flóki and his sheep – don't go yet, Karri,' she added quickly, as I began to stumble to my feet. 'We need you here for a moment, just to talk.' She glanced at Thomas and placed a mug of tea on the table before me.

'I hope this is to discuss allegations of drugging.' I transferred my gaze from Guðrun to Thomas. Thomas laughed over-emphatically. 'Yes, I suppose it is, in a way. How do you feel today, incidentally?'

It seemed likely that he cared at least a little for my well-being, yet given the uneven knit of his brows and the way in which he leaned towards me over the table, the main incentive was undoubtedly a professional curiosity. I was gripped by the feeling that I had been the subject of an experiment.

'Better.' I shifted my feet, reluctant to participate.

'No more terrible side-effects? Nausea, short-term narcolepsy, that sort of thing?'

'No.'

He straightened up, as if unsprung, clapped his hands together and exclaimed, 'Wonderful!' Then he fixed his sunken but still illuminated eyes on me.

'I agree it's wonderful for myself,' I said with a frown. I took a sip of tea. 'I don't enjoy being sick... But what are you so excited about?'

He watched me for a moment. My skin prickled, uncomfortably exposed. He seemed engaged in a debate with himself. 'I am,' he began, quite unable to fit the words comfortably past the contortion of his grinning lips, 'I suppose you might say, a sort of researcher. In a specific field of course; yet more broadly I might be considered a botanist.'

I frowned again.

'You see, Kjartan, I'm extremely interested in plants. They have this fantastic healing power. Now, you're an intelligent lad, I can see in your eyes that you are. And that is why I would quite like to enlist your help.' He fell silent. The grin on his face still filled me with discomfort.

'Err... help with what?'

I heard his words, saw the scruffy, eccentric Englishman sitting before me with his elbows on the vicar's table. I shifted in my seat as his intense gaze bored into my own centre of consciousness, yet I could not locate the correct emotional reaction. I could not locate *any* reaction in myself, in fact. The idea of a French cat wormed its way into my head, causing a spark of thoughts to ignite. A collection of kettles, too many, in a room full of apparatus... The incredible view from the slopes of Tindhólmur: the eagle's eyrie...

'Who are you?' I demanded. 'You live up on Tindhólmur: botanists do not live on top of sea stacks. How did you get there? What are you doing there? And why are you here, now, bothering me and *poisoning* me? You'd better start giving me some bloody answers if you want help.' I had the British garrison to thank for my ability to use bad language effectively in English. I had heard them so often on the streets or at the fish market, or around the card table, conversing with an intense energy: stories, laughter, and brilliantly offensive language.

'I make medicines, Kjartan. Herbal remedies. For instance, that remedy that you drank, err, *accidentally*, is specifically intended to help combat insomnia. I agree that it was a little too effective, but it was really only a prototype, I had not quite determined the correct balance of the ingredients, or the dosage. With your help, however, I managed to perfect it.'

I almost choked on my tea. 'With my help? Is that what you need me for: to be your guinea pig? So you can feed me uncertain home-made substances? *Oh dear, that one seems to have killed him, perhaps I ought to lower the dosage.*'

My poisoner laughed in genuine good humour. 'No, no, Kjartan; that is not my intention. I assure you that was simply an accident – and one that will not happen again. No, what I really desire your assistance for is as a messenger.'

'Messenger?'

It seemed unlikely that this man would have any contact with the village, as the community was small and close-knit; news travelled quickly. In particular, news of an Englishman residing in a small house on the uninhabitable slopes of Tind-hólmur would not only circulate around all available ears at the speed of light, but would undoubtedly travel all the way to Tórshavn. And the garrison would hear; they would swear over it with gusto, laugh at its absurdity, they would marvel at its intrigue... I had heard nothing to this effect. I wanted this man to disappear back to his island, to his cat, taking with him his excitement and his useful remedies. I knew what Magnus would say in response – and it would put even the garrison's colourful words to shame.

Magnus: of course. *He knew about this.* He could not fail to have known, for he had appointed Orri and me to the task of supplying fish. He had carried it out himself when in full health. *Magnus knew.*

I sat straighter in my seat, clutched my sheet with impatient fingers; fixed my eyes on the man before me. *Now* I was intrigued. A messenger.

'For Magnus?'

Much to my annoyance the man laughed again. 'No, no, not for Magnus.' He spoke the name with a hint of familiarity, though he gave away no more clues as to this effect. For a moment the name shone in his eyes. 'Not yet.' He paused. 'Perhaps 'messenger' is not quite the right description... I suppose you might say 'postman'.'

I scowled at him. 'I'm already a postman.'

'Well, exactly. You are a postman, and I require your services. You see, once my work is complete, it needs to be... distributed, I suppose; put to good use around the village.'

'You want to poison the locals?'

Thomas gave another chuckle that caused me to tighten my fists around the bundles of sheet at my waist. Before he had a chance to answer, however, Guðrun interrupted. 'I'm sorry, Karri, that was really my fault. I should not have given you that remedy, it was not my place to do so. But you were so in need of... of *something*; I did not know how else to help.' There was sadness in her eyes.

'I must assure you that my work is of the highest standard,' said Thomas, a rising note in his voice. 'I take great pride in it.

I do not take any risks, Kjartan, nothing I ask you to deliver will be in any danger of causing harm to anyone. I believe I can help people. Of course, I wish for neither my intentions nor my... existence to be widely known, for reasons that I am sure you must understand. Nevertheless, I wish to help others as best I can, and now is the time to begin.'

I could not take my eyes off the man. What did he mean by saying *now* was the time to begin? It was as though it were a plan of action that had been lying in wait for some time, as though he had been working towards this... *how long had he lived on Tindhólmur, right here under our noses?*

'But why me?'

'Because you are the right man for the job. After all, you are the postman – you have already been making deliveries to me. You have been directly, though inadvertently, err, *involved* with my work.' Here, he had the grace to blush slightly. 'And your ability to speak English is certainly of great use. Essential, really... Thus I thought you would be a perfect appointment. You might even think of yourself, now, as a personal assistant.'

I did not react as I might have done those months previously, when Tindhólmur had been concealed, still an infuriating mystery – its obscuring fog, those frequent deliveries of fish and milk to the place I had been sure was uninhabited – plaguing my mind with unanswered questions. Now, I knew what lay hidden beneath the mist. Admittedly I did not know the entire story, not yet. But I no longer wanted to know. The entire set-up was ridiculous: the man with his bright eyes and demeanour; I with my sheet, my sleeping sickness, the escapade in the boat when the sea had been dancing with sparks and colours. The sea was grey. It always had been, and would continue to be, the same shade of grey. The man's grin was sickening.

'Does Magnus know about this?'

'About what?'

'About you.' I could almost have spat the words.

Thomas faltered, the corners of his mouth fell fractionally. 'Well, I suppose he, err... ' The following smile was forced. 'Is that really important?'

'Of course it's important.' I was unsure exactly why, though. Perhaps because of the fact that Magnus had apparently kept this secret, though it might only have been me who had been kept in the dark until this moment. My head had started to throb painfully. The vision in my left eye had begun to blur. I knew I needed to escape, and suffer the oncoming attack in peace and quiet.

'Look, I don't know who you are, or why you have been hiding here without making yourself known; I don't know what you think you are trying to do, or why you claim to need my help. I don't know what Magnus has got to do with all this, or why he has let himself become involved – maybe it was him who sent you to recruit me, I don't know. And I also don't care. Please leave me alone.' I fixed my eyes on the floor and stumbled hastily from the room. I did not glance backwards, even when Guðrun called my name. I was sure the startled sadness I had seen in the eyes of Thomas was genuine but I was not to be turned in my resolve.

I came across my clothes hanging on the back of a chair in the hallway and took them back into the room in which I had awoken, pulling them on with breaths as heavy as my leaden limbs. I desired nothing more than to collapse onto the comforting bed, curl up and close my eyes, but I would not allow myself that absolution. I left the house by the front door. I heard a noise that might have been Guðrun flinging it open after me but I did not turn back to find out.

17

MY FOOTSTEPS CUT a relentless rhythm on the wet road, words in my head creating a marching pattern: *why do you need my help? (Step,) why do you need my help? (Step,) one two three, (step)...*

Eventually the words died down, the churning and the internal music also diminished, and all I heard were my damp footsteps. There were no other sounds around me, even my gasping breath had quietened. Clear raindrops bounced playfully around my feet like tiny balls of elastic. The stone wall before me had turned dark in the rain though the edges of its surface caught the light, and the light caught my eye. I reached out as I walked and ran my fingers lightly along the rough contours of the stone. The world felt altogether too real; so real, in fact, that there ought to have existed some incredible significance behind it, a point to it all.

I left the village and the rain grew heavier, the clouds lower, the air fresher. I followed the curve of the valley behind

Bøur, slipping down grass banks, brushing the sopping-wet hair from my eyes, following the sound of sheep, wet bleats through the spring downpour, forlorn and familiar. Occasionally there would ring out a distant cry, the call of the farmer, and it would echo from the mountainsides as though sounding from every direction at once.

Orri recognised me long before I reached the pasture. I saw his silhouetted figure turn expectantly from the animals by which he was surrounded. In patient silence he watched as I made my approach across the fields. Some metres away, Flóki shouted again to his dog, which barked in echoing response and threw itself greedily into the crowd of milling sheep. The sheep, in turn, increased their noise and bolted haphazardly away from the dog. The newborn lambs skipped and wobbled alongside their mothers with high-pitched cries. They were being rounded up to have their ears marked with one of the special cuts that varied from village to village. On many occasions I had dreamt that my own ear had been marked with the same cut of identification. I pulled at that ear now with a vague discomfort as I strolled closer.

Orri called out, 'You took your time!'

'Sorry,' I called back, my voice enveloped by the rush of the rain. 'I overslept.'

Orri's eyes were uncharacteristically sunken, dark-ringed from early mornings at the post office. Maybe they also bore the marks of the anxiety he must have felt while I was dead to the world. Still, when the afternoon's work came to a halt, he skipped back alongside me to his father's house, now full of energy. Inside, he put the kettle on and chatted to me incessantly until, as dusk approached, I mustered the strength within myself to speak those words that had lain so heavily on my tongue since I had left Guðrun's house. 'There's a man,' I said, 'living on Tindhólmur. I don't know who he is.'

Orri's eyes snapped up to meet mine. Then he looked away and shrugged his shoulders stiffly. 'Just something to do with the garrison, I expect.'

'Has Magnus told you anything about him?'

'I told you, Karri,' he said, and I could hear that he had to strive to sound nonchalant. 'It will just be something to do with the garrison: they do their thing, we do ours, there's no point asking questions.'

'But do you not sometimes wonder –?'

'I don't want to talk about the army,' he snapped. '*Please.*'

I looked at him, surprised by the sharpness in his voice; he would not meet my eyes. Before I had a chance to respond there came a knock at the door. Orri remained stubbornly seated and so after a moment I pulled myself heavily to my feet and left the room without a word.

On the other side of the door I beheld a tall, dark-haired young man with an open face, and another of roughly the same age with blond hair. They both grinned at me.

'Good evening, Kjartan,' beamed the taller one, 'how do we find you?'

'Err... fine.' I was about to return the enquiry but he leapt first into the pause. 'I hear you've been ill. What happened?'

I gave a small scowl and he laughed teasingly. 'Oh, of course: we must never ask Kjartan how he is, must we, Pétur?'

The blond-haired boy gave another grin in response. 'No, we mustn't, Jógvan.'

I gave up, smiling weakly in return. 'Come in, then, if you have to... '

They stepped past me under the low doorway, shaking off raindrops with a lot of exaggerated sighing, the sort that accompanies arrival into a pleasant environment. Indeed, there were few places that could be considered more pleasant than Orri's cosy home with its timbered walls and small windows. I closed the door tightly as Orri greeted the guests. The wave of irritation seemed to have left him; now in the dim light his face was flushed and his pupils were like round planets, shining intensely. He glanced over to where I stood near the door, his expression apologetic, his eyes creased at the corners.

'Is Magnus in?' asked Jógvan, though I noticed he made no attempt to remove his coat. There was always a degree of uncertainty as to the best way to inquire about Magnus's condition.

'Of course he's in.' Orri laughed as he turned his attention to his guest. 'But you could've done with coming a little earlier, Jógvan: he's asleep.'

Jógvan seemed relieved. 'Well, make sure you give him our regards, eh?'

'You and the rest of the town.'

My stomach gave a jolt as I saw Orri reach for his coat. 'Are we ready to go, then?' he asked, addressing all three of us. That was when I remembered, with an uncomfortable wave of nausea, the real reason for Jógvan and Pétur's visit.

'Is Kjartan coming?'

'Of course he's coming.' Orri grinned at me from the web of his shoelaces. 'He'll try to tell us that he doesn't want to, or isn't feeling well enough, or one of his other excuses; but we know he'll come all the same. Won't you, Karri?'

I shifted in my socks and looked from one face to another, took a deep breath and said with a lack of confidence that did nothing to help my position, 'I'm not going... ' As expected, the three of them cheered and broke into laughter before the last syllable had escaped my lips.

18

I ARRIVED AT the town hall wrapped warmly in Orri's grey jumper. Tired and feeling vulnerable, I folded my arms defensively across my chest. It was a dance we were attending, first and foremost, a traditional dance to celebrate our heritage: traditional steps, traditional music, comforting cultural practices in a world that insisted on growing larger and more impersonal by the minute.

Everyone attended these dances, even members of the garrison had begun to make an appearance at them. And yet as much as I was warmed by the excitement and camaraderie, the endurance of it required a certain frame of mind. A desire for solitude does not fit the picture neatly, and it tested my resolve to be caught in a room with so many people. I knew them all intimately of course, I had grown up in their company, yet sometimes they seemed like strangers to me. I came inevitably to feel that night as though I did not belong, as though I, like the troops of the garrison, had arrived from the distance of a million miles; as though I were trespassing. The familiarity, the kindness, the community, did not belong to me; I was a fraud, inexplicably an outsider.

By the time of our slightly late arrival the dance ring had already formed: two steps to the left, one to the right, moving in a gradual clockwise direction with the beat carried by the rhythmic stomping of so many feet. The leader's voice rang loud and clear in the solo stanzas. He was a well-built man with a red face, a large beard and a deep voice to which a man of younger years could certainly not aspire. Confidently he chanted the Faroese words while the villagers clapped hands and stomped feet to the steady rhythm before joining hands – the whole circle – and erupting into the sung refrain as one voice.

The infectious medieval ballads pounded my temples. My own heartbeat adopted the rhythm, attempting to leap violently from my chest with every pulse; a compelling sensation. I ended up, quite without intending to, immersed in the ring of clasped hands. Orri was to my left and Jógvan to my right, for ballad after ballad – for it was not done to sing the same one twice. Each ballad had more verses than could be counted. But I knew all the words nonetheless, I had grown up with them. Even now, as I heard the words and sang them myself, danced the lively circle, I was thrown back to the days of my childhood, some details still fresh in my memory.

The first movements of the steps as a young boy, the excitement brought about by so many of our friends in one place, engaged in one communal activity.

The crashing of the waves near our front door, I smell the rain on the summer grass. I recall the first time I saw a lamb being brought into the world. I feel the swell of the sea beneath the boat. I smell fresh fish at the market.

My father and I stand on top of the mountain, he showing me Sørvágur, Bøur, and the land and the sea around it, stretching back forever. I speak my first words of English. My brother sits at the table, his nose buried in a book, concentrating so intently.

Although it felt as though I had been caught up in the melee of the dance hall for barely a few minutes, by the time I extricated myself for the desperate need of fresh air, thick darkness had fallen outside. I wondered how the hours had passed without my comprehension. I walked to stand some way away from the hall, along the road, concentrating only on the pounding of my heart as it slowed. The rain fell lightly, like snowflakes.

I peered with wide eyes to the place where I knew the mountains stood, and was met with the most wonderful feeling to know that they loomed behind the opaque wall of darkness past which my eyes could not see, so strong and silent, so immovable. I wandered the short distance slowly back to the town hall, hands in pockets, hearing the dull thud of my feet on the damp earth. Despite the chill of the night air my face was heated almost to a fever. I splashed some ice-cold water onto my cheeks from the trough by the side of the building, and in it I caught sight of my reflection. A nineteen-year-old face stared back at me from the rippling surface in the frame of light from the hall. It crept and shimmered on the water. As the image stilled with the ripples, I made out curved cheekbones and dark hair against pale skin. Grey eyes peered out with a troubled sadness that even I found unnerving. *Who are you?* I straightened up once more, pulling the sleeves of my jumper down over my hands with a shiver, and as I turned around I saw someone standing not far away.

She continued to watch me, red hair almost fiery in the light that shone from the doorway. Her skin seemed luminous, her eyes piercing. I tore my eyes away immediately, tugging the sleeves of my jumper down further over my fingers. I tried to speak, but managed little more than a suspension of breath. She took a step towards me, eyes still fixed.

'Where were you going?' Her voice was quiet and husky. I answered equally quietly, mumbling something about fresh air.

'You came back, though, didn't you?' It seemed as though she moved closer to me, though in the flickering half-light it might have been an illusion. 'Did you know I was here?'

I faltered before I had even attempted to organise a response. Of course I had not known she had been standing there; I had not known she had been watching me, or waiting for me. I said nothing, for I knew there existed nothing I could say that would help me. And in saying this *nothing* so emphatically it seemed as though I drew her, by some will of hers or my own, even closer to me. Boldly, she reached out a small hand and brushed hair from my eyes. My entire body shivered. 'You're very attractive, Kjartan,' she murmured, so quietly that I was unsure whether I had heard her correctly.

'Err... thank you.' My voice disappeared into the soft rain.

'I've noticed the way you look at me in the post office.'

I blushed, unable to tear my eyes from hers. Her eyelashes were thick and curled, her lips full and red, parted slightly. Then they were barely inches from mine as she slid a chilled hand around the back of my neck. So close, I could see that her cheeks were decorated with clear droplets of late night rain. Her smell was of a scented warmth, soft and lingering. It made my head reel. The shawl slipped gently from her half-bare shoulders and I saw that they were littered with pale freckles, picked out by shards of light from the hall. I breathed in the scent of her sweet-smelling hair. Waves of its soft redness poured over the gentle curve of her breasts beneath her dress, causing a wave of desire to tighten my insides. My hand wavered uncertainty against her waist, so gently that I all but held it in mid-air. She pulled me in only fractionally. I forgot the rain, forgot how to breathe. But as our lips barely touched she stepped back from me so promptly that the chill of the night hit me with force. Her hands lowered slowly to her sides.

'I just wanted to see if you would kiss me.'

She attempted a condescending smile but I saw the uncertainty in her eyes, belying the self-confidence she strove to exhibit. Her shoulders were tense. She turned her back, graceful yet with haste, and as I watched her walk with apparent calm around the corner to the door her footsteps speeded up. She passed Orri. She did not look at him. Even when she had disappeared from sight I remained motionless. Still able to feel the brush of her lips on mine, my heart was racing, blood pounding in my ears. I curled my fingers into the sleeves of Orri's jumper. Orri did not move as I approached him. His eyes flittered between my face and the imposing darkness. Eventually he spoke. 'I just... wanted to see if you were all right.'

My throat twisted as though I had swallowed a brick. Orri looked forlorn. More than anything I longed to tell him that I was sorry but I knew he would simply smile and ask me why. And why *was* I sorry? I bit my lip, hit suddenly by an overwhelming exhaustion, by a ton of bricks, each as heavy as the one I seemed to have swallowed, and stared at the ground.

'Why did you read in the church the other day?' Orri asked.

I dragged my chin up, missing the movement of his lips and thus feeling strangely as though the words had simply appeared in my head. I answered along the lines that the vicar had been wanting someone to read in English, that was all, but Orri shook his head, silently interrupting my half-hearted explanation. 'That's not what I mean. Why did you agree to do it? Why did you, when you knew it would only make you ill?'

I swallowed and when I spoke my voice sounded weak even to me. 'My own feelings aren't important: the vicar was happy because he was able to hold the perfect service, appealing to the garrison as he's always trying to do. The parishioners were happy because they felt a little more international without having to be tied to the Danish as usual. *You* were happy because you finally got me into the church, got me *involved*, like you've been trying so desperately to achieve for so many years.'

'That's not what I want,' Orri said, looking hurt. 'I know you don't believe in God, Kjartan. So many times you've told me that we have just created Him to fill a void in ourselves, in our morals and in our degree of control. You say He's a "benefactor and maintainer of good fortune, a safety net for our anxieties, and a scapegoat for when everything goes wrong". You said this *conjured existence* strips us of all responsibility, yet still causes us to feel all the more important.'

'So you're angry with me? You're angry because I have lied, because I have disguised myself as a believer, in your church, before the eyes of God? Was I standing at the pulpit *laughing* at all God's lost little sheep with their blind devotion, then, because they believe that praying will stop the war? With God in the picture no one needs to do anything because *God* will clear up the mess, won't he?'

Orri allowed my words to settle before replying. 'No,' he said. 'I'm not angry with you. The only person you are lying to is yourself, Karri. I can't understand this. You say that God is nothing more than a fictitious creation designed to make the world feel better about itself; and you say this bitterly, but then you use God in the same way. And don't disagree with me. You know God has become just as important to *you* as He is to the very people you despise and condemn for that same reason. To you He is a scapegoat. Listen to yourself, Kjartan: you're so angry with Him because of the war; you might be angry because you feel He has allowed it to happen, or that He is simply doing nothing to stop it. You're angry because He is either malicious, or does not exist but either way you still hate Him. You hate Him almost as passionately as you hate yourself.' Another pause. Then his voice was lower. 'So how can you accuse the religious community, the whole world, *me*, of putting all our faith and responsibility in God, when you are just as guilty of that yourself?'

For a moment I stared at him, unable to find my voice. Never had I felt so exposed. I wished, deeply, that I knew my own feelings and could thus express them to Orri's waiting ears. I wished I could convince him that I was not lost, not uncertain, though of course I was and this he knew.

'I don't hate the believers.' I studied my shoes while I muttered the words. 'How can I hate them? They know what they believe, how it makes them feel. They know exactly what to do, and they're never lost; never alone... How can I begrudge them this? They have no doubts or fears, or if they do, then God quells each one; everything can be thought of as beautiful and divine. I don't know how they can be so secure... ' My cheeks were wet with tears, and I turned away towards the hidden mountains.

'Is that why you go to the church in the mornings?' Orri asked haltingly, 'When you take the post... to understand?'

A flash of panic. I did not think he knew this; had Guðrun told him, or had he seen me?

'It's nothing to be ashamed of,' he said. 'Look, Karri, I am not accusing you of anything, or judging you. I just want you to stop tormenting yourself. It's not worth it. I hate to see you like this.'

'Like *what*? You cannot tell me how to think, how to behave. It doesn't work like that.'

'I'm just trying to help.'

'Who says I need help?'

Orri let out a shaky breath. 'I really *care* about you, Kjartan.'

The warmth in his voice melted into the air between us. But

my defences had still not been broken down. 'No you don't. I know you don't. And what's more I know the real reason for your coming out here.'

That brief press of her lips on my own, the tickle of her hair on my neck. The female scent of her body. An afterwave of lust only spurned on my anger. 'You followed Asta out; you followed her out so that you could keep her away from me; so she wouldn't come anywhere near me – you'd really hate that, wouldn't you?'

I caught a glimpse of uncertainty in his eyes. I wanted to expose him, as he had stripped *me* bare. I wanted to accuse him of desiring Asta for himself; though the thought had never occurred to me before. I stumbled upon it now as the perfect catalyst for the emotions that assailed me. Had he and Asta not spent time together in the post office while I lay sleeping? I stood poised on the brink of words, while he took another shaken breath.

'Karri, I've known you for nearly twenty years.'

'That does not qualify you to make my decisions! You may be content with not questioning the world, Orri, but I cannot resign myself to your cushion of blind and blissful ignorance just yet.' Was I referring to the deliberate lack of interest he showed in Tindhólmur's mysterious inhabitant when I had tried to raise the subject earlier? Anger flashed across his face, though he said nothing before he turned and walked back into the hall. I was left shivering with the chill of the night air.

19

I LAY AWAKE, staring irritably at the ceiling. Today I was not going to bother getting out of bed, not going to bother with the post. It could deliver itself or rot in the post office for all I cared – my guilty conscience, however, insisted on coming into play before my duties had even been shirked. I made myself a cup of tea and stared at the walls for a few more stretches of eternity.

I had insisted on returning to the solitude of my empty house for the night. Orri had not spoken to me, had barely looked at me and offered no resistance to my declaration of returning home. So alone I awoke, alone I dressed as the dawn began to illuminate the sky. I left the house, certain that upon my arrival at the post office that morning I would be met with a strange parcel, a delivery of plants or a letter of instruction. Maybe Thomas himself would be standing there wrapped in brown parcel paper, tied with string.

As I cycled absentmindedly into Sørvágur, I planned out

what I might say to the man. Finding him there was an unlikely prospect, though were it to transpire I would undoubtedly say nothing. The words with which I toyed now, granted to me so usefully by the verbal indecency of the garrison, would then sit in the back of my throat until I choked on them.

There was no man wrapped in parcel paper. There was no Asta. There was no coffee, either. I stood in the doorway and smoked a cigarette, watching the world around me begin to wake as Elva apologised for the lack of coffee, remarked that I was later than usual this morning, and fumbled around with piles of letters. There were only a few letters, admittedly. Gásadalur in particular, the hamlet that lay over the mountain, had little cause for piles of the things. 'Ah!' she exclaimed suddenly: 'There's one for you, Kjartan.'

I sprang into immediate animation, arriving by her side in a fraction of a second. Whilst her interest was apparent, I had not realised what poised expectancy I had been gripped with whilst standing on the doorstep feigning indifference; in fact I had been raised on the balls of my feet, tapping my fingers against the door frame, my imagination startlingly active in expectation of something of this kind.

Elva pushed the letter into my itching, waiting fingers. All too aware of her curiosity, I put it immediately away in my pocket. Hoisting onto my shoulder the bag which contained the morning's post I bid her goodbye in as friendly a way as possible so as to counteract the hastiness of my departure. I did not open the letter outside the post office; it stayed in my pocket all the way to Bøur, and even there I did not remove it despite the desperate nature of my anticipation. I did not open the letter until I was looking down upon Bøur from halfway up the mountainside. It occurred to me, even then, that perhaps I should keep the envelope closed, as a bait to compel all my daily actions henceforth.

In my imagination the letter had the ability to become anything. It could be a letter from the Creator of the universe, so elusive to me until this moment, suddenly singling me out and imparting to me the reason and meaning behind all things. And even if in actuality there was a complete absence of meaning, no point, no Creator, I could keep the letter unopened until my dying day. I could toy all my life with the possibility that upon its opening there might still be revealed that elusive secret of all things. This possibility alone would drive the path of my life, conjure motivation as it were. And if in the final moments of my life I discovered the true utter meaninglessness of things – the Creator denouncing His own existence – then I would be upon my deathbed, and it would not matter. In death it would mean nothing to me to learn that my existence had been as vague and as pointless as I had suspected throughout.

Of course, I knew the letter was from Thomas. Had it been

from my father (something that I hoped for every morning, though I knew communication to be impossible), Elva, recognising a Danish stamp, would have announced this excitedly. The Creator of the universe would have used a nicer, cleaner envelope, one that was not stained with tea. And He would have spelt my name correctly. I tore it open.

Come to Tindhólmur before noon, the letter requested of me in spidery handwriting. *Some fish would be nice. And can I have some milk as well? Thomas.*

P.s: deliver your post first.

I crumpled the letter in my hand. Of all the wondrous words the envelope could have contained, I had received merely an inelegant English scrawl on a piece of scrap paper that looked as though it may have been used to clean the table. Upon my last meeting with Thomas I had thought, with his air of grandeur and rushed, glittering whispers, that he had exaggerated his cause but I realised now that it had been me who was guilty of this. I had reacted with unnecessary intensity. The letter, similarly, had roused within me a feeling of excitable expectation. I cursed myself for harbouring such an illusion.

I refused to make any alterations to the routine of my postal delivery. I walked no faster or slower than usual and I practised my English aloud as I always did when I descended the mountain, dropping clean words into the fresh air. I would make no special allowances for Thomas. *The nerve of the man to dictate to me that I must first deliver the post.* I thought about arriving an hour or so later than requested, to prove my indifference; yet it occurred to me that such an action might in fact indicate the opposite. So I wandered around the mountainside in my usual reverie and eventually drifted down through the valley to Birgir's farm. The day was clear and from a distance I could see him pottering about the cowshed in his overalls, with a cup of morning coffee in one hand and a carefree air that indicated he might be whistling jovially to himself, though I was yet too distant to perceive the sound. He waved as I approached.

'Morning, Kjartan.'

It was still too early in the year for the cows to be released from their winter lodgings. Birgir, as a self-sufficient dairy farmer, was in possession of a large and impressive herd and I could hear the animals baying from the shed. With his low voice and slight elongation of the face Birgir reminded me of a cow sometimes. He had dark, moist eyes and a lighthearted disposition. He scratched his greying beard as I meandered towards him, pleased to have a task on which to focus my mind for a few minutes at the very least.

'Morning, Kjartan,' he bayed once more, as if I might have forgotten his initial greeting. 'I suppose you'll be after some milk, will you?'

I smiled timidly. I had known the man my entire life, yet I still felt a little uncomfortable around him, as I did around everyone: what if I inadvertently ruined his cheerful disposition in one way or another? For try as I might I could not match it. 'Yes, please.' I made an attempt at a joke. 'If you are still in the business, of course.'

He guffawed, throwing back his beard, delighted that I should have brought his occupation into the light of a discussion that would inevitably follow. He began by remarking upon the health of his herd, referring to a few names individually and with great tenderness and familiarity. I was impressed that the man was able to attribute so much personality to his animals. Whether or not he merely imagined such anthropomorphic states on the cows' part, he nevertheless knew his herd inside out.

True, I had been known to talk to the cattle when helping out on the farm but always in complaint. Certain that the cowshed contained no life form able to understand my words, I would spill out my anxieties – sometimes in a state of extreme agitation. Pacing the mucky floor, I would throw out my arms in a manner most likely alarming for the bystanding cows and wail rhetorical questions towards every wall. Sometimes my air was more flippant, directing facetious remarks towards the nearest cow who would stare back at me unquestioningly with large, mournful eyes and an apparent interest in my words. In conclusion to my tirade of irritations I would exclaim, 'I mean, you know how it is, right?' Then, viewing the static expression from the static animal: 'Well, of course you don't. You're a cow.'

We did not own a family cow, or indeed any livestock; at home I had to be content, at times of pressing, uncontainable anguish, with shouting at the kettle – the only thing in our possession that appeared to have any life of its own. It would scream as it came to the boil, and I would scream back at it, and invariably feel much better. It was an agreeable relationship, yet the cows were much more understanding.

Birgir considered it a shame that the days of the family cow were beginning to wane. The notion of cultivating the land, he said, of living from nature, supplying for and feeding one's own family, was the traditional way to happiness. I pointed out to him that were this the case, then he would be out of a job. And he laughed and turned towards the farmhouse to fetch the coffee. I did not follow him inside, for I was reluctant to encounter his wife and children. I could not bear the thought of having to make conversation. On the frequent occasions that I came face to face with them I could think of nothing at all to say, not a single word, whether appropriate or not.

I was often called upon in times of bad summer weather to assist Birgir's daughter, Ragna, with the milking. At these times I enjoyed the crispness of the air, the empty wooden milk pails clattering against each other with a hollow sound. I enjoyed being barefoot in the sodden grass of the fields, water between my toes. Orri, too, liked this responsibility: he would skip gleefully across the field when he had been called to help, sometimes singing as he went. And Ragna would run after him, holding up her skirt with one hand, a pail in the other, calling to him teasingly.

Ragna would catch Orri's hand sometimes, wrap her arms around his waist, pretend she was holding him prisoner. His hyperactivity would have him falling about in the grass, laughing incessantly. The girl was seventeen years old, delightfully plump with fair hair and blue eyes like Orri's. She had one of those complexions that was creamy and smooth, always with roses in her curved cheeks. Orri would tease her and make her squeal as he did I don't know what to her – tickle her or something. I was too embarrassed to look.

Needless to say my own experience with Ragna was quite different. On the most recent occasion we had worked together we had sat on our milking stools, finding few words to say to each other as the milk flowed into our buckets. She had sighed occasionally, hardly concentrating on her task, her skirt rustling as she shifted her restless legs. Then she brushed her fair hair behind her ears and finally said, without making eye contact, 'You don't talk much, do you, Kjartan?'

'Um... no. Sorry.'

I had proven her point. After that I was propelled into an almost unbearable discomfort, no longer able to listen to the rain play its melody on the fields or allow my eyes to drink in the mountains and the freedom of the grey sky. I could no longer simply enjoy the silence.

Birgir was not long delayed in his quest for the morning coffee. We drank leaning against the wooden fence, surveying the curves and corners of the open land, the mountains patterned with dissipating snow, like first settlers in a new northern land. The garrison and the industry lay miles south of our isolation. Birgir said nothing of these recent developments; no longer so recent, for over a year had allowed for all necessary adjustment and integration. The British occupation was now part of our daily life, part of the island, and there was little to complain about in that respect. Birgir asked after Magnus, after the success of the current fishing season, after general local matters of ordinary, everyday concern. When the coffee had almost run dry he brought up the topic, smiling all the while, of the shining good health of the village, the winter considered especially. And I thought of Thomas.

20

THE SUN CLIMBED higher in the sky as I approached Tind-hólmur. My small, flat-backed boat threw itself around haphazardly on the waves in a manner that I was barely able to control. Orri, the son of a fisherman, had very little trouble in this respect, come blizzard or torrential downpour. But as the son of a teacher I found myself quite worryingly out of my depth, in more ways than one.

Nevertheless I managed to moor the boat to the iron pole that had been driven into the rock of the shore. There was a small alcove in the rugged terrain of the miniature coastline, and at last I placed my shaking feet on stable land. I looked back towards the coast of Bøur. It watched me from the distance, watched to see what I would do next. I had no idea. I had landed on the more habitable face of Tindhólmur; the other side was a virtually sheer cliff of over two -hundred feet of rough volcanic rock upon which only the birds could settle themselves. I could hear them crying from every direction; screaming above my head and diving over the steel waves. They screeched with such hysteria.

This side of the islet was more hospitable in gradient, but only insomuch as the higher mountainsides around Bøur were, made of sharp rocks and green earth. There was some sparse vegetation above the shoreline, clinging to the rock for dear life. It was not so steep as to pose an impossible climb; nonetheless it would be difficult. I must have somehow achieved it on my previous visit, though I could of course not recall the path I had taken. I was certainly reluctant now to attempt to scale the heights of a mountain I could not see for mist. I was unsure of where exactly I was headed, and whether once my destination had been located I would even be in a position to gain entry.

The house stood in an utterly impractical position; it probably had its front door poised over a cliff. I resolved to wait. For Thomas, for his cat, for Magnus, I did not know, but it seemed a reasonable action nonetheless.

I sat down a little way above the boat, took off my hat, and withdrew some bread from the carefully arranged bag of provisions I had brought for Thomas. My appetite seemed to be returning with a vengeance, for I ate hungrily, something I had not done for some weeks. Meanwhile I examined the plants growing around where I sat. They were small and adorned with broad leaves, a few had dainty, colourful flowers. They grew from the hard soil and the rocky projections with a stead-fast resolve, littering the slope with decoration. They opened hopefully towards the sun that did not shine, and must only do so infrequently. Although the flora resembled the blanket-like vegetation so familiar over all my island, I had seen nothing quite like this before: in size, in colour, in variety, even in this kind of position, so exposed to the relentless torment of the northern weather.

They may have been deliberately planted, and I knew who by, but their distribution bore no pattern or signs of organisa-tion; it was as though they had simply been dropped from the sky. Taking another absentminded bite of freshly baked bread I bent closer to the earth, exploring its secrets. From towards the sky, someone spoke.

'Are you eating my bread?'

I craned my neck and looked up at Thomas. 'I thought if I threw it up to you the birds would get it.' In struggling to my feet I discovered the two of us were of a similar height. 'You're growing plants,' I observed. 'On the rocks. By the North At-lantic. Is that, err... is that possible?'

Thomas did not take his eyes from mine. He beamed. 'Yes.' He closed his mouth, then immediately snapped it open again and called for me to come up and have some tea, and bring the fish. I pulled on my hat and followed him over the rocks. The crashing of the waves grew distant, almost musical, as we ascended the peak by what revealed itself as a well-used route in the earth, curving up around the islet's contours into the mist.

Wet against my skin and clothes, the chill found its way under my outer layers, into my lungs, into my bones, and they shook within me as we climbed further. I watched Thomas's boots on the rocks and tried to copy his footsteps: occasionally they slipped, losing their grip only momentarily on the moss or the damp sheen painted by the mist. I could see no further than his feet: the air was opaque, material, and utterly still, enclosed as walls around us. To one side of us the mountain loomed darkly and solidly, an overbearing presence; to the other there was nothing. Beyond the tread of my feet there existed a ledge of volcanic rock which promptly disappeared into a white void – an unnerving oblivion. All lay deadly silent. In the cold, clear air I felt fragile but did not pause to think. I only climbed higher, my breath coming heavily, until eventually the shape of a house loomed through the mist.

With dark-painted walls and a red roof it stood low, nestled into the rock upon which it was built. It was a small, simple house, Scandinavian in style. Through one of the windows a warm light glowed. Thomas led me up the few wooden steps that ascended to the front door, upon which was fastened a small metal doorknocker, discoloured by the weather. For a moment or two I stared at it, wondering why such a commonplace thing appeared to me now so strange, before I considered that in light of the journey we had taken to get here, the man's visitors must be few, if any. Above the door an oil lamp hung by a chain from the rafters of the roof, completely stationary in the calm desolation of the eagle's eyrie.

Now standing rooted to the spot, all I could hear was the shallow breathing of Thomas as he pulled a key from his coat pocket and unlocked the door. As to why he had felt the need to lock the door in the first place, I did not ask. For the final time I turned back to face the opaque wall of mist and drew a clear, cold breath to the depths of my lungs before following him inside. I closed the door behind me with a satisfying thud of wood upon wood, and took off my boots in the miniscule hallway. My hands were stiff from the cold.

'Don't worry,' said Thomas, peeking his head through a doorway he had entered ahead of me. 'I've lit the stove, you'll soon warm up.'

He disappeared once more, the sound of his footsteps on the wooden floor followed by the cacophonous clattering of crockery, as though he was throwing pans about the room. I could hear him whistling. After vigorously rubbing together my hands, blowing into cupped fingers and stamping my feet, I finally shuffled in my woollen socks past a step-like staircase through the door into what proved to be, with an unpleasant tug of familiarity, the room in which I had awoken on my un-planned previous visit. It still looked as though it had suffered a direct hit in the London Blitz and, again, though outside it was broad daylight, little light managed to infiltrate through the small windows.

Thomas finished trimming the wick of a lamp before lighting it and hanging it from a hook above the table. 'I'll make you some of my speciality tea,' he exclaimed. 'There's no need to look alarmed.' He glanced at me. 'Oh, you don't look alarmed.'

'I'm not,' I said.

'Hmm.' A pause. 'Would you like to sit down?'

I did so, my legs leaden and my head light from the climb. Outside, the heavens opened. Before long I sat in the warming glow of the lamp, my hands wrapped around a steaming mug of tea, contentedly watching the tumultuous gathering of raindrops on the cold glass of the window which was slowly becoming opaque with condensation.

'How old are you, Kjartan?'

'Mm?'

He was sitting across the table from me, observing me with the most relaxed air.

'How old are you?'

'Nineteen.'

'Ah.' He gave a somewhat nostalgic smile. 'A good age.'

'Is it?'

'You'll be getting married soon, I suppose?'

I laughed uncertainly. 'Married? You haven't brought me here to talk about girls?'

'No, I haven't. You're absolutely right, Kjartan. I'm sorry, but after you shouted at me the last time we met for beginning so abruptly, I thought I ought to, err, wean you in a little more, as it were. You know, make you feel comfortable, get you talking... I suppose I didn't manage it too well, did I?'

I smiled. He felt just as unsure in present company as I did. 'No, I'm afraid not.'

Thomas was not to be deterred. 'Well, I don't know,' he gabbled. 'I thought you might want to talk about girls: that's all I ever thought about at nineteen.' He leapt to his feet. 'Wait here, I think I need to show you something... '

While he was gone I sat quietly, listening to the heavy spring rain against the wooden walls, and wrapped myself in the thick wool of my jumper against the chill that lingered about the slowly warming room. *Orri must be out in this weather.* I wondered immediately why the thought of him had sprung to mind while I sat at a strange man's kitchen table, so close to home and yet at such a distance. It seemed there ought to be enough to occupy my attention, for this was no ordinary home visit.

Thomas soon returned with a small green potted plant and an unassuming-looking wooden box. He placed the two items on the table between us and sat down. 'I suppose you've already come across one of these, haven't you?' he asked in reference to the broad-leafed plant, and the sincerity and directness of his query startled me for thus far he had only been frustratingly incoherent. I lost no time in scrutinising the object of interest, and in doing so immediately recognised it as similar to the specimens at Tindhólmur's base. I reached out and took one of its broad leaves between my thumb and index finger, and felt its coarseness and rubbery strength. 'Tear it off,' said Thomas.

I slid my fingers down the leaf's rubbery stem, and found I had to tug sharply and firmly to cause it to tear. I laid it down on the table, feeling as though I had desecrated something sacred. 'This is what I use,' Thomas explained, rolling the leaf between his own fingers.

'For what?'

'For the teabags, of course. You know all about those; but here – I brought some to show you anyway.' With a swift flick of his finger he opened the wooden box to show its contents. 'They're medicinal. If I prepare the correct amounts of everything.' He waved the leaf as though it were caught in a breeze.

'But how do they work?'

Thomas peered thoughtfully into the middle-distance and the leaf danced the tick-tock rhythm of his progressing thoughts until he said wistfully, 'There was a man called Withering.' He paused; I wondered if the explanation had come to an end. 'At the turn of the century,' he added, just before I opened my mouth to inquire. 'A scientist of sorts. And he met a... *wise* woman, as she was known... ' He paused again, knitting his eyebrows, and the lines around his tired eyes deepened.

I fretted that I would fail to understand what he was about to say, whether it be the knowledge he wished to impart, or his use of the English language. I had often been faced with words I did not understand, despite my best efforts. But now surrounded by so many British troops I endeavoured to speak with them at every available opportunity and my vocabulary had improved noticeably.

'Are you aware of the disease oedema, sometimes called dropsy?' Thomas asked.

'Yes,' I answered.

'Are you?'

'Err... no.'

He grinned. I told myself to relax: ignorance was not a crime. Thomas launched matter-of-factly into an explanation. 'Oedema is a disease whereby problems with the heart and kidneys result in raised blood pressure. This in turn means that tissue fluid – bodily tissue? The stuff that all the organs are made of – fails to return to the capillaries – the blood vessels close to the skin. Oh, you know that word. So it accumulates in the feet, in the legs. The organs swell up. Very unpleasant, very painful and eventually the patient drowns as the fluid fills the lungs.' He stopped abruptly. Then, entirely out of keeping with the effect of the unpleasant description, burst into full-bodied laughter. '*Now* you look alarmed!'

(Following his description I had become preoccupied with a sudden aching in my feet.)

'I wonder what the Faroese term is,' Thomas was saying. I admitted that the description did not sound familiar, and as far as I knew I had suffered neither from dropsy nor its Faroese equivalent. Again he laughed and gave a dismissive wave of his hand. 'Ah, well this old 'wise' woman that Withering met was indeed suffering from oedema, or she showed symptoms of the disease at least. But she drank some form of herbal tea that she had prepared herself, and shortly afterwards seemed to have recovered. So Withering took this 'potion' and analysed it and came across twenty or so different herbs contained in it. He called it 'digitalis soup'. It had some very nasty side-effects, one of which was vomiting. So he fed a patient who had heart problems enough of the stuff until he, the patient, was physically sick, then lowered the dosage to achieve the correct amount that did not induce vomiting. And this restored the full, regular heartbeat of the patient, and so cured the disease. Although,' Thomas added quickly to himself, eyes fixed again upon the thoughtful middle distance, 'his next patient – an old woman – nearly died as a result of his experimenting, so he gave up his investigations... But the point of the story *is*, that the active ingredient in the soup was found to be digitalis, which is found in foxgloves.'

'They're poisonous,' I contributed.

'Ah,' Thomas contradicted. "Poison' is a relative term: it relates only to the dose necessary to cause harm to the organism, do you understand?' I nodded. 'You see,' he continued. 'If, at a particular level of dosage, a chemical can kill pathogenic microbes... ' In response to my look of alarm at the English term 'pathogenic microbes', Thomas stopped to explain it in smaller, more familiar words (and I blushed furiously at my ignorance). 'If a particular dose of a chemical can kill pathogenic microbes or malignant cancer cells, *but not humans*, then what is termed 'poison' becomes a potential medicine... do you see?'

'You mean... it kills the things that are doing harm to the person, but not the person himself?'

'Exactly,' Thomas declared. 'So the digitalis – the active poison – in foxgloves, for example, harms humans at a high level of dosage. It causes dizziness, vomiting, hallucinations and heart failure. But in *moderation*, its effects on heart beat make it an effective remedy: in oedema, for example, where the heart is irregular by symptom, the chemical *regulates* it.'

He paused and I watched him in thick silence. 'So you see,' he continued with confidence. 'You see where effective remedies originate from? Natural sources. It's just a brief overview.' The corners of his eyes creased. 'But you see, don't you?'

'Yes,' I assured him. 'Yes, I understand. I suppose this is all about your medicines, isn't it? The ones you told me about at Guðrun's? You're trying to convince me that natural things can't be all that dangerous, for the reason of their being natural, in that positive sense of the word.'

With a smile on his face Thomas accused me of being mercilessly sceptical.

'Can I ask you a question, Thomas?'

He shrugged his shoulders. 'Go ahead.'

'Well, you may accuse me, again, of being a sceptic: but what exactly do you plan to do with these herbal remedies of yours? I mean, putting aside certain inconsistencies such as your actual *growing* of these plants in this environment, and what you do to, err... prepare them, and how you can be so certain of their effectiveness... what happens next?'

'I distribute remedies where they're needed.'

'But will people be... reciprocal? Will they know you're behind this? You know, we have our own medicines. How ill do you think we are? There's hardly a gap in the market.'

His eyes sparkled suddenly. 'Oh, you have medicines,' he said quietly, 'but not like these.' Nothing more was said on the subject and I politely declined the offer of another cup of tea. Thomas insisted on accompanying me back down the rugged path to the boat's mooring, anxious, he admitted, that I might lose my way. We walked in a silence that, though pensive, was not altogether uncomfortable. Eventually we descended from the mist and I picked my way carefully into the boat, though when I turned to bid him farewell I found the man had disappeared.

Thomas had entrusted me with a small collection of teabags intended for delivery by me, his designated helper. After I had taken leave of Tindhólmur I reproached myself for accepting the task without comment; there were many things I now wanted to ask Thomas, questions that I had been unable to formulate whilst in his home, having been muted by the peculiarity of the situation as well as the sheer amount of information with which I had been presented. I resolved to make a written note of those questions which had sprung to mind, but found, having taken up a pen, that I could not locate the words to express my thoughts.

21

Orri and I played cards on the kitchen floor while outside the darkness swelled against the window. In the warm illumination of the oil lamp I squinted at the cards in my hand; the Queen, the King, and a Joker I had forgotten to remove. They repelled me. The king in particular regarded me from his paper frame with a condescending nobility, exuding a dominance that sent a shudder down my spine. I glanced once more at Ásdis as she cleared up after the evening meal. Not once had she turned her eyes in my direction as we ate; when I had thanked her for the meal she had nodded stiffly, forced her gaze to meet mine, so it seemed; when I had offered to help her to wash the pots she had not responded at all, but hurried over to the stove to complete the task herself. Perhaps it was obvious, the desperate way in which I tried to make amends for my evidently ill-timed presence in the household. Perhaps it only made things worse.

Orri sat beside me, his knees drawn up under his chin

and his arms wrapped around them. As his mother left the room without a word and headed in the direction of Magnus's sickbed, I squinted instead at Orri, finding his eyes already fixed upon me. It seemed they might have been for some time, because for a few extended moments there was no change in his attention, as though he had not yet realised that I had met his gaze. Suddenly he blinked and tore his blue eyes away from mine. After another moment he looked at me again and asked quietly, 'Where are you?'

At my evident confusion he gave a gentle smile. 'You're not in this room, are you?'

Heat rose to my cheeks. 'On a different planet.'

'Which one?'

'It hasn't got a name.'

'What's it like there?'

I studied the ends of my fingernails. 'Empty.'

'Of what?'

'Of everything. Of people.'

'Why?'

'Because there can be nothing to worry about with it like that. Everything just is as it is.'

'That sounds awful.'

'Does it? Why?' He was still smiling but it seemed forced, a fragile smile that quivered at the corners of his lips. With his face averted from the lamp his features were bathed in soft-edged shadows, like a painting. The pupils of his eyes looked huge; spherical planets into which the shadows poured. When he spoke his voice sounded deeper in the night's thick silence. 'Well, then what is there to live for?'

'Nothing,' I said pleasantly, 'that's the beauty of it.' I paused, the words lying treacle-thick upon my tongue. Pushed them off. 'Everything just is.'

'You're not at home around people, are you, Karri?'

'Oh,' I groaned, 'I care, I really care; and do you know what? It's exhausting. Everything is a bloody mess; no one's ever happy, for one reason or another. If one thing fixes itself, another falls spectacularly to pieces. There are too many possibilities and difficulties, and relationships and... words. There's no peace. And if that's not overwhelming enough the world goes and starts bloody wars all over the place, as if that might go some distance to establishing solid boundaries around all that we don't understand. It's exhausting.' I pushed a card around with the tip of my finger, then pressed my fingertip into the king's face. 'As a supposedly conscientious person, what am I supposed to think, of a world where the people I care about keep blowing each other up to God only knows what end?'

The silence that followed endured for slightly longer than I would have anticipated. I looked up and found Orri's expression troubled. His eyes were no longer fixed unwaveringly upon me, but bored into the floorboards like a drill, some distance from his crossed, bare feet. As I opened my mouth to offer a too-late apology for my blunt words (for I was now appalled at my inappropriate outpouring), he spoke quietly, without removing his focus from the floor.

'Don't beat yourself up, Karri.'

His voice had come out with such feeling that it flooded me with nausea to know I was the one who had made him suffer. 'Don't beat yourself up because you can't do anything to help the world, to help Denmark or your brothers. There's nothing you can do on such a scale as that. You can help here, though.'

Now he looked at me with a strange expression. Lost – frustrated. He was holding so much back.

'No one can help here.' My inherent pessimism still strove to express itself. 'Not even the man over on Tindhólmur – the one you say must just be a soldier.' At this Orri's gaze seemed to harden, become more focussed. 'He thinks he can help people, but what can he possibly do at a time like this?' I recalled the last time I had tried to talk to Orri about Thomas and wished now that I had not mentioned him. Orri swallowed. 'What do you mean?'

I thought his voice had begun to shake but I could not fall silent now. 'I mean we're not just alone anymore, floating around in the North Atlantic rounding up sheep and knitting socks. The war has come to us, and now our lives have the same sort of worth as every other poor bastard who's involved.

The pace of life has changed; the *meaning* of life has changed.'

Orri's eyes were wide. Black holes in the dark. When he spoke again it was with a sharp edge to his voice. 'You think that he – that *we* should do nothing but sit back and watch everyone die?'

My breath caught in my throat. 'No,' I choked. 'No, that's not what I'm trying to say. It's just difficult to have... *faith* in people when you're faced with this sort of thing. It doesn't make any sense: why do we have doctors when their only purpose is to save the lives of people who've been nearly killed by other people just like them, who have doctors just the same to save *their* lives? I don't understand any of it.'

'Kjartan.' Orri's voice was thick. 'Kjartan, you can't give up, you can't let the world give up. The people who are wounded must be made well again; the cities have to be rebuilt; the people who are ill, dying, they have to be cured. They have to be. No one should be allowed to die. Because then there will be nothing left.' He put his head in his hands and burst into tears.

I shuddered as though the door had just been opened and a sharp draught had crept up my spine; as though with this icy gust the future had revealed itself. The fleeting premonition passed as quickly as it came, but it left in its wake a fearful darkness.

22

I CYCLED FOR the first time into the British Army barracks, my heart straining against my chest and my breath like smoke in the cold air. A small amount of snow remained on the ground but only the tops of the mountains were still swathed in their pure-white blankets of winter, startlingly bright from this distance. Around me the cylindrical, corrugated iron huts stood depressingly grey and unclean beside muddy paths. I had once known this area as fields. Now iron fences had been erected here and there for a purpose that was incomprehensible to the visitor. Discarded bits of scrap metal, wood, weaponry, whatever I understood it all to be, lay around, biting into the slushy spring snow.

Through a labyrinth of undecorated makeshift buildings and uniformed bystanders I cast my eyes about for a familiar face, though it was hardly surprising that with a few thousand men around I could not find David or any other soldier of my acquaintance staring back at me. I stopped outside the building I understood (from the plaque on its grey iron front) to be the headquarters. Barely seconds later, a tall man wearing the neatest moustache I had ever seen appeared. He took delivery of my package of teabags and handed me a clipboard with a piece of paper attached. A pen was pressed into my bewildered fingers.

'But where should I sign?' my voice asked, more high-pitched than normal.

'Just write your name on the dotted line.' He spoke in a clipped formal tone. After I had done so the transaction was complete. Having been dismissed, I cycled back between the barrack buildings with the British occupation surrounding my senses like a thick fog. Soldiers waved and greeted me as I pedalled in the direction of town, and it was not long before, from the sea of voices, I heard a familiar one detach itself.

'Karri!'

The vowels were haphazardly elongated. I pressed the brakes and turned my head in the direction of the call. It was David, his arms outstretched, in one hand waving a glass bottle. He stumbled as he advanced, grinning like a lunatic.

"Karri!' he repeated gleefully, 'Good morning!'

'Good, err... morning?' It was not morning.

'Ah knew you'd come tae see me!' he declared with a note of victory. 'Ah knew you'd come – did ah no say? Did ah no say that I knew Karri Rasmussen would come tae see me? And here you are. Would you – Kjartan,' (looking pleased with himself at his pronunciation skills), 'would you care tae join me in a glass o' brandy?'

'David. Err; it's four o'clock in the afternoon.'

'Yes.' He moved so close to me that I smelt the alcohol upon his breath. 'Yes, it is. But it is also, as well as being four o'clock in the afternoon, a special occasion. And do you know what the occasion is… ?' He winked. 'It's no Christmas, no Christmas. Do you have Christmas here?'

'Yes, David, we have Christmas here.'

'Weeell, it's no Christmas today; it's… ' As he threw out his arms again I noticed that his khaki tunic had not been properly fastened. It lay open at the hollow of his throat, which was as flushed as his face. 'It's my birthday! Twenty-fucking-three! And do you know what that means, Karri? That means that ah can drink brandy for the entire day if ah so wish – and ah do so wish, and ah also wish for you tae join me!'

The bar was dimly lit and hazy under the dense cloud of cigarette smoke that hung beneath the wooden rafters. The soldiers seemed to be taking a well-deserved evening off work, downing pint after pint of beer, loosening their belts, kicking off their boots, lighting more cigarettes. They were laughing raucously and using foul language in animated, drunken discussion. I picked up a few lessons there and then.

I was pushed to sit around a central table with another beer and another cigarette from a soldier named Jack. Before long I heard myself declaring that I f-ing loved the f-ing British, especially in the throes of the f-ing war; that I was so f-ing pleased we had not been occupied by the f-ing Germans instead; that the f-ing English language was so f-ing wonderful with all its words; God bless the f-ing king and all that. The men around the table threw back their heads and slapped their thighs at this speech, in conclusion to which I gestured a little too emphatically and sent an empty pint glass clattering from the table across the wooden floor. Convulsing with spasms of laughter one of the men, known as Marcus, rose to fetch me another drink. David, who sat on my left, threw an uncoordinated arm around my shoulders, declaring with slurred words, 'Karri, lad, you are without a doubt my most favouritest Faroese person. In all the Faroes, and beyond!'

'You should have told me your birthday was coming up,' I replied. 'I would have knitted you a pair of socks.'

The room gradually heated to near-stifling. A pack of cards was laid out and a group of us played. More troops arrived and the alcohol flowed vigorously. David moved to commandeer the piano – an ancient, out-of-tune thing that had once stood in the town hall of Sørvágur. He struck a few flat chords, then, to the delight of his fellow soldiers, began to sing. '*When ah was a wee young lad,*' caterwauling more like. Next he launched into a ballad, heartfelt in its repetition and references to a 'bonny wee lass', which I could only assume to be the name of a famous town or type of beer. I came to understand the true meaning of this strange phrase, however, during the lull between one verse and the next. As David reached for a sip of beer, the man known as Marcus called out across the length of the piano he leant upon: 'You should let Jack give this one a go, Davey: I expect he sings all the time for those sweethearts of his in the village!'

The other soldiers guffawed loudly, and teasingly they nudged the subject of Marcus's remark with their elbows as Jack turned a detectable shade of pink.

'You, Marcus,' he declared with a cheeky grin as the others made suggestive moans and breathless pants of the kind Elva in the post office would have suffered a fit to hear, 'are just jealous.'

'Jealous!' Marcus thumped the piano – much to the annoyance of David, who hit a series of wrong notes – then sighed and stroked his beard, perhaps in mock thoughtfulness. 'Jealous, yes, jealous... Ah, you don't get 'em like that back in Glasgow, ah can tell you.'

His accent was much stronger than David's soft highland tone. In my excitement for the English language I had found myself imitating the harsh way in which the Glaswegian pronounced his words. Marcus had clapped me on the back more than once, declaring that I would yet make a better Scotsman than any of the buggers he worked with. I experienced an odd sense of camaraderie with the man as he again addressed me energetically across the piano. 'You're a lucky lad, Karri: all these lovely Faroese girls at your fingertips! I'll bet you've plenty of lasses tagging along behind you, eh?'

He threw me a knowing wink and I erupted into laughter at such an absurd insinuation. 'Yes, of course,' I replied in obvious flippancy. 'All drawn magnetically to my messy hair and googly eyes.'

'I think he's taking the piss,' chipped in a grinning soldier, whose name I completely failed to recall at this stage of the evening.

'I look like a frog,' I clarified. The remark was met with some hilarity.

'Now, now,' said Jack. 'Lots of princesses marry frogs – we all know that.' He winked at me as he reached into the pocket of his tunic and produced a beautifully made silver cigarette case. He slipped one between his thin lips, one between mine, and lit them both with a single flourish of the match. 'You're destined to become a handsome prince!'

Jack himself was good-looking with straight, strawberry-blond hair that did not fall out of place even when drunk. I could see why he was the subject of some attention amongst the young women of the town. I had seen him before at the fish market. There, in the crowd, his evident charm had been apparent. 'How old are you, anyway?' he asked me once the cigarettes had been lit.

'Thirty,' I lied, determined not to be outdone on the flippancy front.

'He's nineteen,' David shouted from between us, irritated that his piano skills should be constantly interrupted.

'Ah, nineteen,' Marcus echoed. 'Plenty of time yet, I should think: you've barely got yourself started.'

It was true. I found it difficult enough to engage in daily conversation with any other human beings – male or female, old or young. The thought of engaging in intimate contact with a girl filled me with a degree of anxiety that threatened to drown me. I could not see how ordinary social relations could ever be resumed after doing – *it*; sweat pooled under my collar at the mere thought. Yet my insides twisted together and ached in a way that was not entirely unpleasant.

But no. I had never tried to instigate anything, it appeared much easier to simply stay inside on the worst of days and read about life happening to other people. There were, furthermore, few enough girls to choose from in the district – even fewer now that charming, good-looking British soldiers such as Jack had arrived – and I was sure that the girls with whom I was acquainted, Asta (*Asta!*) most especially, detested me or found me repulsive in some way or another. No, no. It was better to focus my mind on other, more constructive things. If life was intent upon happening then it would do so without my intervention.

'Karri here is the same age,' David announced after a few more bars of music, 'as my brother, who is at this moment fighting on the front line in France. So ah will hear no insinuations that he – Karri, ah mean – is too young tae handle anything the world throws at him. Besides,' he added to the listening group, 'he's already got himself a lass.' The others responded with whistles and howls of encouragement.

'Have I?' I asked, bewildered, as David's grin widened. My face heated. 'Hang on, you don't mean *Orri*, do you? Because if you do... '

David gave a raucously sharp burst of a laugh that hurt my ears. It gave way to a look of bemusement. 'No, ah don't mean... what?'

'It's just that sometimes people insinuate that we... that we... err, oh dear. Never mind.' My stomach plummeted. David collapsed in laughter over the keyboard. 'Ah was referring to,' he spluttered, verging on the incoherent, 'that lovely redhead ah've seen you talking to *on more than one occasion*. Eh?' There came another round of friendly jeers from the crowd.

They hadn't seen the cold looks Asta gave me every time we met. I was sure that she was much more likely to lock her arms around a man like Jack. I must have coloured an even deeper shade of red. It burned my cheeks like fire and seemed

unlikely to dissipate whilst I could still recall the face of her...
*The provocative curves of her body under her clothes. The press
of her breast on my chest when she kissed me, those freckles on
her shoulders and the tickle of her hair against my cheek. Not to
mention her lips. Stop it, Kjartan,* I told myself.

'Anyway,' said David heavily. He waved his arms to secure
attention from the rest of us. 'Anyway, look: are we going tae
sing this song, or are we *no* going tae sing this song?'

Still hammering me on the back, the soldiers shouted for
the song. David obliged. He placed his hands upon the keys,
struck the first chord, took a deep breath but then stopped. He
let the breath out and turned his bleary eyes back to me.

'You and Orri,' he said, his forehead creased. 'You and Orri.
Is it true?'

'No! *No*, it bloody isn't. Why are you even asking?'

'Weeell. You know, it wouldnae surprise me.'

My hand jerked up and poured what remained of my beer
over his head. And afterwards I stood dumbly, shocked into
confused paralysis for a suspended eternity. I registered the
hair plastered to his forehead, watched the liquid soak into the
shoulders of his tunic, saw the straggling droplets run down
the bridge of his nose. They fell in slow motion onto the piano
keys, reflecting various sources of light. I saw the inoffensive
contours of his drunken expression widen first to shock, as his
hands rose halfway towards his head in a pointless gesture of

defence, then harden into aggression. Suddenly he was on top of me.

'You little bastard!'

I barely heard. I could taste blood from the blow he had dealt me to the face with such force I was sent like a rock to the ground. Pointlessly I struggled: he was too strong for me. My body was pressed like dough into the cracks between the floorboards, my head ached painfully from the impact. I landed a blow to the side of his face, struggled under him; shouted his name in a panic. When he kept on fighting I saw red as the anger rose up within me. I could smell his sweat and the spilt beer all around us and I *despised* him.

By the time he had finally been pulled off me, kicking and shouting, I was feeling repulsed by the continued beating of my heart. In the heat of the struggle, I had looked upon the fabric of life itself with utter disgust. I hated David for laying himself so open. And for invoking that reveal, I hated myself. I held a hand to my heart, hammering as if it would shatter from its angry pounding.

Outside, my body reacted in its customary way – I was physically sick. While the alcohol and the pain of the unexpected fight took their toll on my insides, I pressed my hand against the drum of my heart, willing it to stop. All around me there was emptiness. I searched for the mountains in the failing light: snow-capped, rugged, they filled my vision with ethereal beauty. I hated them, too.

***

I was driven back to Bøur by one of the lesser-inebriated garrison troops. Too ashamed to speak by now I sank my injured, vomit-scented body into the seat of the car. Rocked nauseously from side to side as the vehicle progressed on my homeward journey, my disturbed mind ranged back in time, stumbling through the void in which my entire childhood had passed.

These days I could recall painfully little of my childhood; rather, I could locate pictures, sounds, other sensory memories, snapshots of particular events, both those of great significance and others of little importance, yet within them I could not place myself at all. I recalled occasional flashes of intense anxiety but the stimulus remained always unknown, lost within the intervening years.

It bothered me that I could not remember what I had been like as a child. Ásdis often spoke of the days of Orri's childhood, not a single detail seemed to have escaped her memory even if it had long since left Orri's. I had no mother to cherish these days gone by. They were lost to me, now. Though I felt certain that having lost my mother at the very beginning, I had never properly begun.

23

Summer 1941.

IN SHOWERS OF rain the summer passed, and each day was gloriously exhausting. The land ached under a perpetual light, for the sun did not properly set in these months. At night it only dipped below the horizon, and with it the sky fell to rest over the mountains. Glowing with a dark, intense gold the peaks rose on the brink of surrealism; softly contoured, the teeth of the bare rocks protruded into the diminished light of the night-time. During the hours in which the sun hung highest in the sky, the lower reaches of the mountains lay a deep green, and in the frequent rain they shone.

It was here that I spent most of my days, tending to the sheep or to the summer crops, gathering golden hay in torrential downpours as it stuck wetly to my shoes, and carrying it to the outhouses to dry. The working day was a long one, and each night-long twilight I fell into bed with contented exhaustion. Orri would resign himself to sleep before his head even hit the pillow.

On free days I could do nothing but rest, sleep, dream of nothing. At first I had been reluctant to work in the fields, for the monotony of the physical activity provided an ideal climate for my mind to wander endlessly. Needless to say, my father's situation in Demark plagued my thoughts continuously. It was not long, however, before my mental capacity was utterly obscured by the demands of daily work. The war was little more than a distant memory now; the anxieties I had experienced upon the arrival of the garrison had long since dissolved.

Occasionally I caught a glimpse of a small group of troops through the hazy, rain-soaked afternoon. With my shirtsleeves rolled up to the elbows, my sheepskin shoes saturated in the grass, I would glance up momentarily to straighten my aching back and brush tendrils of sodden hair from my eyes, and I would see them trudging past, caps low over their weather-beaten faces, each with a khaki kitbag slung over one shoulder, talking together in low voices that rose occasionally in a burst of sudden laughter or in a torrent of obscenities. I was usually offered a modest wave in greeting as they passed, or if they were further away they might wave emphatically in dramatic good humour despite the weather. Sometimes they passed close enough to assure me, through curtains of rain, that the sky appeared to be clearing up a little. Other times they would trudge miserably onwards without so much as a glance in any direction but the one in which they were headed. Occasionally I thought I saw David amongst them, but I could never be certain.

Every moment I longed for the cessation of the working day with delicious anticipation. Without fail, Orri's mother would make sure that Orri and I stripped off our shoes and work clothes, caked in mud and plastered with grass, in the hall-way. We would be forced to stand shivering, half-naked by the open door until she brought us each a towel. Following this we would sit in the kitchen on chairs drawn up to the stove, each cradling a glass of akvavitt for warmth and fulfilment. If the air was not saturated with the onslaught of northern weather we might arrive back to be greeted by Magnus: folded into a chair outside the front door. He would smile broadly at us from his blankets. The summer had been good to him, gentle to his health. The ethereal beauty of constant daylight plunged each day into an atmosphere of calm invigoration, a pleasant wak-ing dream in which to lose oneself. I regarded Magnus through eyes blurred with fatigue when I arrived back, seeing first his hazy red beard under the pale grey sky.

As well as the farm work, my hands were raw from the strain of hauling fishing nets and my clothes were woven with the smell of klipfish. I would lie on my back on the mossy ground outside the house and see nothing but that grey sky overhead, perfectly featureless. Magnus would delight at the aroma that accompanied my presence, despite complaints from his wife. Orri's mother had expressed a desire to have me looking presentable on the grounds that I ought to favour my advantage as *an attractive young man with a good knowledge of books and a conscientious soul.* Orri responded to this with great amusement. He managed to stop the shaking of his body before snatching a bright-eyed look at me. 'He's blushing,' he declared and once more dissolved into laughter, prompting his mother to remark upon her desire for a son who was as good a match in marriage as I. It took Magnus's persuasive reasoning to convince her that she ought to bring us tea outside to prevent the smell of fish invading the house.

On one of these occasions amid the general chatter of conversation and anecdotes, Orri announced, smiling, 'Kjartan's looking well these days, isn't he, Magnus? All this fresh air.' His father scrutinised me with mock sincerity.

'By God, you're right, he almost looks healthy.'

Why would Orri have mentioned this to his father? My cheeks must have fairly glowed with embarrassment at diverting attention from Magnus – he was the one who was ill, not I.

⁂

There was a reason for my appearance improving considerably since I had drifted as a sleepless shadow through the winter; one I was ashamed to admit. True, the nature of summer with its fresh air, long days and lighter skies would have boosted my health anyway, however, I had at last permitted the intervention of Thomas. I dared not speak of this to Orri though: I remembered the upset it caused the last time I had tried. It began in June as the rain lashed and the wind screamed against the windows and I sat at Thomas's kitchen table soaked to the skin from my journey there. When the kettle came to the boil Thomas had handed me not the usual mug of 'normal tea' but one of his natural concoctions. The obvious earthen taste caused me to raise a suspicious eyebrow and he was forced to offer an explanation.

'You look a little peaky, it'll do you a world of good. Trust me.'

As far as I could see I had nothing to lose. Almost immediately I felt better, not just for the concoction I had drunk, but because I suppose I enjoyed the comfortable sensation of being looked after. Although I suspected that Thomas's motivation for his helping hand was largely to advance his research, I could tell he welcomed my company in his home nonetheless. He spoke to me at length of plants, chemicals; different methods of extraction and methods of preparation. He explained the functions of his equipment, telling me of past discoveries, grinning all the while.

Occasionally he would ask me about my own life. I told him of the continued haymaking and klipfish sorting and of driving the sheep up the mountainside; I spoke about the distraction of work in the fields and of Orri's incredible energy reserves. I also dared to talk about Asta, admitting that I was certain she was determined to keep at least one hundred metres from me at all times. After all, why would she want to be around me? I talked freely and honestly in a way I had never done previously. Thomas seemed as keen to listen to me as I was to hear him.

Yet it was not as straightforward every time I visited. His moods were as temperamental as the weather, and erratic. Sometimes he would talk so quickly that I had difficulty discerning the words, he would abandon sentences in the middle and begin new ones. His movements at these times were like a chicken pecking at crumbs. Though he chattered continuously, he did not glance in my direction or acknowledge my presence in any way; it was as though he spoke to some invisible entity. On a few sombre occasions I had arrived to find him collapsed on his bed, fully clothed, rubber-limbed; unresponsive as though he had lain there for hours. Catatonic, his eyes apparently sightless. I struggled to catch enough breath at these times, and my heart fluttered as though it was seeking a way to break out of my chest. I willed myself to stay calm, did my best to coax him out of his stupor: chatted as though nothing was amiss while I lit a lamp, opened a window and brewed a cup of tea. By the time I had resolved to go in search of help, dizzy from anxiety, he would invariably have regained his senses.

Afterwards, Thomas never spoke of these episodes, though when he awoke he would find that I had set the house in order, (for more often than not his apparatus would be dashed across the floor, and I knew he had done this himself). I would clean the windows, wash the scattered pots and pans and bring him water, bread, cheese, milk – all he could need. He never thanked me, but I read from the nod of his head and the half smile he gave me as I left, that he was grateful for my help.

I would sometimes sit on the front doorstep of the house if the proprietor was in no state for company, and if the weather permitted. There I smoked cigarette after cigarette and allowed my mind to wander. I savoured these moments, when the mist hung about the house in a perpetual shroud. I could see no more than two or three metres to any side, thus the world ended in the razor-sharp jut of rock with nothing beyond but dense, white cloud. There might be a sheer drop of a thousand feet, a million feet. And all lay beautifully still and wondrously silent; even the shrieks of the birds could not be heard, nor the crash of the waves.

Once, a cigarette between my lips, my body wrapped up

in wool against the chill, I heard a plane overhead. Tearing through the otherworldly silence, it could have been flying directly next to my ear, such a thunderous shock and a monstrous roar lingered even after it had passed. I heard, when back in Bøur, that it had been a German plane. Later on came the news that a few bombs had been dropped along the coast of Suðuroy, our neighbouring island. Some buildings had been badly damaged but thankfully no lives were lost.

24

Autumn 1941.

SEPTEMBER APPROACHED, AND we heard of bombs raining down on London. Horrifying images filled my head, of castles of glass and rubble gleaming malignantly on the empty shells of city streets, under blood-red skies; sirens screaming as the world collapsed.

I had no doubt that the morale-depleted garrison troops felt it deep within each and every one of their hearts. Some must have been moved to despair, others to rage, yet my own stunted reaction made me believe myself to be heartless, incapable of shedding a tear, unable to fully comprehend what was happening. Sleepless nights threatened me again. Throughout the summer I had laboured so hard that I had become oblivious to the world's incredible, barely comprehensible suffering. Now I suspected the eyes of the garrison to be upon me, detesting me, for why should I live safely in simple prosperity when their people, their own families, were witnessing the tearing of the ground from beneath their feet?

I began to wish that my boat might disappear into the North Atlantic waters, in the throes of an immense storm, or that my bike, whilst hurtling at full speed downhill, might hit an unseen boulder and send me flying over the handlebars. Or that I would lose my footing on the mountainous postal route to Gásadalur and tumble hundreds of metres from the cliff tops. I could too easily believe that in suffering I would be of more use to the world, though I could not articulate how.

'Why don't you just run away to the front line?' Orri said. 'Get yourself killed? You'll be useful as anything, then. The world powers will applaud you.'

I desired to join the mountains of the dead: I did not want to be the one to witness the end of the world. I did not deserve the privilege of immunity that chance had awarded me. After his remark I could hardly bear to look at Orri, so angry was I that he should misunderstand my feelings on the subject of the war, and so embarrassed that he should think me capable of such self-centredness as to seek applause; yet I resisted setting straight his assumptions.

Orri attempted to dissuade me from listening to the wireless, hoping to prevent me obtaining news of the world's latest wartime disasters. He maintained that the invasion of Russia in no way affected either me or my family members in Nazi-occupied Denmark. We none of us, furthermore, lived in London, and so there was no reason to panic about the air raids. When it became evident that nothing he said was having any effect, he then issued an outright ban on my listening to the wireless. The infuriatingly patronising nature of this move led to more than one scuffle between us. We exchanged blows and I gained a black eye from Orri's wayward fist.

'He cares about you,' Guðrun said when I found I had gravitated to her kitchen, my place of comfort as a child. And I scowled, wincing with the discomfort it prompted. 'Well, he has a funny way of showing it.'

***

At that week's Sunday service the vicar informed his attentive congregation that one of the women in the village had recovered from jaundice after a painful, lengthy affliction. I had seen her myself in the preceding weeks. She was now no longer confined to bed and had been blessed with a new glowing pink countenance in place of the former pasty yellow. I knew immediately who was behind her recovery. During the service, however, I was unable to concentrate on the vicar's words for I was somehow (despite it being Guðrun who had persuaded me to accompany her to the church) sitting beside Asta. I willed myself with all my faculties to keep my eyes focussed straight ahead and not to look at her under any circumstance, but of course I remained fully and continuously aware of her presence throughout the service. I could smell the heady mixture of her perfume and the femaleness of her skin; every now and then a stray hair would drift away from the mass on her head and shoulders, aim unerringly in my direction and fasten itself to the woollen threads of my jumper. I sat unmoving, captivated by the rhythm of her breathing, by the rise and fall of her chest at the periphery of my vision. With every move she made, no matter how miniscule, my heart would skip twenty beats, my head reel dizzyingly. I fought a terrible urge to peel off my skin or to run upside down over the arched ceiling, or claw large chunks out of the wooden walls. I almost expected to see smoke rising from my body.

The vicar seemed to have moved on to a different subject but I had not really been listening. Then I saw that all the eyes of the congregation had turned towards me. Looking around in confusion, I caught the end of the vicar's remark that *perhaps Kjartan Rasmussen might be presented with a cure for his bruised eye such as the rest of the community have received for their new healthy countenances.* I felt myself turn what must have been a deep crimson. Ducking my head, I pretended to be feeling particularly holy at that moment.

It was not until after the closing hymn that Asta turned to me. 'Where did you get the eye?'

'I, err... fell over.' Finally meeting her gaze I was met with a pair of huge green, searching eyes that turned my stomach in a very peculiar way. The rest of her features I could not take in, her attention being too much, at this moment and proximity, for my poor heart to cope with.

'You fell over?'

'Yes. During the sheep round-up.' In the silence that followed I made the mistake of thinking I ought to say more. 'I tried not to.'

'Tried not to what?'

'Tried not to fall over,' said my voice. It continued speaking as if it had nothing to do with me. 'The minute I started to fall I thought to myself, *this is a terrible idea, Kjartan Rasmussen: it will only lead to undue attention from vicars, and discomfort every time you blink'*.

She stared at me. I fixed my expression on the back of the nearest pew, until my flippancy revealed itself to be not yet exhausted: 'I won't be doing it again any time soon.'

'No,' she agreed, smiling a tiny bit. 'That's probably a good idea.'

The church was now a moving tide of voices and bodies as the congregation roused themselves and began to gravitate towards the door. We too had risen to our feet. Desperately

I tried to think of something, anything more to say so that I might keep her to myself a moment longer, but by the time it had occurred to me that I could mention the weather she was no longer by my side. I saw her turn her head in my direction before she disappeared through the doors. My body wanted to run after her, to rekindle the conversation, but my nerve failed me. With a groan I sat back down.

25

THE BRUISED EYE, needless to say, caused a great deal of excitement for Thomas upon my visit to him soon afterwards. He dashed about the room, presumably in preparation for something that would cure me. I left him to it, too preoccupied to share in his enthusiasm. Instead I stood staring through the rain-soaked window, again.

'You look a little blue, Kjartan.'

'David's youngest brother was killed this summer,' I told him without turning my head. 'In action, in southern France. He was nineteen years old.'

My eyes watered, fixed on a point atop one of the cliffs now visible through the mist. There was anger boiling inside me, bursting for an outlet. 'David has two other brothers as well, both younger than him and both fighting on the front line.'

'He must be very worried about them.'

It didn't sound sincere enough. Did the man even care? 'Yes. I asked him if he wished he could be there along with them –

I thought I might wish just that in his position. But he said no: he's pleased to be posted here, nowhere near direct action, simply building roads and… training in winter conditions – whatever it is they do. He says this way his mother will have at least one son left after the war.'

I waited for a response but none came, save the frustrating sound of intense rummaging, probably inside a cupboard, by the sound of it. The man's complete self-involvement was infuriating. I drew in a trembling breath and before I had let it out I felt a sudden cold, wet texture against my left eye, accompanied by the unmistakable smell of damp earth. It made me gasp: it was like being hit in the side of the face with a wet fish, or so I imagined. Thomas laughed and my irritation increased. 'Just hold it there for a while,' he advised. 'It should reduce the swelling.'

I put a reluctant hand to the bundle of damp leaves against my cheek, and with my one remaining eye I watched as he busied himself with something else entirely. The words took even me by surprise when I said them.

'Are you a soldier?'

'What?'

'Are you a soldier?' I glared at him. 'Did you arrive with the garrison? Did they station you up here so that you could survey us – assess the strategies of our position and people?'

Just something to do with the garrison, Orri had said. Thomas frowned at me, bewildered, his hands poised in mid-air. 'What are you talking about?'

'Do they pay you to do this work? They must give you a pretty handsome reward for putting in all this effort. Do you even ask yourself *why*? Maybe you are having a positive effect on the war effort – saving lives with which you've never been acquainted; maybe you are here simply as a political stratagem. But what of it? You don't care either way.'

The words had risen in my gullet the way a gannet regurgitates food for its young. Thomas simply stared at me. 'I am not working in the interest of politics.'

'I don't believe you.'

'What would it matter if I *were* working in the interest of politics?' He shook his head. 'Is it a *crime* that I arrived at the same time as the garrison... ?'

I interrupted: 'Because that would prove, once and for all, that you don't care.'

'About what?'

'About anything!'

My hand tore the damp collection of wadded leaves away from my eye and threw them to the floor by the table leg, and I wished immediately that I had hurled the lot at Thomas instead. I wanted him to admit, at this very moment, in all sincerity, that he was not perfect. 'If only it were the case,' I pressed, 'that you were doing all this for the love of another human being.'

'Doing what?'

'Your research. You spend every minute of every day locked up in your impossible house with your foreign cat and strange plants. Every day. And God knows how I wish you *were* working with the wellbeing of others in mind, though you stay as far away from your fellow human beings as possible. How I wish you were simply showing the kindness of your heart, your compassion, your humility, taking a personal interest, in selflessness. But in truth, you are anything but selfless.'

'Oh?' he urged. He had not moved.

'No.' My voice felt thicker in my throat. 'You are researching only for the sake of research: to feed your own greed and self-assuredness. It's enough for you just to *know* you are able to cure people – you don't care about the people themselves, just your own miraculous abilities and self-interest. And with the advent of war, you *whore* your ideas to the military powers.'

'That is not what I am doing!' he shouted. 'How dare you *dictate* to me the morality of your pathetic little assumptions? You are far too young to understand!'

'I understand that you're experimenting on us,' I shouted back as forcefully as my shaking voice would allow.

'Do you want to know *why*?' His shout reverberated as he began to manoeuvre his lanky body around the table between us. '*Do you want to know why I am doing this*? Do you want to know why I am working my fingers to the bone every hour of every godforsaken day? For *you*, Kjartan: for you as an ungrateful representative of humanity. You cannot possibly comprehend the suffering with which our species is faced: the constant stink of disease, the scourge of natural disasters: the inhumane obliteration by war. It cannot even be imagined by a country boy such as yourself, barely out of his teens, sheltered safely on a godforsaken island in the North Atlantic. To you it means *nothing*. But to the rest of the world, Kjartan – to the rest of us, it is a reality, it is *life*.'

'But why do you refuse to have anything to do with the people you claim you are trying to help? Are we just a... a *practice* so you can move on to bigger cities, to more deserving people? Maybe these people here, maybe they *need* you, Thomas: have you ever thought of that? You give them something special, some form of hope, control, support, in a time where there exists very little of the good qualities of life... And they mistake it for compassion and good will.' I shivered with the memory of Orri's tears on the night we had played cards; I could still taste his fear, his vulnerability and I felt, somehow, that Thomas was to blame. My knees had gone so weak I could barely stand up.

'I keep a respectful distance,' Thomas retaliated. 'A *professional* distance. These people are not *children*, Kjartan; they are my *work*.'

'I knew it.' I had pushed him to say it, finally. My stomach was twisted and there was a nauseating emptiness at the back of my throat. 'I knew you didn't care about us... '

'That doesn't mean I don't care. I am offering my help in the only way I know how.'

'You just want knowledge, Thomas,' I insisted, still unsure of why I was bursting with such anger. Had I longed to make accusations like these of the garrison troops themselves, or of the foreign powers that be, perhaps? I was ashamed to the point of self-hatred of the Islands' defencelessness in these times of war. 'You lust after knowledge. You know, some men lust after women – perhaps that's the answer: maybe all you need is a good *fuck*.'

With a terrifying thud Thomas brought his clenched fist down on the table. I flinched, longing to run, but could not move a limb. 'I will not be spoken to in this way by an insolent little boy who has the brainless gall to insist he knows something of what he has never experienced,' said Thomas. 'Get out of my house.'

The door slammed as he left the room.

I shuddered. I had no idea how to get home, how to return to the island, for I had no strength to scramble down the rocky path to the shore; to raise an arm to the oar, or my head to the wind. Instead I slid down the wall to the floor and drew my knees up to my chin. A strong feeling of longing swept through me for Orri, my best – my only friend, and I trembled again as I acknowledged the sadness that had been growing behind his eyes with each passing day since I had brought him to tears. I thought of Magnus, and *knew* that he and Thomas were closely acquainted. The former's illness was as much a reality to the latter as to me. This had I surely known all along... yet to myself I had barely admitted it. And still I could not speak of it to Orri, I could not bring myself to remind him of his father's illness, could not bear to upset him again.

Through my numbness I heard a patter of footsteps and the creak of a door, the squeak of floorboards, and then there was an uncertain hand on my shoulder. Thomas had made me a cup of tea. He sat by my side on the cold floorboards and I did not look at him. For an eternity his breath rose and fell and after a few such cycles a sharp inhalation would precede the beginning of a sentence that each time failed to come to his lips. Eventually he forced out an invitation. 'Tell me about your family.'

I groaned. 'Thomas. Please. Let's not do this.'

'Do what?'

'I patronise myself enough without having someone else do it.'

The rain hurled itself at the windows in agreement. Still I would not look at Thomas.

'I was married,' his voice confided. 'Some years ago. We had a son.' He stopped, or rather his words collided to a standstill. His breathing sounded different. I turned to look at him in the half-light. His long legs, clad in tattered cloth, were also drawn towards his body, his arms tightly wrapped around them. Folding himself shut. He had closed off his body to the world as if he wanted to shrink. It was a vulnerable child's pose.

'He was a beautiful boy, so energetic. Every Saturday we would go to the park to feed the ducks; he would always find the biggest stick his little arms could carry, and chase them all the way down the path.' His breath sounded shallow. 'We lost him to leukaemia. He was six years old.'

I ought to offer my condolences, yet such a gesture seemed empty. He must know my compassion, surely, even if I did not voice it, for I was a human being. I bit my lip. 'Why are you telling me this?'

'You have to trust me. Do you want to know who I am? Well, I'm telling you.' He raised a dry smile: 'If you don't trust me, then God help me, who will?'

My tongue felt swollen in my mouth. 'And your wife?'

'She... ' Again it took Thomas a few attempts to begin before he managed to utter a sentence. 'My wife... passed away shortly afterwards. Anyway,' he continued with seeming difficulty. 'Your family – tell me.'

Again I groaned, and apologised lest my actions and words

should offend him. 'I don't feel comfortable,' I explained, 'sharing sad stories. I don't really see what it will achieve.'

He smiled. 'So that we might understand things better. Face reality.'

'Perhaps we don't want to share all that is in our heads for fear of having to face it.'

'Then how will you know that you are alive?'

I said nothing.

'What happened to your mother?'

'You know what happened, Guðrun has already told you. You've been wanting to ask me for months, I can't think why.'

But I realised that despite my best efforts, the truth (and my feelings – of which I was deeply ashamed) would have to be acknowledged. 'You must understand, you must see, why I don't wish to face this reality you mentioned, admit it like this – because I cannot bear to face the guilt of knowing that it is all my fault. It is guilt that must be suffered; yet I am not strong enough to do so.'

'What do you mean: guilt?'

'Guilt because I am the one who killed her.' I closed my eyes against the hotness that welled behind them, and when I opened them again, when the threatening tears had dissipated, I saw that he had unwound his legs and turned to face me. The look in his dark-ringed eyes was intense. 'Whatever gave you that idea?'

'My brother,' I said bitterly – an emotion that was truly directed towards myself, the guilty one, for my rationality sided with my brother's words. 'He finally decided to elucidate the truth, before he left for Denmark so that he would never have to look upon my face again. *She died giving birth to* you, *Kjartan*, my brother said. *For some sick reason God decided to let you live while she died. And don't you ever forget that.*'

Thomas stared at me. 'He said *that*, and you took it to heart? Did he ever apologise?'

'Of course not,' I answered. 'He said that and nothing else, and the next day he left for Denmark. And I haven't seen or heard from him since, which gives very little opportunity for apologies.'

'And how long ago was this?'

'About six years.' I had long surpassed the need for grievance towards my brother, Kálvur. Now I only harboured facts, as though I read from the page of a history book; exhausting facts, concrete memories that could have happened to anyone.

'You realise,' Thomas said slowly. 'What your brother said is utterly ludicrous?'

I uttered a flat *yes*. But I followed it shortly afterwards with *no*; before settling upon *sometimes*. 'I... I mean,' I stuttered. 'Of course I did not mean for it to happen; I would much rather it had not... '

I had not the emotional strength nor conviction to wail of

the great injustice that I should have lost my only mother, and never have known her. 'My brother's opinions are not ludicrous if he is affected by them. He told me I ruined his life. If he believes that, then it is true. I think he always felt it, even before he understood the cause of his hatred for me.'

'How old was he when she... when she died?'

'Five, I think. So I suppose he'll have memories of her – unlike me, since I never knew her.'

Thomas drew in a deep breath, knitting his brows together thoughtfully. His unkempt beard bristled as he sucked in his cheeks. 'I think 'hate' is a very strong word... '

'No,' I said. 'He really does hate me. With all his heart. I can't say I blame him: he has a good enough reason – one that makes sense to him at least. He has been ruminating upon it for a good twenty years: it would be a pity if all those years of malintent were thrown to waste, after all.'

Thomas was silent. 'You see,' I explained, 'I don't much like to mention my family, for the simple reason that I do not know what to make of them: they've all acted so strangely. I don't understand why my father had to leave as well. It's understandable his visiting Kálvur, but to go at the beginning of a war? I couldn't tell him it was a stupid idea, I wasn't able to lose my temper and tell him that he would only get himself killed; he wouldn't have listened anyway. He'd only call me a pessimist. But how else could I react when my only family members keep insisting on leaving the country?'

'Who else has left?' Thomas asked.

'My older brother,' I said. 'The other one, Georg. When he was my age he decided to go to Scotland – he ended up in Aberdeen – to get an education. My mother was Scottish, you see. That was nearly eleven years ago. And I haven't seen him since. Of course, he met a girl, decided to stay and marry her, raise a family. We didn't even go to the wedding, we couldn't afford to.' I swallowed down a pang of regret. Gaining an older sister would have been a comfort.

Georg had not once returned to Vágar or indeed any of the Islands since his departure. It was true that money – or lack of it – had played a vital role in determining his movements; we had received regular letters in which he had relayed his desire to return home for a visit in the near future. He was, however, as thrilled as could possibly be with his situation in Aberdeen. There lay no end to the variety of exciting things he wrote about, almost illegibly in his intoxicated haste. Yet the visits had not come about. After his marriage, correspondence from him had become less and less. Eventually we could hope for little more than one letter a year. We had never met his wife. Again my eyes prickled with the heat of unshed tears, and I blinked in haste.

Following the sudden German occupation of Demark I had written to Georg, he having sent a letter not long after the war started, though surely he had known already of the situation and had worried for his native people and for his younger brother in Copenhagen? I had told Georg what surely he could not have known: that our father was caught there, and that communication with him was impossible. I had received no reply.

'Perhaps he blames me for the invasion of Demark,' I said, and immediately felt a sharp stab to the heart, for Georg had never held me responsible for anything. I fell silent, struck with thoughts of Thomas's late family, the dull emptiness that must lie behind his heart as it did mine. My heart gave a painful thump. I did not know how to express my compassion.

'I am sure your father and brother are well,' Thomas offered. 'I honestly do care, whatever you might think of me.'

'Thank you. I am sorry about your family, and sorry for what I said, too. I think I would like to go home now.'

26

IN THE LONG, darkening evenings, Orri and I played cards at the kitchen table. The lamps burned low, flickering with the howl of wind. The house itself was silent as the grave; Magnus, I hoped, was sleeping peacefully in the company of his wife, who had taken to retiring to her makeshift bed soon after the sun had set. Perhaps she feared the invading shadows and creeping darkness of the evenings, the stillness that pervaded the house and gave opportunity to reflect, to be afraid.

Orri's hands now resembled those of his father, rough and weatherbeaten, raw from the village fishing which had practically become his full-time job. From endless days spent outdoors his fair hair had bleached lighter still. His eyes showed a marked steadiness, in contrast to his younger years of haphazard excitement. Now they lit up as, dealing the cards, he told me of his most recent adventures in the world of local fishing.

The fishing industry had boomed since the beginning of the war, the small boats and trawlers doing the work of procur-

259

ing huge amounts of fish to be shipped to Britain. It was up to the villagers to muster fish in local waters for their own personal consumption. On their previous trip, Orri told me, they had caught every single fish that swam off the coast of Iceland, upsetting the Icelanders very much, yet before they had chance to convey the catch home their eight-man fishing boat fell under attack from a giant octopus. For three days and three nights they had struggled together continuously, the men hitting with their paddles at the immense purple tentacles. Orri himself had knotted together a fair few of them. Exhausted, weak for lack of water and rest, all had seemed lost until suddenly they heard the sound of a German plane flying low overhead, raining bullets and bombs upon the struggle. Both the octopus and the men of the boat, under attack from a common enemy, had pooled their strength in alliance, and brought down the German bomber.

The octopus, reconciled now to the Allied cause, had ferried all the men back to our local harbour and immediately headed south to France to defend the front line. 'And that,' Orri concluded triumphantly, 'is just how exciting is the world of local fishing.'

His eyes rested upon mine.

'Did the octopus give you his name?' I felt compelled to inquire.

'No,' he answered in unwavering sincerity. 'No, he said he

did not wish to endanger our lives, as he planned to carry out an operation as a spy in Nazi Germany to help the war effort. Anonymity ought to be maintained in such situations, for the safety of all involved. Although,' he added, when I had finished giggling at his ridiculous story. 'We did have to go to Skansin to have our guns checked.' He smiled. 'My mother still thinks it a wonderful initiative of theirs – whoever 'they' might be – to fit guns to the front of every local fishing vessel, then take time and effort to actually train someone to operate them. *You never know when the Germans might attack*, she says: *we all need to be prepared.* Heaven only knows why they'd bother to blow up a harmless Faroese boat with only eight men and a few fish flapping around on deck. Still. I suppose everyone gets bored sometimes. Especially around here.'

Skansin was the harbour at Tórshavn, the capital, which the British had adopted as their military headquarters, and from where they could oversee the approach of any boat that sought entry into the harbour. They had installed cannons – which were anything from six feet long, I had heard locally, to one hundred feet, weighing all of one billion tons. I was desperate to pay a visit, not least to dispel these ludicrous rumours of the weapons' gargantuan size. I wanted to see the hub of the British occupation, the centre from which all organisation radiated, where the military affairs conducted upon our own island were set out. I needed to find out what in God's name was happening.

Pressing Orri for details of his visit there with the fishing crew, I was rewarded with very little information. Either he lacked an eye for details in matters beyond the world of fish, or he was reluctant to share his interpretation of the experience. 'Oh, I dunno,' he mumbled. 'I think it was raining.'

'Well, obviously. But what did you see? What have they built there? Do they have their offices inside those old turf-roofed houses? How many soldiers are there? Is it always busy, or do they live as slowly as we do?'

Orri balked at my questions. 'Bloody hell, Kjartan, I don't know, do I? We only went to get those bloody guns checked. I'm not even trained to use the damn things, waste of space that they are.'

'You must have got *some* impression of it all, or did you hide under the tarpaulin for fear of being enlisted into the garrison?'

'There were just... lots of soldiers everywhere.' He wrinkled his nose. 'They were speaking English all over the place, nudging me and laughing the whole time. Didn't have a clue what was going on.' He moved to put the kettle on the stove.

'You're a useless source of information, you are.'

He scoffed, match in hand above the open door of the peat stove, which appeared to have burned itself out. Before the war, Orri's family had the luxury of burning coal. Now the imported prices were sky-high. 'Where would the world be if we were all as romantic as you, Kjartan? God knows we couldn't feed ourselves with our heads all the way up in the clouds.'

'Romantic?' I had considered myself anything but; often labelled a pessimist, I had compromised eventually by adopting the label of 'realist': I had a pragmatic outlook on life and was prepared always for the worst. Romantic I was not. Orri chuckled at my indignation. 'Romantic, yes. With your wild ideas about these things you have never set eyes on – what are you expecting? Battalions of orderly British soldiers parading around an iron-walled, barbed-wired camp, with rifles slung over their shoulders, shouting about the approach of German warships while a stocky, well-fed general with a moustache like a broom shouts out commands? Oh and Winston Churchill appears only minutes before the commencement of battle to give a stirring, inspirational speech about the essence of Britishness or something, no doubt: everyone cheering and clapping each other on the back and saying: 'Jolly good show, Old Chap'.' He delivered this in his best clipped English accent. 'If you were to go to the British headquarters, Kjartan, you would find nothing more than a couple of uniformed Scotsmen standing about in the rain talking about girls. And not even *romantic* talk about girls.'

'Neither of those pictures is romantic,' I pointed out.

'The first one is,' he protested, raising an instructive finger at me. 'The first one is romantic because it is an accentuation of the grim reality of things, a dramatic interpretation – from which all fiction is born. And fiction is just a collection of romantic ideas! War and squalor and... misery, are just as over-romanticised as love and sex and everything.'

'What do *you* know about love and sex?'

He scowled, perhaps also blushing a little. 'I blame that Wordsworth.'

'For what: your sexual inexperience? Or for the war?'

'For you and your incessant romanticism. *I wandered lonely as a cloud and saw some pretty daffodils,*' he misquoted in English, clanging the kettle against the stove. 'Or whatever it is the man writes about. It's all very well and good getting excited over flowers; you'll find none of them around here at this time of year, we've no place for quaintness. A daffodil wouldn't last five minutes out there.' He pointed at the furious rain that pelted against the window, sounding like an unconducted orchestra. There was nothing visible through the grey slate of early evening save the dim, shapeless outlines of the rugged mountains beyond the hidden fields.

I wondered what words Wordsworth would have penned had he been raised in such a barren, windswept landscape as this. The picture was by no means a lifeless one: the plants were sparse and plain but persistent in carpets of moss and lichen. Birds in their millions beat and shrieked against the backdrop of the limitless sky and hopped over the green-brown marshes. They nested snugly in the crevices of the cliffs and launched wheeling and screaming in flocks into the air, fighting for the necessities of existence. I am sure a poet would have found much inspiration in the calamity of nature, perhaps also in the forlorn, season-changing call of the oystercatcher.

Yet it seemed that our natural world was far removed from the colourful serenity captured by the poet's heart and literary expression. Ours was a world in which the elements presided over all else, in which life thrived and collided near to the edge of the world. Here it could become savage and ugly. Clouds were infinite congregations of weighted skies, threatening to burst with rain; lonely they were not. I communicated this last point to Orri, who laughed openly in delight that I should renounce my apparent tendency towards over-romanticism in favour of the cynical realism to which I was by nature prone.

'Wordsworth obviously never had to dig out his house from under six feet of snow only to find that the roof had leaked,' I added. 'Not to mention the peat dampened and ruined for fuel.'

Orri erupted. 'Oh, go and tell that to Magnus,' he squealed. 'He'll be thrilled!'

He succeeded finally in brewing two cups of tea – without milk, for the household had run out and Orri was not about to brave the rain again, having only just managed to dry himself following the first assault. He had also run out of dry socks, he informed me, still smiling, whilst conveying the cup of hot liquid to my waiting hands. The warmth of his company assured me that there must be a better world. Orri always raised my spirits: he was always laughing. Yet I was filled with apprehension that in return I could only dampen *his* spirits and his hopes, however unintentionally. I was grateful that he put up with me, though I could not say this out loud.

27

I DRUMMED MY fingers on the post office counter in time with the rain. For days it had fallen in torrents, and while I was comforted by its soothing rhythm at nights, I soon began to tire of its daytime persistence. Cycling to work as day dawned over fog-shrouded mountains I was always soaked to the skin, and quickly learned the importance of storing a woollen jumper in the dry tranquillity of the post office in order to stave off fever. I sat now in the lateness of an autumn morning comforted by the confines of such a jumper; my hair still dripping.

Brushing intrusive strands of soggy hair from my forehead, I watched Asta. It did not matter with what she was occupied, I longed only to mediate upon the grace of her movements. Having transcended from the perpetual weather into the material comforts of the quiet room, her form seemed all the more inviting to me for its warmth and sensuality. I was conscious of a distant aching in my muscles that longed for gratification of a kind I could not envisage. I felt alone, removed, but calm in my melancholy.

I was not even aware that she had turned around until her green eyes met mine. As she then tore hers away, I perceived for the first time an awkwardness in her movements. Perhaps, after all, she was self-conscious like me, made of flesh and blood just as I was. She coloured, busied herself rearranging a pile of papers into perfect geometrical order and hesitantly remarked that this morning the weather was not at its best.

I agreed, bewildered that she should now be moved to make conversation after weeks of nearly constant silence. She had always seemed unresponsive to my own limited efforts at small talk; so I tried to look as interested as possible as she proceeded to tell me of the turns the weather had been taking recently, as though I may not have noticed. Eventually, however, she acknowledged my own involvement with the climate, noting my rain-soaked hair. 'You must be freezing.'

I assured her I was not, having had the foresight to leave a jumper on top of the bookcase. She disappeared upstairs, quite abruptly, and for ten seconds my heart ached with the irrational fear that I had driven her away. She returned with a clean towel, and then set about boiling some water for coffee. I dried my hair vigorously with the towel and soon she placed two cups of coffee on the desk, took a seat opposite me and began to help me fold envelopes. I thanked her. My insides felt deliciously warm. For a few moments her white fingers flicked deftly over folds and creases, in the silence broken only by the gentle sound of rustling paper and the thunderous patter of droplets thrown against the building in the wind.

'How is Magnus?' Asta asked, eyes to the table.

'He's terminally ill,' I answered with little thought. I realised then it must have sounded sharp: I was still determinedly on my guard. 'Sorry,' I followed quickly. 'Sorry. I mean he's still getting worse. Nothing seems to help. He's completely confined to bed now; not even the smell of fish downstairs can get him on his feet.'

For a moment she was quiet, unsure possibly of the depth of questioning she ought to attempt. The neighbours often treated me as cautiously on the matter as they would any son of Magnus. 'Is there nothing anyone can do?' she ventured. I shook my head, reaching for another envelope. 'I suppose if it wasn't for the war he'd have been sent to a Danish hospital, but... well, he'd never have consented to that anyway. You know how he is.'

At this she smiled, apparently gaining confidence from the invitation to share in my viewpoint of the man. 'Has he tried cod liver oil?'

'Don't take the piss.' I smiled back at her. Taking a deliberately casual sip of coffee, I was forced to resist the compulsion to pull a face at its bitter taste. Instead I asked, 'Do you have any sugar at all?'

She nodded and fetched me a small bowl, smoothing down the creases of her woollen skirt with both hands as she took her seat, and watched with interest as I piled mountainous spoonfuls of sugar into my mug. I remarked that it was just as well sugar had not been rationed. Following this alteration the liquid was now drinkable and even pleasant as it sent a warm current through my body, and I relished the feeling that I could quite happily have sat there with her in this new companiable atmosphere until the day drew to an end.

If only the door had not opened and let the world (David) in. It closed again with a bang, startling both me and Asta so that her knees knocked against mine. David stood by the door, an untimely visitor. Great droplets of water dripped onto the floor from the hem of his raincoat. He grinned at me, and I felt the girl opposite me shrink a little. It occurred to me that I ought perhaps to translate the conversation that was likely to follow – though I knew she could understand a little English – but I was reluctant to play the role of mediator between the two of them. David approached the table, coat now slung over one arm. He removed his cap and executed a bizarrely elegant bow of greeting in the direction of Asta.

I gaped at him. 'You never take your hat off to me.'

'You're no as pretty as she is,' he beamed. Despite the bewilderment that had passed over the girl's face, along with a faint flush of colour, this was not a remark I desired to translate.

The door opened again, this time slamming against the inside wall in a gust of wind. Hurriedly Jack pushed it shut with a variety of breathless obscenities. Like David, he removed his coat and hat and breathed a sigh of relief. Catching sight of Asta he raised his eyebrows at me, eyes sparkling. I rose to put on the kettle and stayed longer than was necessary in the kitchen, warming my hands above the peat stove, shivering from the sudden exposure to the weather from the briefly opened door. I felt cheated. My safe haven had been broken, and although it had been breached only by familiar faces, the discomfort struck me immediately. As the sounds of chatter and giggles both male and female drifted into the kitchen, the reason for my frustration assailed me all too clearly. I cursed myself for being so fickle. I could not for a moment have the girl to myself – I did not deserve such a thing and she most likely did not desire it.

Returning to the main room, I placed fresh coffee on the post office desk, and patiently sat on the windowsill until David detached himself from the pleasure of female company. He noticed the coffee, delightedly helped himself to a cup and approached the window, yawning widely.

'You're no going tae pour that over ma head, are you?' he said, indicating my own mug of coffee that I cradled in both hands. I could see that there lurked a somewhat bashful smile behind the mock sincerity of this comment. I shook my head, muted by embarrassment as I recalled the alcohol-infused fight at the barracks. I returned his apologetic smile and David took a seat beside me on the windowsill. The air between us felt lighter now, there seemed no need to offer up further apologies.

'Have you heard the news?' he said presently. 'They're planning to build an airport.'

'Where?' How could there possibly be anywhere flat enough on this rugged island?

'Next tae the lake.' He gestured out the window, as though indicating the lake that from here could not be seen. Only the colourful timber walls of the neighbouring houses were visible, comforting in the weatherbeaten wilderness and the grey shroud of war and weather.

'I'm sorry,' David said, when the silence between us had persisted for longer than was comfortable.

'What for?' I asked, surprised, thinking that we had just laid to rest the memory of the scuffle between us.

'You know. Being here, being an occupying force; bringing war to you. All that.'

'It's not your fault,' I pointed out, and though I had to force the meek smile that accompanied this remark, I meant it nonetheless.

✳✳✳

I trailed up to Orri's front door through the slush of the streets and executed the usual procedure: let myself in, shoes off, struggle out of jacket and jumper, announce my arrival. The occupant's voice greeted me hastily from the other side of the kitchen door, adamant that I should not enter the room.

'Why?'

The answer came in a voice marginally higher in pitch than was normal. 'I'm taking a bath.'

Behind the door I rolled my eyes towards the heavens, before pushing it open and entering the room to find him gripping both sides of the tin bath as though he had been about to rise to reach for the towel that hung beside the stove. He abandoned this action and instead drew his bent knees closer to his chest as I closed the door quietly behind me.

'Orri, for goodness' sake. I've seen it all before!' I was careful not to gaze at him directly, and busied myself by draping my sodden socks next to his towel beside the peat stove, which was lit to boil another kettleful of water for the bath.

'Not recently you haven't. It must be a good fifteen years since we last took a bath together.' Orri's ears, visible now through plastered-down hair, had turned a hot shade of red. He shifted his body in the cooling water. Automatically I moved over to the side of the bath and sat down heavily, legs crossed and as I did he let out a sigh of resignation. He asked, 'What's the matter?'

'Mm? Oh, nothing, I don't think... '

Orri watched me patiently. 'Well, are you going to tell me or will I have to beat it out of you?'

'Beat it out of me? With what – your sponge?'

He smiled and leaned forward to wrap his arms around his knees. 'Spit it out.'

I heard how flat my voice sounded when I answered. 'They are planning to build an airport.'

After a moment of contemplation, Orri smiled. 'Of all the worries that float around inside your head, Karri, I expected to hear something of a little more gravity.'

'Does it not bother you?'

'Of course it bothers me. But there's nothing we can do about it, so why worry?' He shrugged, jewels of water slipping off his shoulders. 'Best accept it. I mean, the war has been quite beneficial to us so far.'

'Not to me. I'm an orphan.'

Orri's eyes filled with sadness and I reprimanded myself for making such an insensitive remark. When he spoke it was quietly. 'It's not the end of the world.'

'But what if it *is*?' I put my head in my hands, gripping my hair.

'What do you mean?' Orri asked softly. 'In what way might the world end?'

I murmured that I did not know. 'I'm just scared,' I admitted.

There was a lapping of bath water as Orri shifted again. 'Scared of what?'

'I don't know.'

Another shivering moment passed before he assured me in a hoarse whisper that there was nothing to be afraid of. I did not know what to say. The kettle began to whistle and I rose stiffly at the sound to fetch it from the stove. Orri drew in his knees further as I emptied its contents carefully into the cooling tin bath; then having replaced the kettle I sat back down heavily on the floor, twisting my hands together. With no warning, a feeling came upon me, my whole body itched to unwind itself and wrap my arms around Orri's damp neck, be comforted in the familiar presence of another human being. This particular human being. There was no way to express what I felt. I was trembling.

'Can I stay here tonight?'

'Of course.'

***

The bedroom was empty, Orri's mother was in the adjoining room with her husband. No light shone from under the closed door, no voices drifted through the wall; perhaps they already lay asleep. I undressed quickly and pulled on my night clothes, then moved on tiptoes, found that my feet were guiding me to Orri's bed instead of mine. I didn't argue with them, let myself fall into the wrong bed, pulled the covers snugly around my shaking body and buried my face in the pillow. But still I could not banish the plague of relentless thoughts. I lay like this until the glowing light of the oil lamp in the kitchen blossomed upwards and over the wooden walls of the bedroom, followed by the silhouetted shape of Orri. He placed the lamp on the floor beside the bed, in the dancing shadows he unwound the towel, pulled on his own night clothes and showing no surprise at my presence, slid into bed beside me before turning out the light.

Despite his usual aversion to intimacy, Orri shifted his weight under the blankets and pulled me close, into his arms. His skin smelt of soap; his night clothes were infused with the aroma of peat smoke, having been draped in front of the stove to absorb its heat. I shivered at the brush of his damp hair on my forehead, a sobering contrast to the consoling warmth of his body. I had intended to return to my own bed before he had come to claim his for the night – hadn't I? But I did not, and could not pull away from the solace of his embrace; in silence I leaned into him, pathetically in need of that comfort I had craved earlier.

'Shut up, you daft git,' he soothed while I coughed up apologies and tears, muffled in his neck and shoulder. His fingers caressed the back of my neck and I heard his heart hammering loudly under my ear. 'Everything will be alright. You'll see.'

The next thing I knew I was in Copenhagen, where my entire surroundings were in a state of near ruin. A multitude of grubby Danish shop signs hung from dilapidated wooden walls; discoloured buildings rotted, abandoned – green, brown and grey – they seemed to be dissolving in the trickling rain that leaked from a slate-coloured sky above industrial chimneys. A discarded shoe lay in the gutter, worn to disrepair; I saw a stack of tinned food behind a grimy shop window and a ragged sheet hanging from the open shutters of a second storey. I stood alone, the unevenness of cobbles beneath my sheepskin shoes. Then I heard the striking sound of military footsteps, the clang of weaponry and the crack of a commander's voice. I took to my heels in panic, though it would not do to flee for long down this road for the cobbled enclosure seemed endless. I would have to take to one of the doorways. I flung myself into an alleyway, a narrow space between two towering, dirty buildings and pressed myself there, heart pounding as loud, I feared, as the footsteps from which I fled.

Eins, zwei, drei, vier, *rapped the voice methodically. Hundreds, perhaps thousands of toe- capped boots relentlessly pounded the street in perfect synchronisation. I feared for my life. I slipped inside a doorway and beheld a dirty stone staircase in front of me, coated in soot. It spiralled up above my head, far into the towers of the building, and in the blackened surface of each stair I could see scuffed footsteps. I ran up it, and the higher I ascended the more distant were the sounds of marching. Yet in their place came another sound, too distant at first to comprehend: someone was calling my name and though it grew louder as I pelted up step after step, I never seemed to reach its unknown source. I knew the voice to be that of my father. I flew on and on in desperation. Then, on glancing down at the stone beneath my advancing feet I faltered to a stop. I saw that the footsteps in the soot were my own, many sets of them imprinted over and over again into the black powder.*

'Kjartan.'

Hair tickled my cheek. Peevishly I pushed it away, and found Orri's forehead under my fingers. The bedroom walls glowed, adorned with playful shadows, in the meagre light of an unseen lamp. I lay safe from the German army under folds of blankets and in Orri's warmth. As consciousness set in I saw that an obscured figure loomed over me, reaching across Orri to cautiously press on my uncovered shoulder. I raised myself as best I could in the cramped space, squinting blearily at my gentle assailant, whose face was bathed in shadow.

'Sorry to wake you.'

I pushed myself into a sitting position, head coming to rest against the sharp gradient of the ceiling. 'Thomas? What... ?' I glanced from him to Orri, the faint lightness of his blond head nestling into the pillow. He seemed not to have been disturbed from his coma-like sleep.

'Come into the kitchen,' Thomas whispered. He did not wait for a word of acknowledgement from me, but turned and padded away across the room. The light cast from the lamp that he carried wandered dreamlike over the walls and followed him down the stairs and into the kitchen. As he disappeared from my view it surrounded his figure like an aura.

In the faint glow that emanated from the kitchen I could see enough to be able to extricate myself from my entanglement with Orri's sleeping form; he did not even stir as I climbed over him on the narrow bed, placing my knees and feet and arms carefully, anxious that my movements should not wake him. Setting my feet on the floor, I swiftly followed Thomas's path. As I passed the door to Magnus's chamber it seemed, in the half-light of the room, to be ajar, yet there was no sign of activity.

Thomas was the kitchen's only occupant. He had set the lamp on the table and placed himself on a chair beside it. Illuminated by the flicker of the flame his presence radiated a strange spatiality in this blanketed hour of the morning. It was only as I entered the kitchen that I realised how cold I was, dressed only in my night clothes, my feet bare. I felt them plunge like roots into the icy grip of the wooden floor. The peat stove had smouldered back into earth and lay dormant; the concentrated light from Thomas's lamp was too weak to reach all the corners of the room, and instead lent a spectral emptiness to the space in which I now stood, as though there existed no walls to contain us.

The uneasiness that this feeling conjured crept up my spine, and I shivered. I longed to return to the safety and warmth of the bed that I had just left... My heart skipped a beat: what must Thomas have thought as he coaxed me from the narrow bed while Orri lay sleeping by my side? Was that why he had urged me to get up? I crossed my arms over my chest to try and regain some of the warmth I had left behind, but only the memory of it rose unbidden into my cheeks.

'I have a favour to ask of you.' Thomas's calm tone swept away my thoughts.

'Could it not wait until morning?'

'It is morning. Very early in the morning. I am often up before the birds.' He grinned, and his features contorted with the play of light and shadows in the lamp's glare. 'I am going away for a bit.'

I stared at his attire. The flickering light of the lamp created orbs of gold down the front of his tunic. 'Why are you dressed as a soldier?'

'Oh, this?' said Thomas. 'It simply makes things a little easier.'

'What do you mean? "Things"... ?'

'Oh, you know. Getting around, things like that.' He stood up from his chair and set a khaki cap over his dark hair. Its shadow bathed his eyes in greater darkness. 'Call on Guðrun tomorrow morning, would you? I'll need you to do some deliveries for me again – all the instructions are at the vicarage. Don't forget.'

He offered me a smile – seemingly a gesture of farewell. It appeared unnervingly disembodied since his eyes remained unseen. Then abruptly he turned and left the room, allowing a piercing draught to enter unbidden before he closed the door behind him.

I stamped my frozen feet to thaw them and shuffled to the table to extinguish the lamp. The darkness reclaimed the demonic shadows that its light had awoken. I groped my way, unseeing, back to the bedroom and followed the wall round to my own bed. I pulled back the neat creases of the sheets and blankets, which lay still in place as I had arranged them the previous morning, and curling up into a foetal position on the bed I drew them around me, shivering violently. Although I was comforted by the hypnotic sound of Orri's gentle breathing from his bed opposite mine, sleep was a long time in returning. I buried myself into the bed, unable to find solace from the cold.

I reawoke as the sun began to climb into the sky, feeling as though the bizarre early-morning encounter had been no more than another dream. Orri still slept. In the cold light of morning I pulled on a jumper and a pair of thick woollen socks before creeping quietly from the room. I could hear Magnus snoring behind his closed bedroom door as I passed.

I padded into the kitchen to find that Ásdis had already lit the stove and was arranging socks and coats on the rack before it to dry; the room smelled of damp wool. In the light of the new day I could see now that the tin bath, still filled with water, had been pushed against one of the walls, presumably by Ásdis: Orri was not one for tidying up after himself and I could not imagine that Thomas's spectral presence of a few hours previously would have been concerned with household chores. As I caught sight of the bath something deep within my stomach turned a somersault. I recalled the overwhelming feeling that had come over me as I had sat with Orri the night before, the longing to lose myself in his presence, the comfort of his nearness. And the feeling of completion as I had fallen asleep in his arms.

I swallowed, and bid Ásdis good morning for she seemed not to have noticed my arrival. She did not look up from her task, though she *must* have heard me. Her shoulders were stiff. I had just opened my mouth to offer to make a pot of tea, or to empty the tin bath, when she spoke. 'I think it's about time you went home, Kjartan.'

I closed my mouth again, shocked into silence by the frankness of this address. I *had* been right to think that my stay in her family home had only caused her discomfort; why, then, had I lingered so long? Ashamed, I began to form an apology for having got under her feet, but again she interrupted.

'We've done more than enough offering you a spare bed here,' she said, (with emphasis on the word spare). Her voice simmered with suppressed anger. 'But if you're not going to use it I think it best that you leave, don't you?'

I gaped at her, speechless once more. She must have passed through the room during the night while Orri and I were asleep. Surely she was not asking me to leave because we had shared a bed? It had not been the first time, after all, though on this occasion we had not raised blanket sails or rowed across the bedroom sea using the headboard as an oar. But it was no different now from when we were younger. It was not as though we... *We hadn't...*

I found that I could not voice any of these defences out loud. I longed to set straight her assumptions, yet I could not help but think that perhaps she had reason to doubt, to be angry with me. I felt myself colour deeply with embarrassment. My ears and my cheeks burned. I could not speak.

Ásdis hung the last sock from the drying rack, and without

another word she left the room. Still she did not look at me. I could hear her pulling on her shoes and coat in the hallway, then there followed a sharp gust of wind and the gentle click of the closing door. I knew she would be back soon, she wouldn't want to leave Magnus's side for long. But I would make sure to be gone before she returned.

28

Winter, 1941.

SIX WEEKS PASSED, each colder and more frostbitten than the last, before the return of Thomas. He appeared on my doorstep in the midst of the winter's first heavy snowfall, having grown a full beard and looking rosy-cheeked, bright-eyed and healthy. But he refused to give away any information about where he had been and I was soon forced to abandon my persistent quest for details.

Following the instructions I had received from Guðrun I had paid a weekly visit to the eagle's eyrie in his absence. The cat appeared better at independent living than I, yet I enjoyed the visits with him nevertheless: they were an escape from the suffocation of tight-knit community life, from being ringed in by the frost-scattered mountains around my home. During those same weeks I gave in to my reluctance to join in with the frequent dances for the soldiers and younger members of the village, despite Orri's playful efforts at persuasion. At first I fought the pull of apathy, but I could feel myself sinking back into my usual narrow world of introspection. It certainly did not help that I had returned to the emptiness of my own house: it felt cold and lifeless in comparison to Orri's family home, for most evenings it did not seem worth lighting the stove when I was the room's only occupant.

Instead of telling Orri about his mother's request that I leave, I mumbled an excuse – needing a bit of time to concentrate on my reading or something like that. He accepted my offering without question: it was likely that Ásdis had made her thoughts known to him also. Whatever the reason, my sudden return home and the night that preceded it went painfully unmentioned between us. I could see that Orri felt uncomfortable too. He confessed that his own home also felt empty. Magnus's house had often been a hive of good-humoured activity as various groups of soldiers – mostly the same few – called around of an evening for a game of cards and a glass or two of akvavitt. That was before his illness had worsened. Now the crowds had stopped coming, and Magnus's niche role as the best host had vanished with his health. Of course, he still received frequent visitors but they stayed only briefly to wish him good health and keep him company, the soldiers included. The nights now were darker, longer and colder in all senses.

One of the duties allotted me by Thomas was to help care for a local sick woman, Naina. Spending time with her I did not dwell as much upon the worries that so dominated the time I spent alone. I had known Naina my whole life. She stayed homebound for the most part and appeared somewhat older than her years – indeed, I had mistakenly viewed her as elderly. Her hair had greyed prematurely though she still wore it long, her eyes were dark and, though very much alert, had sunken into the sallow skin of one who suffers permanent ill-health. She had a bizarre preference for wearing the Faroese national dress: full-skirted and made of heavy black wool, delicately embroidered round the neck and bodice, and worn over a simple white shirt. Even indoors she kept on the small, white-trimmed black bonnet that completed the image.

As the rain fell in torrents and the cows bayed forlornly in the barn below the house, Naina would tell me of her childhood in this same village, warming my heart with the colourful simplicity of earlier times. In reality little had changed, she said, at least not before the war had broken out, but the occupation now hung over all of our daily lives and dominated our community in a way that would doubtless bring lasting change.

Each day I presented my neighbour with a full cup of Thomas's strange, fragrant tea, and on each occasion she simply thanked me, gave me a kind smile and made no remark save for 'oh, lovely'. Each day my curiosity swelled to the point where I feared I might soon be unable to stop myself screaming out an enquiry of what on earth she thought I was forcing down her on a daily basis.

'You are good to me, Kjartan,' she said one morning as I placed the steaming mug in her white hands. 'You keep me company. With the night arriving so early these months I receive precious few visitors. Mind you, I've had my patience tested, teaching that lad Thomas to knit. Never in all my days have I seen fingers that are so clumsy with the needles!' Her lips broke into a soft smile. 'He is a handsome young man, though, that Thomas. And always so attentive. His heart is in the right place, though he always has a look of sadness about him.'

I inquired whether she knew of his mysterious whereabouts, but she did not, and furthermore seemed little concerned. I told her that he had enlisted my help in deliveries, and lately with personal visits and such like, in response to which she commented, 'Well, yes, he can't do it all himself I suppose.' I suspected that she had not learnt the true nature – or at least the details – of the work with which Thomas busied himself. But I kept quiet on the subject, and soon abandoned my search for information concerning the man's visits, for each day my imagination ran increasingly wild, preoccupied with imaginative thoughts of the red-headed girl who lived in the post office.

***

Hardly a day now passed in which I did not spend time in the company of Asta for, in addition to our working hours in which we conversed awkwardly over stamps and sorting piles, she had asked me if I might teach her a bit of English. She had blushed as she said it, hoped I did not think her ridiculous or laugh at her for asking, only she knew I spoke the language well and at any rate spent plenty of time in the post office that could easily be devoted to tutoring. Of course I agreed without a moment's hesitation, she could as well have asked me to leap headfirst into the icy fjord and I would have done her bidding.

Given the insatiable attraction that my tutee held over me, diligence in my task proved difficult. I was captivated by her embarrassment when she attempted to pronounce certain words. Her almond-shaped green eyes avoided mine, her ruby lips twisted in self-conscious reluctance to engage with the strange sounds, but she tried repeatedly. This was a new character to the decisive young woman I had formerly perceived her to be. With our increasing familiarity my tongue no longer danced back and forth and my stomach spared me the discomfort of unmanageable knots that had previously blighted me whenever I was in her company.

I now dared to speak my mind when Asta lapsed into bewildered silence midway through an attempted pronunciation. I caught the surprise in her features when I first spoke back, yet she soon seemed to warm to the relaxation of my former inhibitions. Before long we began to converse freely in a way we had not done since we were children in neighbouring villages – and on this topic we reminisced. Anecdotes of picking potatoes and feeding the lambs followed, and we discussed the impromptu whale hunts that ensued whenever a school was spotted close to the fjord. We talked about the harpoons and the blood-red water that lapped the shore and stained the rocks, and the horror and excitement of it all.

I had been a surprisingly good football player, she remarked, and had exhibited an aggressive streak that had surprised her, given my quiet disposition. I pointed out to her that the things we talked about were still very much a part of everyday life: the potatoes still needed to be dug up out of the ground, there were always more sheep to be seen than people and the whale hunt had lost none of its excitement in the ongoing years. In fact it was entered into with just as much enthusiasm these days, the garrison troops notwithstanding. Indeed it was a blessing to have so many helping hands, while the entire village looked on at the churning waters and beached bodies with thrilled anticipation.

As for the football, well, I had played a routine game with

some of the soldiers only last week. It had been an unofficial, friendly match: the islanders versus the occupying force. I had nearly come away with a broken leg, not to mention frostbite. Yes, my alleged streak of aggression had its place: I had scored a lucky goal after all, and Orri had scored two.

Asta laughed, her lips curling deliciously, her eyes shining so close to mine as she leaned towards me over the desk with the open English book between us. 'You are not managing to impress me,' she smiled, 'try as you might.'

But it was Orri who was unimpressed by Asta and he lost no time in warning me of the mess I was sure to get myself into. Exactly what the problem was he did not seem keen to elucidate, insisting only that she was *not right for me*. When I pressed him further he pirouetted round to face me on the low tidal rocks across which we were hopping like the mute turnstones that dipped their beaks into the silt around the shoreline. Orri almost lost his balance. His nose was purple from the bite of the sea breeze.

'Well, for a start,' he declared, 'she is far too attractive for the likes of you, with your goggly eyes and sea of freckles. Honestly, there's so many of them they are forming their own constellations. And who could feel romance and everlasting love whilst staring into your colourless, frog-like eyes? I swear to God I have seen prettier amphibians than you.'

I frowned at him, rubbing my hands together vigorously.

'They are not colourless,' I objected; 'they are grey. Grey is a colour.'

'And you're just so terrible at making conversation,' he continued. 'I mean, she must think you're a lunatic, and if she doesn't already then she'll realise soon enough.'

'Realise?'

'And what have you got to offer her anyway, apart from your knitting skills? Honestly, Karri, you haven't got a hope in hell.'

Orri had raised his voice above the rush of the waves and the wind, for we stood exposed to the open sea, buttoned up against the winter. Turned now towards me, and close enough to reach out and take the ends of my scarf in his fidgeting fingers, which he did – Orri's eyes shone with what seemed a wild urgency. 'And even if you had that hope... if you were... you know, the two of you, then... then she's just not *right* for you.'

For a fleeting moment I wanted to push him off the rocks. My stomach knotted uncomfortably. *Who* was *right for me?* I swallowed. 'You've said that a few times.'

'Well, that's because it's true. She's rude and vain. And just... aloof.' He thought for a moment. 'And she's a redhead.'

'What has that got to do with anything?'

'You *know* what,' he retorted, his eyes wide, 'You *know* that it's bad luck to see a red-headed girl just before a fishing trip. You know – and yet you won't admit it, I *know* you: you'll tell me it's all a load of superstitious nonsense and we should know better in this day and age.'

He fell silent. 'Of course it's a load of nonsense,' I snapped. 'And that's a terrible excuse. You don't want her for yourself, do you?'

'No, I bloody don't.' He seemed furious at the suggestion. He turned away into the wind and I noticed how his shoulders sagged. 'Have her if you must – what is it to me? Just don't say I didn't warn you.'

The wind carried away the last of his words over the fjord. To his back I shouted, 'When what?' but he did not turn to answer, simply picked his way over the remaining rocks that lined the shore and walked away in the direction of the village.

My longing for Asta instilled in me a frustrating combination of lethargy and restlessness, and a desire to cycle down the road to the post office as fast as possible; yet the stronger the desire was, the more I coveted my bed and its feeling of safety and comfort. When I was not with her the effort of moving – even picking up a book or rubbing my eyes – required an intense amount of willpower and concentration. I struggled to swallow even a mouthful of food, though concern for my health made me try to take in a decent meal every evening.

Just as I thought I might die from this terrible affliction there came a moment one grey afternoon when our eyes met, as they had done so often before, over the books from which

I was teaching Asta. Before I knew what I was doing I leaned forwards, placed my hand on the back of her neck, and kissed her. She stared, red-cheeked, seemingly as amazed at this sudden transcending of personality as I was myself. We were both astonished that I could be so bold.

She said nothing though, watching me, and in the light of a lamp over our work I found the colour of her cheeks so warm, the light so tender and her fixed gaze so calming that I kissed her again. In fact, all paralysing lethargy vanished in that moment, and with my hands on her shoulders I pulled her towards me. My heart beat surprisingly tranquilly as her warm lips melded into mine and her hands threaded themselves into my hair, and gloriously, I lost myself.

29

IT WAS AROUND the time that Asta and I shared this un-expected kiss that Thomas returned from his mysterious absence: a uniformed, bearded visitor on my front doorstep. I beheld his arrival in disappointment, as I had of course anticipated that the person knocking on my door might be Asta. When I first saw him I mistook the visitor for David or Jack or one of the other soldiers as, in the heavy rain I saw before me a khaki tunic, a kit bag and a soaked cap.

Thomas manoeuvred past me into the house without being asked, flung his cap from his head and grimaced. The rainwater fairly cascaded from his beard to his chest. I gave him a towel and patiently made tea while he dressed himself in dry clothes which he dug from the depths of the kit bag.

'Much better,' he announced when this had been achieved. 'Much, much better.'

I was rudely awakened from my reverie, sitting dreamily on the bed, flung back to reality when all I had desired was to be allowed to dwell in my own little world and relive the sensations I experienced when I kissed Asta. 'How hospitable you are,' he remarked, grinning, as I gave him a cup of tea and something to eat. 'You wouldn't mind just washing my, err, uniform, would you?' he added hopefully. He gestured to the discarded pile of sodden khaki fabric on the floor. 'There's no rush, I won't be needing it again for a while.'

I shrugged my shoulders. 'Anything for a northerner who wanders around in the rain dressed as a soldier.'

For a while we ate in silence, Thomas somewhat greedily and as contented as a man can be when eating. It was indescribably strange to behold this man in my own house, putting away large quantities of my homegrown potatoes, boiled on the stove, drinking my tea and stalking around the floor peering in contented interest at this and that, whatever caught his eye. It was as though a being from another world had landed in my house. Eventually, he said, 'So where am I to sleep?'

I looked up from my forkful of cabbage.

'You can't very well expect me to travel back home in *this*.' He got up from the table and threw open the door to reveal the torrential downpour outside. In apprehension that I might be expected to transport him back to his turret in the clouds as an alternative to him staying in my home, I offered him my father's bed, for it seemed unlikely to be taken by the rightful occupant any time soon. I showed him the extra blankets and pointed out the chamber pot, which I strongly suggested he should use, as my elderly neighbour had a habit of complaining whenever I went in the fresh air of a morning to empty my bladder around the side of the house. Having left him to his preparations I busied myself with the cleaning up, and when next I turned from the stove, barely minutes later, my guest lay fast asleep, breathing gently, his face young in the soft, dim light.

The next morning I was shaken gently into wakefulness. Thomas moved, already dressed, as a murky shadow in the small room while outside the winter sun had barely cast its light over the horizon.

'Why?' I murmured from under the blankets after he had declared that it was time to get out of bed.

'Because we have work to do!'

Bleary-eyed, I sat up and watched him inspect the contents of the kit bag. 'But I have to go to the post office.'

'Not this early. Work first, post office later.'

I pulled on some warm clothes. Due to modesty, as Thomas was still rooting around in his kit bag, I went to relieve myself outside, reasoning that it must surely be too early for the old woman next door to be up and about. The morning was clear and still, the mountains basking in the watery glow that emanated from the sky, casting long, transparent rays of light over the valleys and village, interspersed with stretched shadows.

The varying shades of the patchwork fields were exaggerated in the light of dawn, so stark as to appear black and white. The fjord below lay calm and grey with not a wave on its surface. Overhead a pair of ravens called harshly to each other through the suspended animation of the landscape.

Just as I was buttoning up my trousers, I heard the usual scolding from my neighbour on her front doorstep, her face shadowed unsettlingly in the half-light.

'Ah.' I hoped that my spreading smile might be interpreted as apologetic, rather than as amused. 'I, err... have a visitor, you see.' But she only scowled and turned her back on me.

When we left a short while later, the Englishman caught sight of the woman still standing wrapped in a shawl at her front door. He offered her a nod in greeting which she returned. It was a nod of acquaintance, surely, yet yawning too widely to question it, I turned to follow Thomas to Naina's.

It was the vicar's wife who opened the door to the two of us, for a sick woman who cannot walk requires a helping hand around the house. She embraced me warmly and led me into the kitchen where Naina was knitting under a pile of blankets. She looked strikingly thin and pale in the light of the morning.

Thomas wanted me to act as translator, though he must have managed perfectly without me in the past – maybe I was here to release Guðrun from the duty. Thomas asked a few simple questions concerning the woman's health, her digestion and such; she in turn replied to a positive effect, always looking directly at Thomas while she spoke, so that I supposed my presence to be largely unnecessary. I was in no doubt that the man knew more than a few words of his patient's native language. He took her pulse, her temperature, all manner of tests for which I was required to pass him the various instruments and general paraphernalia from his kit bag, while Guðrun pottered around the stove and soon served Naina a steaming cup of, unmistakably, one of Thomas's strange concoctions.

With the light of dawn and the few candles around the kitchen, it was as though we were conducting some sort of secret ritual. Barely anyone spoke. Eventually, the sun had risen fully and voices could be heard from beyond the confines of the house, and my presence was no longer required. I kissed Guðrun goodbye and emerged into the real world, whose fresh air and natural light was a welcome contrast to the atmosphere of the quiet kitchen. Gripped by invigoration, I fairly flew down to Sørvágur.

It had begun to snow quite heavily. The sky lay comfortingly low over the rooftops, the ground was a greying white. Asta stood calmly at the door of the post office, red hair against an open red door, both dusted with snow. She watched as I positioned my bike against the wall and I sensed her eyes on me.

Feeling more clear-headed than I had felt in longer than I cared to remember, I walked calmly to the step on which she stood, pulled her close to me and kissed her warmly and deeply. She relaxed into my arms, slipped her cold hands around the back of my neck and pressed her body even closer. The feeling almost made me pass out with the wonderful strain it inflicted on my hammering heart. Asta blushed a little when I released her, most unwillingly. 'I knew you couldn't keep away from me,' she said. She took my hand and led me inside.

We dispensed with the day's English lesson, having little concentration to spare for intellectual pursuit. Instead we revelled quietly in our newfound mutual affection. Asta made two cups of coffee, bitter but gloriously red-hot, such that when our lips next met the tender warmth spread to my stomach and my fingertips. I broke away from her in embarrassment as her mother walked into the room, but Elva only smiled knowingly as she caught my eye. She continued to smile to herself as she fetched a wad of documents from a drawer across the room and soon tiptoed out again, evidently not wishing to disturb us.

As Elva closed the door quietly behind her, Asta giggled, perhaps noticing the crimson hue that the heat in my cheeks indicated was there. 'Don't worry, you know how much she likes you!'

Asta seemed to have recovered from the brief setback of shyness that had gripped her during her English lessons, having now regained the self-assuredness so true of her character. I no longer worried that I was below her expectations or under her feet. I was Asta's equal and I smiled contentedly even as she informed me that I was in dire need of a haircut, that I read far too many books, and that it really would not hurt if once in a while I came down from the clouds, for my absentmindedness could be irritating. I sipped the bitter coffee and continued smiling in wonderful thoughtlessness, while she spoke to me about this and that. But my bubble of contentment was burst by the door banging open, letting in the cold grey daylight.

Orri entered hurriedly in its wake, half-skipping to the post office desk. Ignoring Asta, he placed his two hands flat on the desk and leaned forward, his eyes fixed on mine. 'Karri, the Japanese have bombed an American naval base called Pearl Harbour, and now the Americans have joined the war.' He paused, breathing heavily. 'Allied cause, of course.' He was actually smiling. This boy, who would purposefully refuse any information pertaining to the progress of the war on the grounds that it was not his business, was seemingly animated now by this momentous news from across the globe.

An explanation for his behaviour soon followed, however, for barely had the words escaped his lips than David made a rushed entrance through the open door, equally as breathless and pink-cheeked as Orri. Orri wheeled around and, pointing at the gasping, uniformed figure, exclaimed in slurred English, 'Aha! I told him first, David. I told him first: that means I win!'

30

I WAS NO longer appalled by the immense impersonality of the wide, tortured world, but now accepted my existence within our tiny pocket of it. In the enclosure of the post office I would often find myself drinking coffee and playing cards with Orri and David and the red-headed girl whose existence and affections encouraged me to get out of bed every morning. Previously I had not noticed how good Orri's English was becoming. Or the way in which Asta's freckles were distributed across her nose and in the corners of her eyes, but not on her plump cheeks. The details of my life were sharpening.

I also noticed that the days grew shorter through December, and the darkness would settle over the mountains long before the day had seemed to run its course. Heavy-footed fisherman would return from an opaque sea to an endless evening; the garrison would drink and make merry, or else fall exhausted into their bunks. The monotony of these long evenings was avoided somewhat by the approach of Christmas: a common goal made it possible for the days to become separate, directed towards this landmark – though of course the war would still be on.

As the sun began to sink behind the silhouetted mountains we played football until the falling darkness was too thick for the ball to be seen. We frequently organised matches, the home team versus the occupying force. And it was impossible to allow the melancholy of winter to overwhelm a person at these times: he who stopped running after the ball would freeze. The spectators kept themselves warm by shouting and gesticulating in the failing, snow-tinted light, bundled in woollen jumpers and hats, cheering no matter which side had scored.

David sometimes invited Orri and me to an impromptu gathering in the barracks after the football. Over a game of cards Orri, already light-headed from the number of hyperactive goals he had managed to score for the home team, would inevitably succumb to the influence of alcohol. Once I had to all but carry him home. Magnus had broken out in coughing-laughter from his pillow to hear his son, red of cheek and grinning, singing slurred folk songs in the kitchen.

Orri said little of the situation between Asta and me, even when he was drunk and reeling. However, he did declare irritably that he risked looking inferior to his peers and now had no choice but to go out and acquire a girlfriend for himself. I grinned broadly and suggested Birgir's daughter, Ragna: she would jump at the offer of marriage to him, were he to ask.

At first Orri had scowled at me, though he had promptly taken the girl to the next village dance – I had managed to avoid the discomfort of attending by feigning a mild cough. When I called in the following morning to ask how his evening had gone, he only complained that Ragna was unfortunately prone to giggling at everything he said; he found it irritating, also, that the girl insisted her hair was pinned back flawlessly at all times; and to top off her faults, she kept kissing him at every opportunity. Following a comprehensive list of faults and grievances concerning Ragna from his son, Magnus laughed croakily before assuring Orri that, as a fisherman, he would be unlikely to see much of his wife anyway, whoever she happened to be.

***

We walked together to church at New Year, chatting companiably, Ragna hand in hand with Orri. My friend dreamily surveyed the mountains with a small, private smile on his lips, and occasionally contributed a remark or two to the conversation. It was a startlingly vivid winter day, clear and crisp. The new January sun of early evening fell over the snow of December, its cold winter light displaying the full height of the mountains in clear definition. The cold penetrated every woollen jumper and seeped into the bones of every person present so that we all ached and flexed our stiffened muscles in complaint. The church was filled with a chorus of foot-stamping and blowing into cupped hands until the congregation were sufficiently warmed to endure the chill of sitting still, at which point we squeezed into the pews in our coats and scarves and looked expectantly towards the vicar.

He was a vision before the altar this evening. He welcomed his congregation, saying we all ought to be thankful to be alive on this the first day of January, the year of our Lord, 1942. There was a strange illumination to his features, excitement trembled in his voice. I saw the glint of a secret in his eyes and sat up straighter. Throughout the short service I listened eagerly in case he might give something away, utter any word or phrase that was different to those in his standard speeches. Then, when old Naina was invited to approach the altar, my heart leapt into my throat. I placed my finger on the erratic pulse there while I scanned the congregation for a glimpse of the Englishman I knew must be present. But in the tiny church Thomas was nowhere to be seen.

The sick woman looked resplendent in the Islands' traditional dress, as everyone was accustomed to seeing her. She was wheeled to the front by Guðrun, who in turn took a modest seat nearby. All eyes in the church were upon Naina but no one spoke. In the silence of breath-held expectation, the woman, contrary to speaking out as all of us must have anticipated, gripped the sides of her wheelchair. With all the strength of her slender arms she raised her frail body to its feet and took a few tentative steps.

I leapt to my own feet along with the rest of the congregation. A chorus of gasps rang out, followed by a cacophony of chatter. It is difficult to say what happened next. I know only that I turned to look at Orri once my eyes could be torn away from the newly-walking woman, and found that he was not there. Through a barrage of exclamations – *unbelievable, praise be, it's a miracle* – I tracked his passage through the crowd and out of the church doors with my eyes, then swiftly I squeezed my physical presence out of the pew and followed him.

Orri cut a solitary figure in the grey atmosphere of the evening. Behind him the sea rolled in quiet waves, birds reeled over cliffs hung with mist, and when he turned to look at me a strange mania was in his blue eyes. 'Don't you see?' he burst out. 'Don't you see what he's done... *what he can do*? He's made her walk, Karri. It's all possible, I know that now!' He was laughing wildly, brimming over with hysteria. I told him to calm down but was met only with indignation. 'Calm down? But Karri, if he can do this, he...I won't have to watch my own father die.'

'You're not suggesting... ?'

'What, that he can cure him?' His eyes hardened. 'Why is

that so impossible? You've seen what he can do – of course he can cure Magnus. This is what it has all been leading up to, Karri.'

Was this why he had kept so quiet on the subject of his and his father's apparent dealings with Thomas? Perhaps he had not wanted to invite my scepticism, or tempt providence. The secrecy of such an important experiment must have lain so heavily upon his heart all this time – and I, oblivious and self-centred in my indignation at being left out, had let him struggle with it alone. Now I did not know what to say. There could be a shred of truth in his words, given what we had just witnessed in the church. A strange fire ran through my veins, threatening to engulf all reason. But Orri's manic anticipation kept my emotions in check: such violent enthusiasm set off alarm bells. Still... I could not explain the scene in the church.

The congregation spilled out. Orri vanished. I cast my mind back to recall every word Thomas had ever spoken about plants, about Magnus, about his work. Surely somewhere in the tumult of memory I could find an answer. My head began to buzz, my thoughts cartwheeled in all directions at once as though I had only just awoken, and while I had lain sleeping the world around me had gradually adopted a shape which had eluded my simplistic understanding.

Suddenly I knew where Thomas could be found. He would not have wanted to miss this dramatic culmination of his doings for anything: *what it had all been leading up to*, as Orri had said. Slipping through the tides of oncoming parishioners, I moved back through the church door and took the wooden staircase to the left of the vestibule. It was wide enough for only one man and so steep that I had to use my hands on the steps above to steady me as I climbed. On the balcony at the top, two pairs of eyes greeted me expectantly. *Thomas and Orri.* Orri looked crushed. When I had taken in his expression a surge of hatred for Thomas coursed through me.

'What did you do to her?' I kept my voice level.

'He cured her,' said Orri, quietly. He cast his eyes over the interior of the church far below, dim in the grey winter light filtering through snow-coated windows. I looked down too, over empty pews, the old pipe organ, bare walls. I turned to Thomas. I sensed arrogance in the smile playing about his lips. He had not yet uttered a word.

'But how did you do it? Why did you... That woman hasn't walked a step in thirty years. What gives you the right to play God?'

The corners of his mouth dropped. 'Play God? Kjartan, this is *medicine.*'

'Didn't you hear what they were saying? They're calling this a miracle, an act of God. You can't just prey on people's weaknesses like this, toy with their emotions.'

My voice reverberated in the empty church. Orri was staring at me, his expression shocked. Thomas frowned. 'What's the matter with you? Since when did helping the sick become such a taboo subject?'

'Helping, curing, Thomas, is one thing. But how dare you convince people that you can save the world?'

'What do you mean?'

I glanced at Orri. 'He thinks... he thinks you can cure his father.'

'And who's to say I can't?'

My stomach turned. 'No one can cure Magnus. No one. We know that, we've accepted it. Then you come along, all grandeur and outlandish claims... We'd *accepted* it, Thomas. How can you do this to his family?'

'Don't you trust me?' he asked quietly.

For a moment I held his gaze. I thought of everything I knew about him and all that we had been through together. 'No.'

A second later I lay on my back, my rib cage bursting, head spinning. Orri had delivered an iron-hard fist to my stomach. 'You ungrateful bastard!' he shouted. 'What's wrong with you? How could you wish my father dead?' He fell onto me. Gasping for stolen breath, I could not answer; with his knees on my chest I could not move nor fight back. Dazed, I saw Thomas try to pull the boy from the attack, but pushing the Englishman away, Orri removed his own weight from my bruised body and swore at me once more. I heard his footsteps receding quickly down the steps.

For some time I lay helplessly on the cold, unyielding wood of the balcony floor. Thomas lingered just long enough to make his deliberate silence heard before following Orri down the stairs. He had a right to be angry and Orri had been right to hit me – he should have hit me harder. I was only an obstacle to the happiness of others. I saw this clearly now as I lay in agony, guilt seared under my skin by Orri's blows.

It was Asta who helped me to my feet – ignoring my pleas that I ought to simply be covered in compost and left to rot for the benefit of all concerned. It was Asta who took my hand and led me home through the snowdrifts of a bleak world; Asta with whom I spent the night. She had no ears for my heartfelt insistence that I was no good, that I was bereft of morality and malicious in nature. She blocked my attempts to extricate myself from the glorious warmth of her embraces and wander back out into the snow and die. She refuted my insistence that I did not deserve an angel such as she was.

Asta held me close and kissed me until I found comfort in her arms, and feverishly I whispered that I loved her and would never do to her what I had done to all the others I had cared about.

31

February, 1942.

TIME SEEMS NOT to pass in the depths of winter, a sense of place cannot be uncovered from beneath the deep snow. The days roll by one by painful one and they are monochrome, featureless, on an endless loop. There is more darkness than daylight. In those few hours of visibility the observable world stretches off into the distance, always the same shade of grey-ing white, to the north, to the south, each view a suffocating eternity. The cold inhabits all places: curls its claws through the cracks in the door, slips under the bedclothes; finds its way into all areas where the meagre fingers of flames from the stove do not radiate their warmth.

The cold spread such hopelessness in me that it consumed my spirit and passion. I confined myself to bed, in the weari-ness of a shivering world. I forsook my duties and sought comfort in the enclosing arms of feverish dreams and thoughtlessness. The colours of the world seemed so distant that I realised I could not regain a hold on anything that lay beyond my front doorstep. I dreamt of birds and oceans, of machinery and cinders, of the spilling of dawn upon snow, and of the oblivion of the battlefield. The nights were dark, and the days were like the inky depths of Arctic waters.

I ran through memories of my father in every waking minute of lucidity. In my imagination I saw his face, pale and indistinguishable as rocks under shallow water, and like a child I retreated into the self-made den whose walls I had known each time my nearest brother had fought with my father, or blamed me for our mother's death.

At some point within the featureless flow of fatigued routine, when I sat fully dressed on my bed after Asta had insisted I get up, Orri knocked on the door. I knew it was him: he had a peculiar little skip of a knock. I said nothing as Asta rose to answer, though my stomach twisted sickeningly with those three little taps. I heard Orri and Asta exchange civilities, hushed but friendly, and I closed my eyes to capture the inexplicable comfort that had crept over me with the sound of Orri's voice.

I heard the rustle of a coat, his footsteps; when at last I opened my eyes Orri was peering down at me. He was swathed in a hat and scarf, his cheeks pink from the bite of winter and the flush of the warmth indoors. He smiled meekly before leaning across the width of the bed to put his hands on my shoulders and his frosty cheek to mine in greeting.

Despite my reluctance to leave the house Orri insisted on dragging me outside for some fresh air, remarking that I looked as white as the untouched snow on the mountains. I allowed him to lead me a little way up the hill between our village and the neighbouring hamlet. We followed the postman's path – a route I had not taken for some time. I had not even bothered to enquire who had taken over my duties, and in turn Asta had not bothered me with the information. With our heavy breath translucent in the northern air, Orri and I sat ourselves down on a flat boulder overlooking Tindhólmur. The islet gazed back submissively in the thick white air, a large bulk of inanimate rock.

'I wonder if he can see us,' Orri mused aloud.

I did not look up to see if the house was visible, did not care one way or the other. I drew my knees in against my chest and sank into the warmth of my many layers of clothing.

'I'm sorry,' Orri said suddenly. I looked at him, at his eyes shining with what could have been the threat of tears. He swallowed, gazed out over the sea. 'I'm sorry I wouldn't talk to you about... *him*. It's just that with Magnus and... he said he thought he could help, and I was *scared*. Scared to trust him, scared to put all my hopes into his promise, and scared to admit to trusting him... I couldn't tell you. I thought you might be sceptical; I thought you might say something that would make it all seem... impossible.'

I gulped down a wave of sickness as he spoke these words. This was what he had thought of me. 'Orri –,' I began.

'You did, though, didn't you?' he interrupted, and as he turned to look at me directly I saw that his gaze was hard, accusing. I heard the sharpness in his voice. 'In the church, after he made Naina walk... you said you didn't trust him; you said that no one can cure Magnus.'

Sitting with my shoulder pressed against his, I longed to turn and wrap my arms around his neck, to apologise until my voice ran hoarse, to promise that I would never hurt him again; but it was the wave of self-hatred that stopped me. It coursed sickeningly through my body and collected deep in the pit of my stomach, rested there like a stone, weighting me to the rock on which we sat. I felt the distance between Orri and me to be so great I could have cried. Again he turned his gaze to the stony sea, leaving me even more bereft.

'I'm really sorry for what I said in the church,' I managed with difficulty: there was so much I could *not* bring myself to say. 'You know I could never wish Magnus dead. He'll... it will all be alright.'

Without turning to look at me he nodded – a mute acceptance of my awkward apology. Then taking off his woollen hat he rested his elbows on his knees. He ran his fingers through his hair and sighed deeply. 'But I should have told you. Right from the beginning.' He shook his head, the wind catching in his hair and carrying the renewed strength of his voice out over the fjord: 'Why didn't I tell you?'

I shrugged, tried to give him a smile. 'I never really asked.' Catching my eye, he too smiled meekly. He lit two cigarettes, one for each of us, and it was only when almost half of the one I held had crumbled into ashes and smoke that I realised we had lapsed into a heavy silence. I stole a look at Orri and beheld a pained expression on his face, one of a man lost in irresolvable thoughts.

'There's something else I have to tell you,' he said when he noticed me looking. 'I, err... might have done something a little stupid.' He swallowed hard, pulling at the fingers of his woollen gloves while I waited. 'It's Ragna. She's, err... she's going to have a baby.'

I stared at him, feeling after a minute or more of deep silence that I ought to say something in return. Anything. 'I didn't know you'd... '

'I thought you would be ashamed of me.' His voice shook a little.

'Ashamed?'

Another long pause followed. 'It seemed like something I should do,' he said flatly. 'Something I should *want* to do. Oh, Jesus, Birgir's going to *kill* me!' He put his head in his hands despairingly, and the wind continued to play with the back of his white-blond hair. I reached over and put my hand in Orri's coat pocket, pulling out the packet of cigarettes. I withdrew two and lit them. Orri took the cigarette gratefully from me when his face had finally surfaced from his hands. 'I suppose I'll have to marry her.'

'Do you love her?'

A cloud of smoke from our two outlet breaths was caught in the wind and swept away, dissipating over the sea.

'I'm quite fond of her. I like her company.' For a brief moment his face lit up in animation, though the flame soon puttered out. 'But I prefer yours.'

I had started to laugh but when our eyes locked I saw that there was something terribly poignant about the expression in his. Heaviness sat like a rock in my stomach. *I don't want him to marry her.* 'I'm not going anywhere,' was all I said. After a moment, Orri smiled. 'Do you promise, Karri?'

'Of course I promise. What are you on about? Where would I even go, the other side of the island? And you love children,' I reminded him. 'I really don't see what the problem is.'

He gazed out to sea. 'You'll have to knit some clothes,' he ventured, as the wind caterwauled over the heather: 'You know – for the baby. If you're going to stick around you might as well make yourself useful.'

***

It took Orri another few days to pluck up the courage to ask Ragna to marry him, during which time he would frequently turn up at my door and pace around the floor in his socks, a cup of tea in one hand, imploring me to convince him that this action would not irreversibly change all things for the worse. And when finally he came to me with the news that the offer had been made and accepted he was not joyful nor brimming with anticipation, as a man in his position surely ought to be; rather he appeared detached. It stirred a deep unease within me and I struggled to hold down my own feelings on the matter.

The family, at least, were thrilled with the arrangement. None more so than Magnus at the prospect of his first grandchild, whether or not he were alive to welcome it into the world – as he himself pointed out with no hint of self-pity.

A series of gatherings between the two families of the betrothed followed in the sparse and simplistic comforts of Magnus's dining room. I watched with enjoyment as Orri's mother put a comb to his head and forced him into a clean, ironed shirt. Moments before the guests arrived he popped out, as usual, to put the chickens in for the night, and returned drenched and disarrayed by the winter's wrath. Thus he spent the evening dripping under the scrutinising displeasure of his mother, throwing grinning glances in my direction when she was not looking.

Birgir was disillusioned by his daughter's condition, of course, but did at least appear reconciled to it, mainly because the deed had been carried out by one of Magnus's relations. Birgir had of course great respect for the fisherman, and it must be a matter of plain fact that all the desirable characteristics Magnus possessed would also be present in any grandchild of his.

And as for Magnus himself: well, it was obvious to all that his condition was improving. I was torn between shame at the behaviour I had exhibited in front of Orri and Thomas, and the calm understanding of this recovery being inevitable. No -one spoke of Magnus's health – even though he was now able to leave his bed for small periods of time and join the gatherings in the dining room – for who speaks of such things?

On the first of the gatherings in his house the fisherman remarked tactlessly (as was his usual tendency) that he would not have thought his son had it in him to 'knock up' a young lady. Orri and I both choked on our coffee and Orri's mother shot Magnus a warning glance. Ragna turned crimson. An awkward silence followed. Drunk on the warm thrill of Magnus's sense of humour at the table again, I raised my coffee mug in a toast. 'To Orri, more of a man than any of us could ever have imagined.' Magnus's blankets and beard shook with laughter; his wife left the room in a flurry, and Orri threw me a surprised glance before grinning delightedly.

I cannot help noticing how his cold-chapped cheeks glow pink and his hair a dull gold in the lamplit room.

I feared I was about to lose him, despite the promises we had made.

'Ásdis!' Magnus called to his wife, 'More coffee for Kjartan!'

32

March, 1942.

IT WAS ONLY shortly after Orri and Ragna's betrothal that David stopped by, early one evening, to tell me it was time for his regiment to leave the island. 'There'll be other squadrons tae come,' he assured me.

'Wonderful.' Gloom descended on me, though from my front door we were watching a glorious sunset. David stared fixedly ahead, his expression thoughtful. I hazarded a question, though I was sure the answer would console neither of us: 'Where will you go?'

He shrugged his shoulders loosely. 'Who knows? The Eastern Front; the moon; Glasgow? Wherever they send us.'

'At least you will be a little more useful in any of those other places,' was my flippant response. 'I mean, what have you achieved since you've been here? Precious little. Even Jack went and knocked up one of the local girls. You've not even managed that.' *Jack and Orri both.*

David snorted. 'That daft bastard,' he muttered, half to himself. He took another prolonged drag on his cigarette.

'I suppose he'll not see the baby; Jack, I mean,' I said. Orri would, of course. David did not reply.

Clouds were darkening on the horizon, their tops gleaming, their edges defined sharply against the clearer twilight-pink area of sky stretching over our heads. I pointed towards the illuminated peaks and crevasses, up there in the sky.

'Just for a moment, if you concentrate on it, if you leave your body, forget the island, forget that the Atlantic stretches on forever, you can imagine the world that would exist in such a place as that. Sometimes I think I could walk there: take my coat and walk until my shoes fell apart and the cold stopped hurting. And when I arrived there everything would be different, beautiful.'

'What are you talking about?'

I sighed, having discovered within me an intense longing to have both my feet upon solid earth. 'With all this in existence, you'd never know there was a war on.'

After I had watched his khaki-clad figure amble away into the falling darkness, I was struck by the thought that I had forgotten all about the uniform that Thomas had left with me to be washed. It was still stuffed in the kit bag which lay discarded on my father's bed. Curiously I pulled out the creases of heavy fabric, wondering why he did not wear the uniform all the time, as did the other garrison troops – if, indeed, he was a soldier after all.

I heard the rustle of paper in the chest pocket of his tunic, and from there withdrew a wadded document. I opened it out: it looked official, and bore a stamp in black ink, though I could not make out what it said. There was a black and white photograph of Thomas, unsmiling. His full name, nationality and date of birth had all been written in the allocated spaces beside the picture, as well as some brief information on his appearance: *height, 5ft 8ins; hair, dark brown*. I looked again at the photograph: it had faded somewhat, and ill-defined as the picture was, his face appeared younger. Oddly, I imagined I could have been looking at a photograph of myself.

Just something to do with the garrison. How I had wondered at the mystery. I could not see that it mattered now, where the man had come from. The occupation had become an inextricable part of life, after all, it had come to dominate all of our lives, perhaps in more ways than we realised. All at once I ached with exhaustion. I put the identity card back into the tunic pocket and folded the uniform back into the bag for now.

***

I made no effort to travel to Tindhólmur to see Thomas. I thought about it, almost every day in fact, yet concluded invariably that I would no doubt run into him on my next visit to Orri's, given the Englishman's evident preoccupation with Magnus's health. This, I supposed, would be a much more desirable situation in which to offer my long overdue apology and return his uniform, now washed and dried. I did not wish to appear drenched and exhausted on his distant front doorstep and have to face the weatherbeaten journey back home immediately were he to refuse me entrance to his house.

But he remained elusive despite my best efforts to catch him by surprise. Orri, however, lost no time in expressing his curiosity as to why I had developed the habit of turning up in his kitchen a few times every day and lurking apparently pointlessly around the house and the chicken coop. His mother seemed increasingly displeased at the frequency of my visits – her attitude towards me had grown no warmer since I moved back home as she had requested. Orri's offer of marriage to Ragna had evidently not quelled her suspicions about me, though naively I had thought it might. More than once I was informed stiffly by her that her son had responsibilities to attend to, given his recent engagement and expected child, and could not be at my beck and call every hour of the day.

In my heart I knew that this was likely true, and had many times been unable to bring myself to extend an inquisitive knock to his front door for fear of impinging upon his duties or time. Yet I was still upset by the unfriendliness in his mother's voice.

I waited until I knew she would be out of the house before visiting again. The daylight was drawing to an end, the landscape had sunk gently into the purple shroud that hovered over the mountains. The fields were cut into long shadows and the roaring sea seemed suspended, muted in ethereal light. The days had begun to lengthen again as winter relinquished its grasp, yet the evenings were still long and I welcomed their quietness with an insurmountable anticipation. I felt safe and calm in the blankets of the eternal twilight in which the world was lulled to sleep.

I desired nothing more than to spend time with Orri, playing cards in the welcoming light of the oil lamp with the kettle boiled and ready for our tea, the weather banished and the world forgotten, Orri's eyes bright with brimming laughter.

Only now Orri's eyes were not so bright; since his betrothal to Ragna they had begun to dim. Day by day, thought by thought it seemed, the weight of realisation descended on him. He would not tell me what he was so afraid of.

On this evening I all but ran to his front door, unsure of the reason for my haste. I knew only that in the morning he would be off to sea before most of the town had arisen and when he got back he would marry. And what then? I was heady, perhaps, from Asta's brief visit as the sun had begun to sink below the mountains. It had been a passing tryst of intertwined legs and her red locks entangled in my dark ones, and I, though shuddering and breathless, had been able to think of nothing but the look of sadness in Orri's eyes while my body played its part in its interactions with hers.

The snow on the mountaintops had all but disappeared, hardened now to frost. It was bitterly cold. I let myself in, for there was no need to knock when Ásdis was not at home. I discarded my boots and coat and tried to steady the uncertain rhythm of my breathing. I found Orri sitting on his bed, eyes downcast. He seemed a mere shadow in the gloom of the house. He offered me a meek smile as I entered, waited in silence as I lit the lamp. I hung it on the wall next to the bed and sat down beside him. The house was comfortingly warm from the peat stove and my mind was a little giddy. Perhaps I should not have come and disturbed him.

'Magnus is asleep,' he whispered.

I nodded. 'How is he?'

'He's much better, Karri.' He met my gaze for a second.

'He should be well for the wedding.' I strove to sound light-hearted, but Orri groaned. I noticed that his jumper was beginning to unravel at the base of his neck.

'Do you not think you'll be happy with her?'

He shook his head wordlessly.

'Why not... ?'

'Oh, for God's sake, Karri, is it not *obvious?*'

I bit my lip. My head swam. Was it obvious? If I should be witness to the anguish of my closest friend yet remain wilfully blind as to the cause I could never forgive myself. If only he would meet my eyes and reveal the workings of his soul. But he would not look at me. Perhaps also I was as ready as he to tear my gaze away the moment his began to lift. There was both heaviness and elation within me – feelings so strongly feared I could not face their meaning. Maybe neither of us could face it.

'She's not all that bad... '

But of course the character of the girl was not the obstacle to his happiness and as I had anticipated he sighed heavily and dropped his head further, into the cup of his hands. 'You'll be away at sea for half the year,' my voice continued. 'And for the other half she'll be too busy with the baby to pay you much attention.'

He raised his head then and let his hands fall into his lap. 'You are such a cynic, Kjartan.' A small smile played about his lips though, and as his eyes finally met mine a ripple coursed through me. It *was* obvious what the doubts were that plagued him.

'I'll lose everything if I marry her.'

I shook my head. 'Don't be stupid.' My hand reached to brush a fallen lock of hair from his face and lingered there.

He let his forehead come to rest against mine and the gentle, hypnotic rhythm of his breathing, so close to my skin, was the only sound, the only movement in the low light of the bedroom.

'I think you'll be just fine, Orri,' I whispered. He nodded, or shook his head, it was difficult to distinguish which. When he spoke again it was as though his voice had drifted through to my senses from another time, another world, another conversation. 'Could I not just spend the wedding night at your house?'

I had not heard the sound of the front door opening, nor footsteps through the kitchen or up the steps to the bedroom; it was only when I shivered from the sudden, invasive chill of the wind that followed in Ásdis's wake that I saw her in the doorway. I pulled my hand away from Orri's cheek and he whipped his head up. Not a word, not a breath made itself known in the stillness of the room, until Ásdis resumed her path along the floorboards, her lips pressed together. With hurried, suppressed steps she threw open the door to Magnus's adjoining chamber and entered it, closing the door behind her.

Orri and I sat motionless for a moment longer, then I, too, was on my feet. I crossed the bedroom floor and almost fell down the steps, ran through the kitchen into the hall and thrust my arms into my coat and my feet into my boots. Orri called after me from the kitchen doorway, quiet and imploring. I did not turn back but plunged straight out into the sobering cold of the evening, my cheeks flushed, my head dizzy and my heart pounding.

From the look on his mother's face I understood fully, now, her animosity towards me. It was a flush of shame with which my cheeks burned, hot as a fever, but I also shook with defiance. I had committed no wrong towards her or her son. *It wasn't as though we were... We hadn't even...*

Once back in my own house I found I could not keep still. I dared not sit quietly for fear of the thoughts that would assail me if I gave in to contemplation. Instead I fervently tidied, swept the floor and washed the pans, stacked up the peat stove and tidied my various piles of knitting on the spare bed. I half expected Orri to appear through the door, frost-bitten and windswept, but in reality I knew he would not.

It was only when the heat of the fire found its comforting way to my chilled bones that I realised I was exhausted. I put a kettle of water on the stove to boil, and sat on my bed and drank tea until the oil lamp had burned itself out. Then I laid my head down to sleep, and dreamt of everything, all at once.

33

AS THE NEW day dawned I cycled to the harbour to see Orri off. It was a grey morning, heavy with overcast skies, made bright by the bustle around the boats. I made my way through coiled ropes and tattered nets, discarded fish heads and rusting hooks. There were shouts and peals of laughter and the chatter of many voices. Orri was alone by his crew's boat, re-threading a worn net with white-and-pink fingers. I watched him for a while, content to stay back from the bustling activity of the working harbour. The atmosphere was thick with the aroma of fish, the soundtrack was the lively breaking of waves on the rocks and the caterwauling of the gulls; those that reeled overhead and others hopping amidst the flotsam and jetsam of the harbour, seeking an easy meal. My cheeks were chapped from the bite of the sea breeze.

Glancing up to swap a few words with Jón the fisherman, Orri caught sight of me. He smiled and waved in greeting.

'I was just pointing out to Orri what a pity it is that he's not got a wife to wave goodbye to him as the boat leaves,' Jón said teasingly as I arrived at their side. Orri grinned, not taking his eyes from the intricate mending of the fishing net. 'I told you, Jón, we're not holding the wedding until Magnus is better: he can't miss it. He's promised to bring his beard along.' He swore suddenly as a knot slipped from his stiff-fingered grasp. 'Here, Karri.' He passed it to me. 'You're good with these things: see what you can do.'

I took the net willingly and held it up for scrutiny. Through the coarse webbing, the faded red body of the fishing boat behind Orri rocked gently on the swell of the tide. Its mast and rigging rolled in the grey haze of the sky. The two of us joked together as usual, as though nothing had to change. I kept my fingers busy with the net, while Orri struggled into his waterproof dungarees and his thick fisherman's jumper and anorak.

Eventually he stood grinning at me, planted in his oversized gumboots. I could not help but laugh at the picture he presented in his working attire: these were, of course, Magnus's clothes for the job, and hung from Orri's lithe frame like laundry from the drying line. With the ends of the trousers turned up and the sleeves rolled to allow his pale hands to peer from beneath, the overall effect was that of a child in the first stages of adult life, lost in the folds of his future uniform. Orri scowled at me good-naturedly as I continued to laugh at him. 'Magnus says I'll grow into them.'

He had recently given up on what he deemed the 'luxury' of shaving in favour of a blond stubble of a beard which, when teamed with the anorak and gumboots every fisherman wore, was entirely in character. Despite his mother's complaints he had asserted that he would be much warmer in the winter, would save money on shaving soap and, most importantly, could carry out a more accurate impersonation of Magnus when the situation called for it.

My newly bearded friend pulled at the cuff of his woollen jumper which protruded from the folded sleeve of Magnus's anorak. A growing hole had appeared in the knitting. With a tug of my stomach I remembered noticing, as I had sat next to him the previous evening; that the stitching was also in a state of unravel at his neck. 'This jumper is falling apart,' Orri complained, in line with my thoughts. He worried again at the loose thread and all of a sudden he looked up at me and beamed mischievously. 'Will you knit me another one – for when I get back?'

'Is that not something your wife should be doing?'

He scoffed, as though I ought to know better than to suggest such things. 'Ah, come on. You always knit my jumpers. Nothing has to change.'

He met my gaze only momentarily before glancing to the boat as Jón summoned him. He put out his hands and took the mended net from my numbing fingers, brushing against them. Again I felt that painful lurch in the pit of my stomach. I opened my lips to speak but nothing would come out. Orri's eyes were over-bright. Lifting his free arm, he wrapped it around my neck, pressing his wax garments and roped net to my woollen jumper and his cold-chapped cheek to mine. His hair smelled comfortingly of salt. It stirred as the wind rustled through it playfully. Time stilled and the cacophony of the harbour and the birds dulled to the gentle pulse of my heart against his, through all the wool and wax of our clothing, through the webbing of the net.

He released me a little awkwardly and moved to climb up to the waiting boat. For a painful moment I feared he might not look at me or speak to me again, that he would simply disappear into the throng of preparation. I kept my eyes fixed on him, still felt the cold press of his cheek on mine.

Then, once on board, he gripped the side of the boat and faced me. His slender hands were blanched a mottled pink with the cold. He leaned over the coarse, aged wood.

'Just nothing khaki!'

It took a beat or two before I realised he was referring to my offer of knitting him a new jumper. 'I know you, Karri: you'll knit me a camouflaged tunic *just in case* the Germans turn up on our doorsteps. And a gas mask.'

Beside him Jón paused in his unwinding of the heavy mooring rope and shook his head, a smile on his face. I grinned back at Orri and needed to raise my voice considerably above the commotion for him to hear me shout, 'How about a chest pocket for your fish hooks?'

The peals of his warm, familiar laughter spread and carried like smoke through the clear air as the chugging boat moved away from the harbour wall. I did not tell Orri to watch out for himself and he did not ask me to look after Magnus.

34

I SPENT A large amount of time during the following weeks at Magnus's bedside, experiencing utter indifference from Ásdis as she came and went from the room seeing to her husband's needs and comforts. She appeared to have resigned herself to my presence now that her son was not at home. Magnus and I kept each other's thoughts occupied, discussing whatever topic came to either of our minds. Every now and again we speculated on the possible hour and day that the boat would come home.

When it did not appear around, and then after, the expected date, I was there at Magnus's door again, too consumed with worry to fear what Ásdis might say at my returned presence. Installed at his bedside with a cup of tea that had been handed to me by his wife rather bad-temperedly on this occasion, Magnus and I joked together about the possible reasons for the boat's delay; many of them involving Orri being too scared to come back and marry the girl he had landed in trouble.

'Perhaps my son is more virile than I thought and has a girl in every port, and this is why he has not come home.' Magnus let out a burst of laughter but it stuttered prematurely to a stop when I failed to uphold my side of our unspoken bargain to keep our spirits up. I could hear Ásdis banging pots in the kitchen below, and felt sorry for her. As much as Magnus, she would be unable to bear it if the only surviving one of her children was never to come home.

I had finished knitting the earthen-patterned jumper that I had promised Orri, and still the harbour remained quiet, the horizon empty. As the days slipped by and the wait elongated beyond the point of discomfort, a hard lump made itself felt in my stomach.

When I was with Asta I did not speak of the missing boat. She made a visible effort to stay by my side and to talk to me of this and that – anything that was not related to fish. It would seem she sensed my desire to withdraw, and I suspected from the way her hands twitched in her lap that she longed to reach out to me. Yet I could no longer find comfort in her arms.

I again began to neglect my daily duties, always returning to the harbour. There I passed hours scanning the churning, end-less waters for a dark blemish upon that faceless grey surface – but in vain. The late winter days of our island life were so featureless, so poorly lit and silent that my imagination could make no move to envisage what could have happened. Upon thinking, as I did throughout most days, of the missing boat I pictured only a masted object standing stationary on an infinite grey plane, silhouetted by the unchanging face of a colourless sky. No waves rocked it onwards, no wind billowed in its lifeless sails; it seemed to me that it brooded silently in this vacuum, in a stone sea beyond the horizon's mountainous clouds.

***

In late March the news finally reached us, that the little boat whose return we had so restlessly awaited had disappeared somewhere off the coast of Iceland. Sunk, it was suspected, by an enemy submarine; hit by a torpedo – a neutral boat in neutral waters: and a crew of twelve.

Again I stood fixated at the sea's edge, staring at an unfaltering view of slate waves. I shivered, cold to the very marrow as I tried to imagine the sequence of events that had taken him away. The boat could not have simply disappeared from the face of the earth – a stone-cold fury was kindled within me that its fate could elude even my imagination.

Orri's fate. I thought only of him. I tasted the panic of the attack; saw him running across the deck in his over-large boots. I heard the hoarse shouts of danger and the prayers of those who rightfully saw no hope in the ocean's icy open arms.

When this image had faded, everything beyond it was unthinkable. How long had he struggled in the paralysing bite of the water before his heart had given out? Was he the first, the last? So many times I closed my heavy eyelids and tried to imagine where his body now lay, and I could not. How could I picture the true depth of the ocean floor, feel the weight of fathoms of water bearing down upon his breathless lungs? The utter blackness and silence of his eternal grave was unimaginable for me, for my own senses were still awake in the living world.

35

Spring, 1942.

THE WATERY SUN peered mockingly from time to time through the heavy sky, the birds' screams echoed and were amplified by the wetness of the barren landscape below; the air carried all sounds into the far, far distance. As usual, rain fingered the thick fleeces of the roaming sheep and the woollen jumpers of their two-legged wearers caught in the shower. Yet still, darkness threatened the lengthening days, a blanket that dulled the sharpest senses. The mountains closed in, curved in an arc around the village. The grey of the sky was oblique, unbearable. My thoughts were terrifying and insistent, too material to ignore.

It was barely three days after we had received the news about Orri's boat that I sat by Magnus's bed as I had done so many times before. My heart beat with laborious pain, while the heart of Magnus had stopped. I looked upon his lifeless body and felt nothing. His face still retained a portion of its colour. Illuminated by the sparing evening light; his eyes were closed and his lips were parted slightly. He looked tranquil, safe in his own home. His wife sobbed loudly downstairs but it did not bother me – I had grown used to the sound – it had gone on for days.

Magnus was at peace and I felt no pity or despair for him. It was good that he had not suffered for too long.

***

Once again the world clawed with its blackened, frost-bitten fingers at my soul. The wounds in their deep-set hurt woke me from whatever sleep I managed to catch or sink into feverishly. Drained of all strength I lay powerlessly within the folds of blankets, my dead eyes fixed on the knitted jumper intended for Orri which lay instead upon the cold wood of the floor; and I wondered only why, of all colours, I had chosen grey – the colour of desolation, of lifelessness and of my own eyes.

When Asta turned up at the door, her eyes swollen and red-ringed from the tears she had shed, I felt only unspoken anger towards her – why should *she* mourn Orri's loss? She had made no effort to hide her animosity towards him after all. My heart softened when I remembered, in her renewed sobbing as she fell into my arms, that her own uncle had been aboard the boat, and I reproached myself bitterly for my fleeting hostility. She lit the stove for me, and spent the night, yet I found to my shame that I could not comfort her in the way she wanted, in the way she tried to comfort me. And after she had left me alone again in the morning I felt even lonelier than I had before. The stove had burned itself out but I ignored it; once more I pulled the warmth of the blankets around me and curled into a foetal shape on the bed.

Eventually my door was opened and determined footsteps crossed the floor. It was Guðrun, of course. Through her usual kindly forces I again found myself in her maternal care. She put me to bed in her spare room, the one I always occupied on my frequent stays in the comfort of her home. I had taken only the jumper with me, too disorientated to settle upon any other necessity; what else could matter?

I clutched the jumper to my shivering body as once more I lay, attempting to find solace, to escape reality, under the folds of heavy blankets and in the gathering arms of slumber. The bedroom door had been left open, the frame filled with the pale golden light of the oil lamp which illuminated the kitchen and Guðrun in her evening tasks. I heard the distant clattering of copper pots, the hiss of a kettle, heard low voices pouring like water into my ears.

Feverish, perhaps from the lack of food – for despite

Guðrun's offerings I could swallow nothing – or perhaps from the fatigue of shock, darkness quickly washed over me with such unstoppable vigour that I felt as though I was falling quite literally into its absorbing, horrifying oblivion.

Suddenly I was a bird in flight. The wind rushed through the dancing feathers of my wings and I saw them flutter as though I were now an onlooker, felt it as keenly as though I had become the wind itself. On this upthrust and resurgence of power I soared effortlessly. I bent my black head downwards, pointed my beak towards the sea far below, seemingly smooth as glass from this dizzying height. Even the tumultuous waves that careered and crashed against the rocks of the shore were nothing more than mere spray – white pockets that divided up an otherwise uniform surface. Below me and around me rose the mountains in their serene glory, bare now of snow and exposing instead every rock, every hewn cliff and bouldered slope, every sharp precipice and each green-brown living thing growing from its soil.

I dropped and dove over the angular shapes, plunged over cliffs and raced along fjords to the point at which the two banks met in steep collision. I circled the Islands, both in the cloudless height and at the level of the crashing sea. Occasionally I would drop and lose height with such startling suddenness that my stomach thrust into my throat, my wings resisted every urge to flail wildly. Yet always I would regain my flight and the rush of the pure, cold air through every fibre of my being. The heart-wrenching majesty of the world proved so invigorating, so glorious that my heart strained with the weight of its unchecked beauty.

When I awoke, Orri was sitting at the end of the bed. The light in the kitchen had long been extinguished, the darkness settled comfortably beyond the open door. Outside the wind howled like one lost in the wilderness, whistled through the cracks in the window frame. But for the light cast by a waxing moon the ghostly figure at the foot of my bed would have been obscured by the night.

I sat bolt upright, but this sudden movement provoked in him no response. He was sitting with his back hunched to the watery shafts of moonlight through the open curtains. His hair in the faint light was no longer golden; it lay lank, plastered across his forehead, the colour of dead seaweed. It took me a moment or two to realise that it was wet, dripping with salt water. His clothes, too, were saturated and gleamed dully in the night's allowance of light. He did not look at me, seemed not to look at anything of this world for his eyes were hidden in shadow. Yet the air of melancholy, of despair about his whole presence, filled the room with an ice-cold dejection. Even fully clothed, I shivered under the blankets.

So many times in the previous days, even the preceding weeks, I had thought of the way in which he had embraced me on his departure, desperately trying to recapture each detail in my memory. I wanted to be able to recall it at will and once more feel his hair upon my cheek and his arms safely about my neck. On continually scanning the clouded horizon for signs of the returning ship in the after days of its lateness, with my anxiety building, I had imagined how I would greet Orri, embrace him in relief. I swore to myself that we would laugh together again and I chided myself for fretting, for assuming that the worst had happened.

Yet this figure which sat on the end of my bed, so changed and so despairing, provoked no such longings within me. I could not move. I tried to say his name aloud but I could only produce a whisper. It did not rouse him. I could not tell whether his pale, glistening cheeks were damp with tears or from the salt water in which he was drenched. It was a soddenness contained within his immateriality: my bed remained dry.

My bones shook violently. In shock my mind was clear of all else save the dreadful clarity of his presence. My very soul lay naked upon the bed, the blankets mere transparency; my body disengaged from its unstable physicality. The cold reached deep within me – a cold which was bred in the existence of darkness that has never once known the warming light. Orri's silence was that which lies behind all life in this world.

I struggled to regain the warmth of the winter night I had left behind but my eyes, ears and lungs felt full of death. I turned violently away from the apparition, my head buried under the blankets, my eyes squeezed shut.

***

Awake again: the room appeared to darken under my gaze; the few items of furniture which inhabited its small dimensions seemed heavy as the earth, immovable and looming. A pressing need to relieve myself had awoken me and, still in confusion, I used the pot in the weak, thick half-light of early morning.

My blurred vision caught a glimmer beyond the open door of the room. It was as though the wan dawn had concentrated its most intense, gathering light upon this one spot. On unsteady feet I stumbled across the floor. Facing that point of dancing, glimmering interest from the doorway, I beheld something that troubled me. It was a face. Neither young nor old, happy nor sad. An oval-shaped face, lacking definition. It appeared grey, like bread left unbaked. The face was framed by an untidy mop of dark hair; it was obscured by a dark beard and inlaid with two oceans of eyes.

I stared, transfixed. Cavernously the eyes stared back, great round windows into an emotionless vacuum. I came to my senses and reacted by springing back, yet it still seemed that the mask of a face remained in place. It was a mirror on the wall. I turned my back and stumbled into the kitchen. The light of day scratched at my eyeballs, and as I stretched my eyes wider open I saw that Thomas was sitting at the kitchen table. We stared at each other. I felt sick.

After the long moment of mutual recognition his down-turned lips twisted themselves into a pathetic smile. 'How do you feel, Kjartan?' His voice was weighted, like damp cloth.

'You,' I choked. 'You've got some nerve.' I struggled to draw breath.

Surprise flickered across his sallow features. His eyes adopted a vague quizzicalness, though he averted them quickly. I wished that he would leap from his chair and promptly declare his innocence, admonish me for the accusations I was bound to make upon his morality. I longed for him to reanimate, regain his power of conviction. Why couldn't he show some spirit in this world of dead objects? Instead he turned his eyes flatly towards me. 'Why don't you sit down?'

'No. Why should I – with you?' My heart welled like the ocean. 'Thomas – you let them die.' I took a shallow breath, hoping in vain to steady the violent shaking of my hands. Still I did not look at him, addressed the floor. 'How could you...? How could you, after all you've done for us? We trusted you – *I* trusted you... and you let them die!'

His hand gripped the edge of the table.

'You promised Magnus would get better – in all but words you promised. I admonished you for your arrogance and still you showed no modesty, so I *believed* you. How could you just let him die like that after all those promises? And Orri. *Orri.*' I swallowed another sob. 'He was twenty! His child will grow up without a father and you did nothing. *Why*, Thomas, why couldn't you save him?'

'Because I cannot work miracles,' he said.

'Then why did you convince us all that you *could*? The outsiders, the people from the corners and the shadows, like me, and you, with your lies – we go on living. But not him. He was real.'

My throat seemed to be obstructed. Blackness began to creep into my vision and before I could right myself I slipped into a swimming darkness. Instinctively I gasped his name in panic, and when I came to, barely a split second later, I found Thomas had caught me before I hit the floor. I struggled to keep my feet and grasped unsteadily for the door handle. Again the blackness threatened and fighting for consciousness, this time I fell hard onto my knees, my burning forehead sliding down the door frame.

'Come on, lad, I'll warm us up some soup,' said the voice of Thomas. His hand took hold of my elbow and pulling me to my feet, he led me over to a kitchen chair.

We ate in silence, though it was obvious that neither of us felt hungry. I did not look at my companion, only at the thick liquid in the bowl as the spoon coaxed it around. Tears were falling into what was left of my soup. I hoped Thomas had not noticed but he must have because after a minute or so he said, 'It won't hurt forever.'

I nodded, pushed the bowl away and let my head fall into my hands. I heard Thomas rise and stoke the peat stove, fill the kettle. There was a swelling pain behind my hot eyelids. Thomas sat down again with a scrape of chair legs on the floor. It was comforting to know he was there, yet anxiety still grew in my stomach. A well of guilt, of sorrow and dread. Outside, the first oystercatchers of spring spread their wings. They reeled and sang in the freshness of the day.

**

He was there again in the night. I cowered against the headboard and he sat unresponsive, seeming to drip seawater onto the bedclothes. I prayed only that he would not turn those terrible dead eyes on me. As the moonlight flickered under strips of clouds, his skin took on a greyer hue. The shrouds of fisherman's fabric that he wore shimmered with an eerie glow. The pounding of my heart caused explosions of lights behind my eyes. I blinked and as my night vision improved, the apparition's hair grew darker and he began to fade from sight.

'No!' I scrambled from the bed, tripping in the bedclothes. 'You mustn't leave. Don't go away and leave me like this. I don't want you to be so alone. I won't let you... I'll come with you. I'll go to the cliffs, it couldn't be simpler!'

I ran for the door and wrenched at the handle. It rattled as if the wind were at its hinges, but it would not open. I knew he was preventing me from leaving. 'Let me out!'

When I turned back to look at the bed there was only a soft glow where he had been sitting, the vestiges of a dissipating fog. Now the door handle turned in my hand but what use was it to me if I did not know where he had gone?

'Don't go,' I whimpered a final time. 'Don't leave me. I don't want you to be alone.'

36

AFTERNOON SUNLIGHT AGAIN broke through ominous clouds. Its warm rays fell across the coffin lids and brought light to the surrounding faces of the mourners. I stood apart from the rest of the community, aware of my untidy hair and appearance, evident to all, and of the blackness within my soul that cast a long shadow only I could see.

The dark dress of the mourners cut a stark contrast against the deep, earthy colours of the mountains and the tumbling grey-blue of the sea. Only the garrison troops in attendance were dressed in their smartest khaki. Sunlight bounced on their polished buttons, their caps shadowing their eyes as they sang while the coffins were lowered.

How bizarre that only one of those coffins should be occupied, that only Magnus should lie as he was supposed to in there, placed to his eternal, peaceful rest. The other twelve were empty. It seemed a mockery, for why must pretence be made of laying bodies in the ground when they have been lost

in the ocean's godless arms? Yet the mourners stood by duti-
fully and tearfully: wives with children in their arms or at their
feet and the mothers, fathers and siblings of the lost. And the
distraught pregnant girl whose eyes I could not bring myself
to meet.

I wanted to be with them, to stand next to Ragna and Ásdis, to comfort them; I wanted to share their grief and tears.
But I was not a part of the family and never had been. I was
little more than a charity case, a lonely orphan taken in and
sheltered. How could I claim to mourn Orri? I was not his
father or his brother; I had not been his lover. And I was not
Magnus's son.

My thoughts turned, as they did so frequently, to my father.
I realised quite suddenly that over two years had passed since
I had last seen him, since I had waved a miserable, frightened
goodbye to him at the harbour. It was before the garrison had
arrived there in their battleship fleets; before the German army
had marched into Denmark and taken the whole country and
my father prisoner. I had become accustomed to his painful
absence, had stopped sorting, heart beating with frantic expectation, through the morning letters at the post office, searching
for his handwriting on an envelope. Yet as I looked with tired
eyes upon the congregation and the empty wooden coffins I
could not help but wonder if I ought to be laying one out for
my father, too. I was as unsure of his fate as indeed I still was

of Orri's – his I had learnt of only through word of mouth, for I had not been a witness.

Perhaps my father, too, had fallen from the face of the earth, only no telegram could reach me before the war's end. I shuddered violently with a sudden chill. Thomas placed a comforting arm around my shoulder. Maybe he felt as alone as I did, rootless in a changing world, for he, too, was an outsider. Together we watched as the garrison began a new song: sombre and harmonious. With their caps politely clasped before them, they lifted their voices into the clear, still air – wheeling birds the only movement, the only sound the chirping of the oystercatchers.

A thick fog began to crawl over the rocky slopes of the mountains, engulfing the sheep in the fields together with their early lambs. It spiralled about the church roof in a strangely comforting veil over the stark revelations of daylight. It rolled down to the sea shore and hung over the waves, narrowing all vision of the world. The air dripped with a cold moisture which soon glistened upon the cheeks of the congregation and soaked the bare heads of the garrison so that their hair clung to their foreheads. I saw David amongst them.

Thomas lifted his head. 'They hate me.'

I cleared my throat. 'Why should they hate you?'

'Because I couldn't save him. Magnus.'

The guilt with which he rendered this statement startled me:

I realised that the accusation, when it came from his own lips and not mine, was blatantly a false one borne of emotion, not reason. Of course it was not his fault that Magnus had died.

'You weren't to know this would happen. It was the shock that killed him, you could never have accounted for it. And you did the best you could for him, no one could hate you for that.'

His gaze softened. 'I could have done more to help him.'

The vicar began to read another verse from the Bible, the content or significance of which I could not say, for I found all words customarily proclaimed in public use devoid of all meaning. Nonetheless the characteristic voice of the vicar carried clear as a bell into the crisp, sodden atmosphere of late afternoon.

'What would you say to him?' It was the more subdued voice of Thomas close to my ear. 'If you had the chance?' Then he added, 'Orri, I mean.'

My vision filled with the cold, snaking arms of the fog which had claimed the afternoon daylight and was snatching its onlookers from view. I closed my eyes against the disturbing way in which it exacerbated my light-headedness; closed my eyes to the black spots that began to dance before them. 'I think I would tell him not to be afraid.'

'You don't feel compelled to follow your own advice?'

I looked at him blankly. He said, 'I know a frightened boy

when I see one, Kjartan. You think you hide it so very well, but it's there in your eyes, plain as daylight – no amount of politeness can hide it.'

I dipped my head.

'But why,' he persisted, 'with all that fear within you, would you tell Orri that he, and he alone, should not be afraid?'

I could not meet his gaze. 'The vicar always talks of heaven,' I murmured, as the voice of the man in question rose and fell with the wind, 'as a place of peace and happiness, where the dead are reunited, fulfilled, love each other, you know? But how can that possibly be? After death there is an unimaginable nothing. Something like this, where we are now. Hidden in fog, as though we are blind, silent save for distant voices like memories. The voices of those we knew in life. And the cold feels like glass in the bones, but it is constant, and soon we become numb.' I flexed my fingers in the chill of the fog. The vicar was still speaking and one or two people close to Thomas and me had begun to cast irritated glances my way, so I lowered my voice to a whisper. 'And now we are alone, truly alone, unreachable and unfeeling. What is there to be afraid of? Nothing can happen. The dead cannot become cold, hungry or lost; they cannot feel loneliness or longing or sadness, or the pain of others.' I shifted my feet on the cold, damp ground, realising that I was no longer talking about the kind of death that can only occur after mortality is finished. 'It is when the daylight breaks, when the day begins and we fall again into our bodies after the safety of dreams that we become afraid.'

'But what are you afraid of?'

'I don't know.'

The thud of clods of soil falling on wood. The escalation of sobbing and wails from the bereaved. The sodden earth was being set back in place now, folded like bedsheets over the final sleeping place of Magnus. Now the empty coffins were also embraced deep within its heart.

Silence.

'Orri would ask me too what I was so afraid of,' I began again after the pause. 'He talked of excitement rather than fear – the thrill of the unknown. He said that was what could make us certain we were alive.'

The gravestones and the stirring congregation were as insubstantial as ghosts in the swirling fog. I screwed shut my eyes. 'It's just not fair, is it?'

'Kjartan,' said Thomas. 'No one is more deserving of death than anyone else.'

I only nodded in response: I did not wish to talk anymore.

***

Guðrun's house filled with the mourners. Red-eyed they conversed over coffee, swapping condolences and praising the conduct of the vicar.

Thomas and I sat outside on a low stone wall, remaining on the peripheries of the gathering. We had set ourselves apart and had now grown comfortable this way. We did not need to fill our silence with anything except the regular surge of the sea, the forlorn cries of the oystercatchers and the wash of blended voices that flowed dreamily from the house. For this I was grateful. I broke the peace only to offer him a cigarette, which to my surprise he accepted. In the cold drizzle which fell continuously we smoked and sipped our tea, and looked out upon the sea and the islet with its turret of clouds and its concealed settlement. My heart was heavy. I had not shed a single tear in the midst nor in the aftermath of the funeral service. I feared this numbness even more than the gravity of emotion.

'My cat misses you,' said Thomas.

'I miss your cat,' I confessed. The trickle of rainwater down the back of my neck set me off in a bout of uncontrollable shivering, and I excused myself. I planned only to go quickly to my room and fetch a coat; I did not wish to forsake the soothing peace of our silent exchange just yet.

37

I PASSED UNNOTICED through the house and once at my destination, I stood for a moment, cold, wet and shivering, staring at the place on my bed where the apparition had sat. Truth be told I had thought of little else but him all day. *The boy I knew to be dead, sitting at my feet in despair.* In the poorly-lit room with its musty atmosphere and its bare, gaping walls which emanated cold, I was again gripped by the encounter, as though I had only just awoken, sick and bleary-eyed, shaking still.

I heard the door close gently behind me and turned, still half in the experience of the night. Blinking, I registered the red hair, the freckled white skin and the overwhelming scent of Asta's perfume before she had fastened her arms around my neck. Her lips felt hot as she pressed them against mine.

'Poor Kjartan,' she said when she took them away. She stopped and looked at me and then drew more kisses over my mouth. 'My poor Kjartan.'

In the scented envelopment of her embrace my mind fell into a comforting absence of thought and at once I began to relax. I cupped my cool hands around her face as I kissed her in return; pulling her down, feeling the woollen mattress beneath me and her slight weight pushing me gently against it. Her fiery hair brushed my cheeks. Her hands left a shock of cold on the bare skin of my stomach, and I found myself thinking, as the wonderful emptiness of mind brought about by the unexpected encounter began to abate, of how she must only just have come in from outside. I wondered why I had not seen her, and if she had followed me into the house.

Her fingers were manoeuvring the buckle of my belt, the buttons of my trousers; and my mind was becoming clearer and sharper. The thought of Orri pushed its way to the surface. Again I recalled his likeness, sitting dripping at the foot of the bed, as real to me as Asta was now. He would be watching as the two of us made love, Asta and I, barely centimetres away from him. He would see us and in his sadness he would say nothing.

My foot had come to rest against the bed post. If I were to move it but a few inches to the left I would touch Orri's side...

With a sudden jolt in my stomach I sat up, pushing Asta away from me. 'No, I said hoarsely. 'Not like this.'

Her forehead creased. 'It's all right,' she said, fixing me with an intent gaze. 'I can make it work again, you know I can.'

Her fingers played in their familiar way about my body and she watched my expression, as unwittingly my body started to respond. The corners of her lips moved in the tiniest of smiles. 'Let me warm you,' she offered, pressing my face down to her breast, her hand at the back of my head. And I wanted to, she was so comforting and warm, she could make me forget.

I breathed. She wound her stockinged legs about my waist, pressed herself closer up against me; kissed me harder.

I couldn't breathe. Gently I pushed at her shoulders so that her lips came away from mine.

'It's not right.' I was breathless with an anxiety which was rapidly transcending to panic.

'Shhh.' She brushed my hair from my forehead. 'Just relax, Kjartan. It's not like we haven't done it before. No one will hear us: they're all busy talking. And besides...' She shifted her weight to one side. 'You need to be comforted.' As someone determined to complete a task, she cupped her hands on either side of my jaw, her thumbs against my cheekbones. Again she pressed her crimson lips on mine, whispering, 'I can make the pain go away.'

No. I could not bear her proximity any longer. I pushed her from me with force this time and jumped to my feet. Pulling my clothes back into place, I paced back and forth alongside the bed.

'Just stop it.'

She rubbed her arm, looking hurt. Maybe I had pushed her too hard but she should have listened to me in the first place. She watched me, tight-lipped now. Her stunned expression gradually gave way to one of obstinacy, her little-girl helplessness to the scorn of threatened pride. Still pacing, my heart pounded in a panicked beat. I focussed my attention on the path along the edge of the rug by the bed and back again but I could see, from the corner of my eye; that she was rising from the bed with as much grace as she could muster. She smoothed her black skirt down against her thighs.

I made my head turn and look at her. Her eyes glittered and there were high spots of colour in her cheeks. 'Even now I can't compete,' she said in a shaking voice.

My feet resumed their unbidden march, my head reeling. Her words meant nothing.

'I don't see why I always have to be second best, after all I've given you. God knows I deserve more in return. I'd call you selfish, Kjartan, but I know that for Orri you would have done anything. And you wonder why I never liked him; why he never liked *me*. He still means more to you than I.'

Breathe, I told myself. *She will be gone soon.* I concentrated on slowing my footsteps, on making myself stand still and facing her, showing her that I was listening. It might make her leave sooner.

'Just look at me, Kjartan: do you not see I'm alive? And yet

I still have to compete. Anyone would think the two of you had been *lovers.*'

So she can hurt me. 'Shut up,' I said. 'You don't know what you're talking about.'

'Oh, I do,' she replied.

An unpleasant feeling, it startled me to realise I could call it hatred, started to uncurl in me. All the parts of her person that had so entranced me seemed cheap now and distasteful in such proximity. I wished she would leave. I did not want to have this conversation.

'I know because I've seen it all,' she said. 'All that time the two of you spent together, you were never as awkward with him as you were with all the others. With him you were always so intense and *happy.* And when you are with me you barely say a word. It's like you're on another planet, all misty-eyed and thoughtful.'

'I've told you enough times you could get better conversation from a brick wall.'

'But you were never like that with *him.* I don't suppose anyone else means *anything* to you?'

'Not today, no. You see, this is a funeral reception. Here the dead have priority.'

'So I mean nothing to you?'

She seemed to have lost all her professed desire to comfort me in my loss. I shook my head sadly as she waited, her hands wrung together. 'Oh, Asta, how could I have been so stupid?' I breathed out. 'You said yourself: you can't compete. This shouldn't be a competition, or a game, you shouldn't be trying to claim me as your prize only to prove that you can have me as your own.'

Asta was closer to the door than I. She looked up at me, her eyes burning with the onset of tears; sucked in her lower lip, and turned to grasp the door handle. I took in a deep breath and held it for as long as I could. 'I won't keep you any longer, then,' she managed to get out through her tears. 'Sorry to have wasted so much of your time.'

**

Still shaken, I took my leave of the funeral party after giving Thomas the remainder of the English cigarettes and thanking Guðrun for her hospitality. More to the point, for her patience and kindness. These, she assured me, smiling, were by no means exhausted and added that I ought still to stay with her for the majority of the time, rather than be left to myself in the emptiness of my own house.

I approached David to bid him goodbye, for this night was to be his last upon the island, but the words would not rise to my lips. He lit two cigarettes and we stood for a while side by side. We smoked in silence, looking out to sea, and it was not until he had extinguished his cigarette under the toe of his boot that he spoke. 'Look,' he said, turning to me as though he was about to make some great demand. 'Maybe when the war is over I can drop by? Come and visit – you know, and we can go walking over the mountains again.' With a swelling feeling behind my eyes I nodded. He continued speaking hurriedly. 'And if I don't meet some pretty young lass to write letters to, then maybe I'll write to you instead.' He forced a grin. 'Every soldier needs someone to write to. *Anybody*. Just to keep him sane, you know?'

I nodded again and we parted with a melancholic handshake and all wishes for good health and a safe journey.

38

CONSCIOUSNESS CAME TO me like a blow to the back of my head, I was falling; a thousand foot drop into a deafening silence.

I sat up in bed. Aided by the dim ration of moonlight I was quick to ascertain the absence of ghostly presences at the foot of the bed or anywhere else in the room. There were none, yet on this dark morning I had awoken with an unusual sense of determination. In the chill of the early hours I moved robotically, as if my body knew what it was doing. It threw back my blankets and dragged off my night clothes, standing on the floor in the middle of my house. From Thomas's kit bag I withdrew the clean khaki uniform with its shiny buttons. I stood with it in my hands, tracing the cold metal accessories with my fingertip.

When I put it on the tunic was a little large for my skinny frame, but layered over the grey jumper I had knitted for Orri it fitted like a glove. Into the emptied kit bag I stuffed a few possessions I thought might come in useful – dry socks, underwear and a book (though it seemed unlikely that my haphazard concentration could ever be tamed enough to read even a page). I buttoned up against the morning damp, pulled the uniform cap down over the top of my face and closed the door behind me, pressing the palm of my hand to the familiar wood, before I turned away.

By the time I had pedalled all the way to the town of Miðvágur on the opposite coast, the morning had dawned properly. I laid my bike down by the side of the road and left it there – I would not need it again – and continued on foot to the jetty, sweat cooling on the back of my neck. Leaning against the fence I lit a cigarette to try and steady my nerves while I waited for the ferry boat that would take me to Tórshavn. Seconds passed like hours until the small boat approached over the glassy sound between the two islands. My heart hammered painfully. Surely I was mad to think that this would work...

The ferryman greeted me in English and I was relieved that I did not recognise him. My trips to the capital had been few and far between, after all. Our journey passed in a respectful absence of conversation; he whistled jovially as the boat rocked on the gentle swell of the tide. I was the only passenger. I kept my gaze down.

When we finally reached the other side I bid the ferryman a hasty goodbye before hurrying off towards the town. There the cluster of houses would swallow me up into insignificance – just another man in uniform. I waited in sight of the harbour, trying to look as if I was not simply caught in the act of waiting. My chest felt so tight I could barely breathe; my heart hammered, my fingers itched restlessly. It was not long, however, before the scene began to swim with the arrival of soon-to-depart garrison troops. Thousands of them, so it seemed. And at this point, unnoticed in the organised chaos of the operation, I joined the crowd.

The ship loomed above the busy harbour, swallowing the troops one by one. I remembered looking upon such a ship for the first time on the day the army had arrived, Magnus and Orri by my side. *Magnus and Orri.*

This time I dared not look up at its imposing height for I must keep my head down. Step by step I moved ever closer with the movement of the throng. When it was my turn to show identification I drew the papers – Thomas's papers – from the pocket of the tunic and handed them over with as much confidence as I could muster. They were given back to me almost immediately; no questions were asked, no rough hands threw me back to the island where I belonged. I stowed the stolen papers safely back in my pocket. There was no turning back now. Dizzy and nauseous, I gripped the handrail as I boarded the ship, and clutching Thomas's kit bag I followed the stream of soldiers.

Such a strange world this was, in which a man's identity was marked only by a few pieces of paper – and how would Thomas manage without them? Guilt washed over me like nausea. But I had to get to Aberdeen, I had to reach my brother; I did not know what else to do. Once there, perhaps, I could sort out papers of my own. Georg could help me, he would have no choice for he could not send me back and he would not turn me away. Perhaps I could explain I had picked up Thomas's papers by mistake, in desperation to reach my brother. Perhaps I could play the fool, plead insanity. Perhaps...

I did not even watch as the hills and valleys of my home, the only place I had ever known, retreated slowly, oh so slowly, into the greedy distance in favour of the ever-present deep and sullen ocean. My legs were shaking violently. Around me upon the deck, now at ease, the troops milled conversationally, though I spoke to no one. Possibly a few suspicious glances were thrown my way but the soldiers mainly ignored me. The ship rocked sickeningly. The scene swam in front of my eyes. How had I even got this far?

Instinctively I clutched for the man beside me as I gave way at the knees. There was a scuffle, then I heard helpful voices. A small crowd had gathered to see the commotion. Through the thickness of massed bodies I yearned for a sight of someone familiar. Someone from my own community – yet there was no way in which I could return to that which I had forsaken.

'The lad's seasick.'

'Daft old thing.'

'He'll have just left his sweetheart back on the shore!'

'Ah, bless his little heart, hahaha!'

'Who is he, anyway?'

I was offered a cup of water which I accepted shakily. Sitting back on my heels, I drank to quell the sickness of my stomach. The biting ocean wind, at least, blew away what little shred of doubt still marinated in my bemused conscience. I could live no other way, now. I had felt myself to be a lost, wandering soul even before I had forsaken my home. I had no regrets; my thoughts were stark and surprisingly clear; before me awaited only the oblivion that had beckoned in so many ways – I was anxious no longer, only warmly satisfied that I had finally laid aside my struggles. The tranquillity that overcame me on the deck of that boat was perhaps heightened by the draining fever of malnutrition and troubled sleep but I welcomed it.

Light broke from the pregnant clouds and fell sharply on the slow movements of the figures around me. Everything was bright, so bright, cut with an incredible clarity and freshness, both sight and sound. Human voices, engine noises, the cries of gulls, all could be heard distinctly and crisply, and my skin tingled. My heart ceased its perpetual frantic hammering and settled down.

When I looked up to thank the man who had offered water

to the shaking idiot on his knees on the deck, I caught the eyes of Jack. His familiar face peered down at me in scrutinising disbelief. I watched his surprise harden as the gaze lengthened, slowed by realisation. 'David,' he called, not deviating his eyes from me. 'David!'

David appeared. I did not see his expression even alter as he loomed towards me and grabbed me violently by the scruff of the neck, hauled me to my feet and pressed me up against the wall as though attempting to push me through it. I did not struggle. One or two of the onlookers, surprised by this sudden aggression, exclaimed loudly. But David only asserted his full strength and glared upon me in outright anger.

'What the hell are you doing here? Ah knew you were mad, Karri, but ah didnae think even you could be this stupid. What in God's name do you think you're playing at, eh? This is not your war! You won't last a minute, not a *minute* out there! Don't think you know what it's like – you don't; by God, you don't know a *thing*!'

Jack, never one to lose his head to anger, succeeded in coaxing David to loosen his grip. I was left shaken, though my shortness of breath seemed to stem more from the shock of the confrontation than from its rough physicality. When I felt sufficiently restored to address him, I whispered, 'Don't patronise me, David.'

'So you're going tae become a hero, eh? Is that it?' He stood sickeningly close. 'A brave soldier o' the front line – is that what you fancy yourself to be? A naïve country boy come tae prove himself, eh, change the course of history? Well, how lucky we are tae be in such fine, noble company!'

'I just have to get to Aberdeen,' I said, striving to keep my voice steady. Red anger had gripped me that he could be so presumptuous and so wrong. No one need tell me I was naïve and youthful: this I knew already, and I despised myself for it. That he should think me driven by the vanity and blind arrogance of heroics, or even martyrdom, was an insult, and the worst I could imagine. I glared at him, my fists clenching instinctively.

He continued as though he had not heard: 'Of course, you've no training, no experience – you might no be a virgin anymore, Karri, but that doesnae make for anything. You stand even less of a chance of survival than the rest of us.'

'Well, I'm glad!' I spoke with all the force I could muster, too angry to explain or defend myself further. 'The sooner the better. And if it would come as such a relief to you, too, David, to be rid of my existence, then it's nice to know I wouldn't be being totally selfish.'

He stared at me, apparently speechless. 'What are you playing at? You cannae just march out and get yourself killed... '

'Why not? Even if I planned to: what difference would it make to you, to Jack, or to anyone else, if I went out and got myself killed? I can't go on being a spoilt child, milking the cows, cutting the peat – all those meaningless things – how can I when everyone I care about is caught up in the war or dead? You've no right to play the brotherly role to me, David, you can't take the place of anyone this war has taken away from me.'

'Ah don't want tae see you dead!' he shouted, 'No one deserves tae lie in nameless pieces on a foreign battlefield. Now, *we* don't have a choice, Karri, we are sent out to die; but you –.' He made a visible effort to steady his voice, 'You condemn yourself to the worst fate of all.'

'*I just have to get to Aberdeen,*' I repeated.

'Ah might as well be a brother tae you,' David said angrily, again ignoring my remark. His voice caught. 'After all this time. And you doing such damn stupid things – ah've a right to be upset, like anyone else you've left behind. What would your father say, eh? He's caught up in the war through no fault of his own and you go throwing yourself into it like a bloody idiot. What will he think, eh, when he finally manages to get home and finds you've been blown tae pieces somewhere in Europe through your own wishes?'

'*If* he gets home,' I said. 'If he's still alive.'

David ignored this remark, too. 'What would Orri say?'

My stomach jolted and my eyes saw red. My cheeks flared up in unmistakable heat. Instinctively I raised a clenched fist to punish David for uttering the name aloud. *Blasphemy.* The name was forbidden. But instead I was seized by exhaustion. Overwhelming helplessness paralysed my muscles and my hand only fell to my side. I leaned my head back, closed my eyes and felt the cold wind playing with my hair.

'Well, go on,' the Scotsman pursued. 'You knew him well, didn't you? So what would he say?'

'David,' said Jack quietly.

David glanced at his friend, his mouth going slack, then fell silent.

'I think he'd be pleased,' my voice said slowly, 'if I enlisted.' The clamour of the engines and drowning wind seemed to diminish. I heard the swell of the sea, the cry of the gulls, and pictured a glorious, clear emptiness where no voices spoke, no machinery roared. I felt the first drops of cold rain on my face. 'He'd be pleased I was coming to join him. He won't leave me alone.'

A silence so profound followed this that the organic world must have stopped for a moment. My pulse quickened. In sickening guilt I perceived the wrong I was committing unto David, to his ideals, to the pain of his losses: his search for understanding. To be faced as he was with a damaged idiot such as me (even though he seemed to have misunderstood my intentions as far as I was aware of them) could be no less a cause of despair than his helplessness in the face of his young brother's death. In no way could David understand the motives for my stealing a man's identity and my assumption, my welcoming, even, of defeat – whichever form it might take.

39

DAVID PURSUED ME at a near run through the wet streets of Aberdeen. Even his heavy footsteps were inaudible in the deafening rush of the city. Hurrying along cobbled streets and in the shadows of towering stone houses which were joined in endless rows of blank faces, I did not wait for him. The din was incredible: multitudes of voices were raised in summons, in greeting or in passing conversation. There was the roar of a thousand engines, tyres rattling over the stones of the streets, then David calling out my name over and over again, urging me to slow down.

The cacophony of the city sent a frantic rush through my veins, and it was in a focussed panic that I continued to hurry, paper in hand, searching for the address upon it. I passed khaki-clad figures with rifles held to their shoulders, some who nodded at me as I flew by. I looked upon shelters piled high with discoloured sandbags, I trampled over discarded newspapers and once I almost stumbled in front of a motor vehicle, blinking and dazed.

The intrusive blare of a horn sent me jumping with shock, and in an instant David had me clasped by the shoulders and steered to safety in a side street. He admonished me for my recklessness, insisting that this was no place to rush around heedlessly for one as unfamiliar as I was with such an environment. But I brushed away his warning hands and my feet continued hurrying along the pavement. Exasperated, David kept at my heels.

I had dreamt of cities. Never of one in particular: having no model by which to run my imagination by, I was adept only at composing an indistinct scene which was not a welcoming one. I had never pictured trees, such as I saw now on the streets; never imagined how busy the roads would be. In my dreams the city's cacophony had been no more than a melee of voices, alarming in their number, offensive in their volume, yet a mere background chorus to reality's unfathomable roar.

It was a maze. I marvelled at the force of the city, yet could not take it in. I rushed past road signs and street corners without really looking to see where I was. Careering around the corner of one indistinguishable building I realised that David was no longer at my heels. It stopped me in my tracks and sent a cold rush through my bones; for the first time I was aware of my dependence on him in this place. I had drawn strength from his friendship and from his conviction in me. His presence in itself was a comfort.

I stood alone now on foreign soil, lost and shivering. My heart beat like a drum as I retraced my steps. I needed to pay more attention to my surroundings and try and locate him. I feared he might give up and simply return to the barracks as his brief period of leave within the city was coming to an end.

Then I saw him standing a little way back along the street out of which I had just hurried: a residential street, now that I looked closely, lined with terraced brick houses and with one or two stationary cars. Two women stood chatting in a doorway, one with a child in her arms. They nodded at me with obvious curiosity as I passed. A group of giggling children in the middle of the street sent an old leather football careering in my direction, and cheered excitedly as I sent it back with a deft, instinctive kick.

David turned his head at the commotion and pulled an impatient face. He motioned me over to where he stood in conversation with a tall man wearing an immaculate black uniform. 'You need tae show him the address, Karri.'

'What?'

'On the paper there: the address you've been running around looking for all afternoon. Come on, hand it over.'

I stretched out my hand to the stranger. He smiled at me from his open, middle-aged face. He had dark eyebrows and creases of good humour around his mouth and the number of his chins was doubled by the strap of his tall helmet. The helmet bore a silver emblem on the front, and for some reason this consoled me. The policeman took the scrap of paper from my fingers and, seemingly struggling to decipher my handwriting, finally looked up.

'Aye, lads, you're on Fisherrow Street,' he said brightly. He raised a chubby finger to indicate one of the red-brick houses on the opposite side of the road, not three doors down from where we were standing. 'That there's number eleven: the one with the blue door, see?'

I thanked him. David continued to exchange a further few words with the man but I did not listen. Gripped by curiosity I had turned to survey the house in question, but before I could draw any conclusions somebody tugged at my sleeve. I looked down to find myself surrounded by five young, grubby faces, each turned upwards in curiosity. The owners of these faces were clad in torn shirts and scuffed shoes. Their slackened socks revealed scratched kneecaps and skinny legs browned by the outdoors. A muddy football was thrust against my stomach.

'Will you come and play with us?' inquired the girl who had pulled at my woollen sleeve and still held onto it. She peered at me boldly. She had round grey eyes above a nose steeped in freckles; her dark hair had evidently been brushed into plaits at one time or another, though now they lay all but decimated on her shoulders, clumps of hair sprouting out of them.

'Not just now,' I said. I smiled regretfully at her look of intense disappointment. 'I have to go and see someone.'

'Who are you going to see?' piped up a blond-haired boy at my other sleeve.

I pointed across the street. 'The man who lives in that house, there, with the blue door.'

'Do you know him?'

I explained that I knew him very well, yes, but had not seen him for many years, at which another voice chimed in, 'You talk funny.'

I grinned. 'I'm not from around here.'

'Then where?' demanded the blond boy.

'Further north,' was all I could think to answer. I stumbled unsteadily on my feet as I was prodded and pulled at by two of the boys, who seemed to take great interest in the buttons of my oversized tunic and the pockets of my trousers.

'Do *you* have a gun?' demanded one of them. 'Can I have a go on your gun? Do you have one? Please, do you have a gun?'

David appeared at my side, also grinning. 'Who lives in the house with the blue door?' he asked my tormentors. I had told him nothing of my intentions – save for my desire to reach Aberdeen – perhaps for the plain fact that I did not know how to reconcile myself to the questions that would undoubtedly follow, or to the required explanation were I not to find what I had been looking for.

'Do you have a gun?' repeated the boy, turning upon the Scotsman and yanking at his belt.

'Ah'll tell you what,' David said quietly, in a secretive act of bargaining, 'if you tell me who lives in that house there – the one with the blue door – *then* ah'll let you have a go on my gun.'

'The doctor,' shrieked the child immediately. 'The doctor lives there. He's got a car and everything.'

The grey-eyed girl shuffled in front of him and, puffing out her chest with pride, she declared, 'The doctor is my daddy. He works in the hospital.' Again she tugged earnestly at my sleeve. 'He's from further north, too.'

David shot me a glance so laden with calculation that I avoided his gaze. The heat in my cheeks made me light-headed; I felt transparent. It was with a sense of wrongdoing that I allowed the freckled child with the unkempt hair, my new found friend, my *niece*, to lead me by the hand in the direction of her family home.

Behind me David, pestered and hemmed in by the insistence of small boys confronted with a real soldier, plunged his hand into his pocket and drew it out carefully with his index and middle fingers extended and his thumb bent above them. In utter sincerity he offered this 'gun' to his audience with the end effect that each and every one of the half-amused, half-outraged children followed us, shrieking, to the house with the blue door.

It was an unassuming façade, no different from any other house on the small, quiet street, and yet my heart hammered like a bell as we approached. It seemed as though the path might lead to a castle or a palace. There was neither grass nor greenery in sight; only a few plant pots stood around the entrance, empty of life, following a harsh winter.

A cold, light rain began to fall from the slate sky – the same sky, I thought, a lump rising to my throat, that must hang over the Islands that I had left behind – and the steps leading up to that expectant blue door gleamed modestly. I did not dare ask the name of my young companion; I only blushed in the gaze of the windows, the interiors behind them obscured by lace curtains. I instinctively held my breath, and doubted the purpose of my coming here. I had not seen my oldest brother in over eleven years. Our last direct contact had been the letter which I had sent following the capture of Denmark and our father's disappearance. That letter remained unanswered.

It was perhaps for this reason that I now stood on Georg's doorstep, shaking with nervous apprehension born from a desire to confirm his existence and re-establish our relationship. I would look upon the face of the one family member who was not lost in this new darkness, that faceless oblivion that had so recently claimed Magnus for its own and had wordlessly swallowed up my dearest friend.

Orri was in my mind now, as always. I pictured the way in which his lanky frame would have been drowned by the jumper I had made for him and which instead hung loosely from my own body, hidden by the borrowed khaki tunic. I thought of how he would have worn it anyway, worn it gladly and gratefully. If only he could be standing with me before this blue door, then I would not be so afraid. I was eternally grateful, of course, for my present company, but David could not keep the creeping evils that plagued my anxious mind at bay, nor the fluctuating darkness. Not as Orri had always done.

The blue door stood solidly closed. The girl, having found it locked, proceeded to pound immodestly upon its scratched paintwork with a grubby fist. The accompanying children fell curiously silent, and with bated breath we waited. Standing so still, my heart was the drum which in grim ceremony continued its marching beat.

Eventually the blue façade gave way, and in its place appeared the slim figure of a young woman. Her face newly illuminated by the rain-drenched light of late afternoon, she looked surprised to behold the gathered group upon her doorstep. I, too, was taken aback, for she seemed to me startlingly beautiful with her green eyes in a face of dainty features. The face was framed by neat hair, dark blonde in colour and as fine as the wind. I found I could not meet her eyes, though it was not from sudden shyness at the sight of her beauty but because I was struck by the indignity of my knowing her, whilst she knew nothing of me. Here she was, faced with two uniformed strangers.

In hesitantly polite tones she enquired how she might help us. My life blood beat so loudly in my ears that I barely heard her, only studied the neat hem of her apron and despised myself as usual in the uncomfortable silence.

'We're... looking for your husband,' said David, following a furtive glance at me and thus ascertaining that I had indeed lost my tongue. 'Is he at home?'

I kept my head down, hearing the courteous smile in the young woman's voice as she answered in the affirmative. But before any further invitation could be extended I heard light footsteps on what sounded like a wooden floor and the feet of another figure appeared beside those of the woman in the doorway. A man's voice demanded rather gruffly, 'Yes, how can I help you?'

I instinctively raised my head at the sound. Our eyes met, mine and the man's, and our gazes locked. The look of recognition which passed between us was slow: he appeared at first taken aback, then bewildered, then calculating all in the one long glance. His eyes were like my own, grey as the endless sea. My head ceased swimming and my fiery cheeks cooled. An icy stillness solidified in my stomach as I looked upon Georg, unchanged for the many years that had passed since he left.

'Daddy, the soldier's from further north, too,' said the girl at my side, whom I had forgotten. Evidently certain now of my identity, my brother's eyes at once filled with joy, then sorrow – a simple acceptance of our filial relationship.

Moments later the energetic squeals of children made themselves known to me again and I realised that our entourage, long bored with the proceedings, had run back out into the street. They had resumed playing, oblivious to us, with the worn football.

'Please,' said Georg hoarsely. 'Come in. Both of you.'

As we stepped over the threshold, David and I, the grey heavens opened. Through a curtain of rain the houses across the street all but disappeared, the children ran screaming joyfully for shelter, and the air breathed and rang with the music of raindrops upon cobbled streets.

About the Author

Holly grew up in Derbyshire but has always been drawn to the sea. Writing from a young age, she began with fantasy stories and poetry. Her love affair with island landscapes started on a brief visit to the Faroe Islands at the age of eighteen, en route to Iceland. She was immediately captivated by the landscape, weather, and way of life and it was here that she conceived the idea for *The Eagle and The Oystercatcher*.

Holly went on to study Icelandic, Norwegian and Old Norse at University College London. She sought escape from busy city life by working on the novel and knitting Icelandic wool jumpers. She also studied as an exchange student at The University of Iceland (*Háskóli Íslands*) and spent a memorable summer working in a museum in South Greenland.

After graduating from UCL with a first class honours degree, Holly decided to start a family. She currently lives on the west coast of Scotland with her husband and two very young children. Holly values simplicity, community and creativity, and eventually hopes to attain the dream of self-sufficiency. She also hopes to take part in Viking re-enactments.

On the rare evenings that the toddler goes to sleep, Holly works on her second book, a folktale-inspired novel set partly in Greenland. She types one-handed, sitting on the settee whilst breastfeeding the baby, balancing a cup of tea on a cushion. Progress is slow.

Lightning Source UK Ltd.
Milton Keynes UK
UKOW02f0007040716

277645UK00001B/1/P